Bang

Steven Atkinson

Published by Ophidian Books
www.ophidianbooks.co.uk

ISBN 978-0-9573554-4-6

1st edition paperback
Original publication date – 30th July 2012

To find out more about the author and his upcoming
works, please visit
www.stevenallinson.co.uk

Acknowledgements

A huge thank you goes to my wife and the rest of my family for enduring me during the process of writing this novel. I could not have done it without you.

A nod goes to the three guys I met outside High Royds Hospital. I'm not sure what you were doing there at that time, but your help in allowing me to do my research was invaluable.

Thanks also go to my sister Samantha, Nick and Neil for doing such a great job of reading (and re-reading) the book for me. Your assistance and feedback will never be forgotten.

Part One
SOLITARY

Chapter 1

Bang.

A solitary figure awoke to the cacophonous roar of hell tearing asunder. The wind howled and the ferocious sting of seawater lashed at his skin, searing exposed capillaries, and frosting blood. Bolts of lightning raged down from the shattered sky and peppered the buildings, which lay in the harbour surrounding the figure. And the thunder that accompanied the onslaught, the likes of which Thor himself would run from, threatened to smash the heavens into their constituent pieces.

The figure rolled over onto his front and tried to push up, but found his faltering strength unable to comply with the request. He looked out towards the sea where, intermittently lit by the sparks of fury released by the clouds, the smashed remains of a ship lay beleaguered against the jagged rocks of the shore.

The derelict clipper, grounded on the jagged volcanic rocks that lay either side of the stone jetty on which the figure laid, loomed out of the night, an enormous hole clearly visible in its facing side. The Brechin, he thought, unsure as to what part of his mind recovered the detail. As he wracked his psyche for further information, wicked, tormented fragments of memories surged through his subconscious and flared out across his mind's eye. Horrid, twisted scenes of torture and pain rose up, and sent waves of fear and panic through him with every anguished scene.

Eventually, the flurry of images subsided, and left him alone with the storm.

He composed himself and looked back beyond his feet. Looming out of the gloom, he saw an immense building. The Institute, his mind told him. It reared out of the black, its dank, granite construction littered with spires and grotesques. At the end of the jetty leading to the building, a long flight of stone steps wound up to where the building lay, perched on its bluff above the sea. A heavy wood and iron door, in its near face, clattered in the swirling winds.

He began to crawl, cold and desperate, as he strived to reach the security of the building.

Then it came to him, a name. It was difficult to pick out through the distant mists of his memory, but he could tell it was his name. He ran the memory repeatedly, desperate to extract anything it contained. Was it Alter? No. Maybe Lestaff-something. He concentrated hard and tried one last time. Walter, the figure thought, my name is Walter Wagstaff.

For ten arduous minutes, the newly realized persona of Walter scrambled toward the doorway. Once close enough, he sprung through, and into the presumed safety beyond.

The polished stone floor of the building was awash in rainwater and he found himself slipping and sliding, as he struggled to close the door and keep the elements at bay. Eventually, the wind conspired to assist him in his task, and flung the door back into its frame long enough for him to push the bar-lock into its socket, holding it firmly shut.

His mind exploded in joy and triumph. The relief he felt, as he collapsed to the floor and leant back against the door, unbridled. He laughed aloud, unable to restrain his emotion at being safe.

He wiped his face of and began to appraise his surroundings. He sat in a wide entrance corridor, lit with a

3

series of spaced oil lanterns, many of which had blown out in the raging winds. Just enough light remained, from those still pouring forth their orange warmth, to make out a wooden clerk's desk to his right. Behind that, a bank of numbered pigeonholes contained an assortment of neatly stacked mail. The Institute, his mind repeated, sending an involuntary shiver down his spine. He did not like the images that meandered to the surface when he thought about the place.

He stood, holding the lip of the desk to save from tumbling to the ground, and looked down at the floor where water lapped his bare toes. Even through the half-light of the interior, he could see something. A vague swirl of crimson was interspersed with the water. Instinctively, his eyes traced along the corridor. Each foot further away, the tendrils in the water grew darker and more numerous, until his eyes found the source.

He howled like a wounded animal and turned away from the gruesome scene, but was sure he could still feel the stare of the body in the corridor.

For its part, the body simply laid, his lifeless eyes directed toward the door, and his brains slowly drooling out across its once pristine, white shirt and on along the corridor of its previous employment.

Chapter 2

Doctor Levi Thaddeus bolted upright and shook his head in amazement. He felt stunned, somehow distant, and yet free. A strange ambivalence of thought, but it pleased him greatly. He stared at his surroundings, unsure of what recently transpired.

He sat in a simple room, about fourteen feet square. A single, iron barred window flashed with the light emanating from an electrical storm raging outside. The walls were bare and reassuringly white, and the floor covered in smooth, porcelain tiles. In front of him, a slightly ajar, iron-barred, oaken door led to a flicker-lit corridor.

Other than this scant array of pointlessly irrelevant data, his mind was unfortunately blank. It was a situation he knew could only be remedied through empirically gathered information. He picked himself up and went over to the door, striding carefree into the corridor beyond.

Just outside on the floor, was the body of a Caucasian male, maybe thirty to thirty five years of age. He knelt down and flipped the man's head over in his hands. Extensive bludgeon marks ran down one side of his face and the man's right eye hung loosely from a broken socket. He dipped a finger into the pallid ichor situated behind the eye and remarked of its scent. The smell was relatively sour, but was not yet effervescently rancid, indicating a time of death within the last twelve hours.

He noted the information and looked around. The corridor ran forty feet in either direction, marked with equally spaced, iron barred, solid oak doors. At either end of the corridor was an iron grille, presumably locksmithed of some fashion, and intended for keeping this corridor separated from the rest of the building. He smiled. It was a curiosity to be determined for reason later.

He arbitrarily picked a direction, headed to the next door, and glanced through the metal bars. It was empty. He repeated the process three times, before he found an open door. There, on the floor, was the naked form of a twenty-something woman. He crouched over her, turning the body onto its back and moving the hair away from the face.

Even from a cursory inspection, it was clear she had been dead a while and her bruised legs were covered in a conspicuous pattern of purple blotches. He reached out to confirm his suspicions; male hands made the marks. From the frequency of other scars and abrasions about her person, it was possible some form of sexual abuse befell the woman before her death. He ran a hand between her legs, parting her womanhood, and dipping his index finger inside her. He removed his hand, brought it close to his face, and inspected it. The crusted juices he managed to extract were a mix of creams and reds, and the smell was one of soured milk and almonds, suggesting festering trauma. He placed the finger into his mouth and licked the substances from it, being careful to give the flavours time to roll around his palette. Even through the heavily rancid texture of rotting flesh, he could make out the unmistakable taste of salt, a clear indication of the presence of semen. He looked at her face. It was pitted and broken, and her nose was smashed. Even so, his experience told him she was quite a comely woman at one point. He looked at her wrists and found them covered in the tell-tale marks of repeated suicide attempts. Perhaps her abuse was habitual, he reasoned, as he absently squeezed an exposed breast. Pausing only to lick the skin of her neck, he made his way out and continued his search of the area.

After a summary review of the next cells, he eventually reached another of interest. Inside the scant space was a figure, probably male, but sporting long hair and laying on his front. The figure was moaning softly, beginning to writhe with the first stirrings of consciousness. He tried the door. It was locked. He looked at the figure again and noticed he was clothed. Until that moment, he had not noticed he was naked. The fact eluded him as inconsequential, but now appeared strangely relevant. He felt cold and noticed the tumescence he experienced in the previous room had subsided; an obvious result of the temperature of his external capillaries. It was time he was warm.

He searched the next few rooms and eventually reached one with a clothed body. A man, probably in his early fifties, lay face down on top of another, naked man. The naked man had a small knife, perhaps a scalpel of some kind, protruding from his ear and the clothed man bore the unmistakable bruising of attempted asphyxiation by strangulation. It was clear these two men died whilst attempting to kill each other. He tossed the clothed man off the pile and began to remove his garments.

What he took consisted of a well-made set of undergarments, mildly soiled with the release of seminal fluids at the moment of death, a pair of well-tailored wool trousers, which hung well around the waist but were perhaps an inch or two short. A set of fine wool socks that comforted his feet, a simple white shirt, and a basic, heavy-linen doctor's jacket, which although comfortable around the shoulders, was conspicuously too short around the arms, completed the ensemble. He appraised the situation and found himself happy to roll the jacket sleeves back to the elbow, to hide any issue in length. His one problem rested with the sturdy, black-leather, laboratory boots the man was wearing. They were at least three sizes too small and lined with a substance he could only assume was a derivative of sand. After trying to walk only a few strides in them, he angrily tore them off and flung them against the wall as nothing more than useless. What he could now use for footwear he was unsure. After a few moments thought, he rummaged through the pockets of his newfound jacket and located his solution with a reassuring metallic jangle. With a high-spirited, tuneful whistle, he made his way back to the locked room.

The man inside was now fully conscious, as he smiled through the bars at him.

"Who are you?" the man stammered.

"My name is irrelevant." he said, trying each of the keys in the lock.

"What... What am I doing here?"

"Is it not obvious?"

"I can't... I do not remember how I..."

"Calm yourself. Do not bother your mind with irrelevancies at this moment. It serves no purpose."

"But I cannot... My head feels like it... What happened to...?"

"You are babbling like a child when its master beats it for misbehaviour. You do not wish to be thought of as a child, do you?"

"I do not want to... I do not know what I am to do... Can you help me?"

"My dear boy," he said, as the lock finally gave to one of the keys and the door opened, "I am only here to help you. But first you must help me."

"What must I do?" asked the man, terror covering his face.

"You must give me your slippers."

"My slippers?"

"What have I said about babbling incoherently? You are only delaying what you know to be true."

"Why do you need my slippers?"

"Because my feet are cold." he said, closing in and grabbing a handful of shirt.

"Please!" the man screamed, suddenly seeing the intent in his eyes.

"If my feet get cold," he said calmly, as his first blow landed on the side of the man's head, "then blood will leave my extremities. This trigger is not localized to my feet, however." he continued, as another blow shattered the man's jaw. "Blood will flow from my skin's surface to my core, meaning that I will also lose blood flow to my hands, as my body attempts to keep my vital organs warm." he said, as the next contact sprayed his face with blood. "But the lack of fine motor control and the reduction in my athletic ability is the least of my worries." Cracks began to sound from the man's skull, as his onslaught continued. "My concern stems from the fact that blood flow to my brain will be reduced, impairing my ability to reason and thus to find a way out of this predicament." He left the last fist embedded in the side of the man's shattered cranium. "Surely, you must understand I cannot allow this to occur?"

He stood and looked at the corpse created. Blood still streamed from the mangled remains of the face, as the heart fluttered through its final beats.

He removed the man's slippers and felt the warmth and comfort of them against his feet, as somewhere out in the corridor a faint crackle sounded out, startling him into action. He jumped to his feet and peered round the doorframe into the void beyond. There was nothing.

Ignoring the noise and continuing to whistle his merry tune, he wandered out of the room and down to the end of the corridor.

Somewhere out in the distance, a howl broke the still of his locality as another crack of thunder lit up his surrounds with hellish fire. Fumbling with his keys, he unlocked the bars blocking his path, and followed the sound, unsure of what he may find.

The corridor snaked through the dark building to a descending staircase. He could see the delicate flicker of a moving torch deep below and decided a location in the depths of the building would give him sufficient cover from the storm.

Marching down, he peered along the intersection, and to his surprise, spotted a figure he recognised.

The small fellow moved furtively from door to door, lantern in hand, checking each room he passed.

"Wagstaff?" he said, unsure of where the information to vocalise the thought came from.

The figure twisted, startled by the sound, and nearly dropped his precious oasis of light. "Doctor Thaddeus?"

"It is you, Wagstaff!" he said, happy to be able to place at least one item of information. "Do you know what is happening?"

"Oh dear. I was going to ask you the same thing. There are bodies everywhere."

"Ah." he said, realising his malady was not a localised event. "Never mind that now. Let us find ourselves suitable refreshment and see if we cannot discover the finer detail of our situation."

Starting his whistle once more, he set off with Wagstaff in tow. They would find an appropriate provisioning area and discuss their situation like gentlemen. And, if his newfound companion proved unhelpful, at least he would have somewhere with running water to dispose of his body in a sanitary fashion.

Chapter 3

Alouicious Tirney sat up and felt the lump on his head. He was in a well-appointed bathroom. He considered the fact for a moment and concluded he did not need to relieve himself. He did not feel right. His memories were gone.

Leaving the room behind, he shambled into a stone corridor, littered with fallen forms. Some wore blue pyjamas, some white coats. At his feet lay a nurse or female orderly of some kind. She bore long, curly, ginger hair, and her cosy-looking, woollen jumper had a silver pocket watch attached to it. He leant down and sniffed her. She smelt bad. He removed her jumper and bit the exposed skin of her back. The torpid flesh squirmed with juices, and the rancid liquor that exuded from the marks his teeth made caused frightful delirium in his mouth. Why do women always let themselves go when they find gainful employment? The fucking town bulls! he thought, tugging at his hair.

He wandered off down the corridor to explore his surroundings. Whatever building he was in was large and, save for the decaying detritus of death littering its many stone walled corridors, it appeared cleanliness was a priority here.

The corridors contents made him very excited. Even though he did not know where the feeling came from, he greatly enjoyed the experience of exploration. All too soon into his voyage of discovery, his eleventh finger, the one that felt good when it explored, was tired and sore, so he made his way back to the bathroom to bathe and cool it. Whilst there, he checked himself over for injuries and noticed he

was beginning to feel hungry. He toyed with the idea of heading in the direction of some of the low murmurs heard on his wanders, but he quickly decided something cooked, preferably sweet, was what his heart desired more than something fresh, and resolved to locate a pantry or food store.

He set off, ignoring for the most part, the many items of interest his fingers wished to touch, as he tracked his way across the building. Eventually, he reached a flight of stairs and, understanding only casually why, descended.

Once downstairs, he felt strangely at home. As if following some invisible trail of breadcrumbs, his legs led him to a long corridor beset by heavy, oaken doors. Food! He was not sure how, but he remembered being taken down this corridor by nurses. Trussed up and shackled in his chair. Bridled like a fucking horse by a bitch in a white overcoat. Fucking whore fucks! he thought, pulling his hair so hard his scalp tore and blood oozed out.

He ran down the corridor and burst into the room beyond. The mezzanine area was just how he thought it should be. Rows of polished tables, sat surrounded by chairs lined with fine, vermillion cloth. In the occasional seat was a fallen figure. Glancing around the room, he recognised one of the dead and his heart began to soar. One of the bitches who used to bring him here to feed him had fallen unconscious into her bowl of soup and drowned. The sweet irony! The delicious joy the sight brought!

Alouicious unbuttoned his britches and began to whoop and bay for all he was worth. He flapped his arms and leapt onto the table by the woman's side. He dipped his burgeoning excitement into the bowl by her face and began to prod and poke her all over with it. He was free, and the goddamn slags that once tied him down were gone forever.

A stern voice from behind him cut his exuberance short.

"Remove yourself from the table Mister Tirney!" the voice boomed, with audacious authority. "That is no way to treat one of your former hosts. Do not make me force upon you the manner of your wickedness."

Alouicious turned to see a strangely familiar man bearing down on him. He wanted to call him Doctor Thaddeus, but his gut did not like the name his mind ascribed. With a growing sense of foreboding, he decided it was in his best interests to do as the eccentrically attired man requested. He replaced his eagerness in his trousers and stepped down from the table, his head hung.

"That is much better Mister Tirney." said Thaddeus. "Now that you have exhibited some measure of restraint in your actions, I feel obliged to act accordingly. Myself and Mister Wagstaff are about to enjoy a brief sojourn of afternoon tea. We are arranging an assortment of fine cakes from the larder and are mashing a pot of Ceylon for our indulgence."

Without further pause, Alouicious skirted around Thaddeus and ducked into the kitchen. All further explorations could wait.

Chapter 4

Somewhere in the dank recesses of the Institute, a lone soul hammered plaintively against the iron bars that confined it. It awoke, an indeterminate amount of time ago, to the terrible sensation of being atop a pile of corpses. Ever since that first, skin crawling experience, it searched in the dark for an exit. It fumbled, often its hands or feet sinking into the fetid mucus of some rotting form, in a desperate attempt to understand its surroundings by touch alone.

It was in a circular room, at least a hundred feet across, circled by iron bars. It located a door, but even though it searched, often through gut wrenching sensations of oozing fluids, it could not be prised open, as exquisitely made for its niche as it was. So, it hammered on the bars and screamed for all it was worth.

Eventually, in piteous and forlorn acceptance of its fate, the figure sagged to the floor and began to weep, its attempts to escape at an end.

Seconds, minutes, perhaps hours passed by, as the figure languished in its solitary oblivion. Before somewhere, just out of range of full perception, a low rumble began.

It started, almost unnoticed by the figure, in the blackness of its iron prison. There it found voice and slowly, insipidly, the noise began to muster in the dark.

Soon the figure could feel vibrations. The first stirrings of audibility appeared and quickly, a dolorous throb resounded in the void.

The noise picked up pitch, droning out in long, oppressive thrums across the space. The blare so low and tortured, it forced the fine hairs on the back on the figure's neck to stand on end.

Rising to bellowed crescendos with each pulse, the reverberation hung in the air in front of the figure and tugged at its trembling gasps for breath. Even through the blackness, the figure could almost pinpoint the source of the noise to an area in the centre of the room. It struggled furiously against the bars, as an eerie terror began to foist itself within its soul, clawing at its faltering heartbeats.

Another crescendo, much louder than before, boomed out into the space, this time accompanied by a flash. Instantaneous and brilliant, it illuminated the dark and gave a fleeting glimpse at the figure's living hell.

It was in a domed room, circled by a series of metallic bars. Bodies, many just eviscerated piles of flesh, lined the space. A hundred, perhaps more souls perished, their brightly coloured clothing scorched and burned to what remained of their forms. There seemed none other saved alive. Most puzzling of all, was the core of the room, where three metal orbs dangled in a column from the ceiling.

The bars began to rattle with each pulse and the flashes of light drew closer together, as the sound grew louder and sharper. Soon, the noise was so intense the figure had to cover its ears to prevent its brain rattling loose.

The figure noticed, through excruciating pain, the light emitted from tendrils of white fire running along the surface of the orbs. The sakes of light danced and twirled, as they drifted along the edges of the polished metal.

Tighter and tighter. Faster and faster. Louder and louder. Jericho was upon the figure and the walls were crumbling. The air fizzed and hissed, as its mouth filled with an acrid, almost metallic taste.

Almost at the point of fracture, the noise rose to a cacophony, an exalted height of vicious ecstasy that blasted out across the room. The sound froze in the strained space, as a brilliant shaft of silver fire bolted from the centre of the room and sprang toward each bar.

With vile indifference to the helpless figure, the jets streaked across the construction and leapt at it, hurling it back.

With its last, dwindling strains of vision, the figure slumped into an unconscious embrace with the rotting remains of its fellow occupants. Its nostrils now full with the smell of charred flesh.

Chapter 5

Jennifer Grahams sat and waited for her fiancé's return. She busied herself with darning his socks and attempted to take her mind off the terrible row they were ensconced in that very morning. As she lovingly sewed up the delicate seems, her mind drifted to how different things were only a few weeks ago.

She met her love around a year ago. Walking through the park, the hazy crimson shades of autumnal leaves drifting through her vision and distracting her actions, she accidently walked into a man coming in the opposite direction. Jennifer did not believe in love at first sight, but there, with the harsh autumn wind a long forgotten foe, she suddenly realized what it was.

Their romance was a joyful ride. They spent hours talking. She discussed her maritime upbringing and her love described his wealth of education. They discussed what they wanted from life and how they would go about getting it. They talked about what they thought the future would hold and how, as long as they were together, they could bridge the impossible. She never felt so safe, so secure, or so loved.

When asked, she eagerly moved into her love's house. She knew to be together with your betrothed before marriage was not to everyone's liking, but theirs was a love that would not wait. They hastily made plans for their wedding day, with Jennifer happily taking on the lion's share of the duties required to organize the venue and their guests. However, all too soon, their early eagerness faded.

Her love's work, something about which he bore a bracing passion, began to encroach upon their time. It started with the occasional long night, a late return a week perhaps. From there, it escalated to a few days, and then to whole weeks spent away.

The last month was an excruciating drift apart for the pair, one that tore at their bonds of companionship and love. That morning, after he returned from a particularly long time away, Jennifer noticed something had changed in her love. Foolishly, she pressed the matter and he was not able to contain his emotion. He exploded with passion and trashed their bedroom. He stormed out of their house into the raging gale, which howled around the harbour in which they lived. She cursed herself for acting as she had, belittling as it was to their love. She resolved to wait, to entreat of his courtesy when he returned and to accept what his work meant to him. It was her duty as his future wife.

The storm raged on, banging the shutters of the windows and snarling out into the open sea beyond the harbour wall. Jennifer sat and busied herself as best she could, as time passed by. With each hour, her anxiety grew, fearful her love might never return. Eventually, just as her arms tired, her head began to loll into the soft cushions of her chair, and the last flickering embers of the hearth's once radiant fire began to cool, the door finally opened.

The wind whooshed into the house, fluttered the curtains to her side, and roused her into action. She righted, straightening her clothes, and put on her bravest smile. Heading out of the drawing room and into the hallway of their home, she froze.

Before her was the unmistakable silhouette of her love, picked out against the violent night. He stood in the doorway, the random flashes of distant lightning illuminating the space and sparking her trepidation. His hair was thick and matted. Its long, carefree curls wrapped and jagged by the beating winds outside. Hung loosely in his grip was a handsaw clumped with flesh. Spots of ochre bathed his pristine coat, and his brow drooled with crimson goo, thinned by rainwater, in rivulets down his wide cheeks.

"Levi!" she said, aghast.

For his part, Doctor Levi Thaddeus pushed the hair from his face and raised his bloodshot eyes. "I am home, Jennifer."

Chapter 6

Walter startled in his chair, a half-eaten apple stuck to the teeth of his bottom jaw. He was still in the kitchen. He felt woozy and his skin crawled with feverish excitement. He had been unconscious again. He looked across the table to where Thaddeus sat, but he was gone. That thought troubled him. He could remember after the blackness this time. Something had changed.

As he sat and looked around the room for signs, the doors of the kitchen burst open and a rancid looking fellow darted into the room. He howled and climbed up onto the table, as the shambling form scurried through the room and darted into the pantry.

As he peered after the strange form, from his safe perch on the table, Thaddeus returned through the open doorway, striding confidently and smiling.

"You have awoken Wagstaff." said Thaddeus, moving over to the oven. "Do not just crouch on the table like a stray cat. We have a guest. Get the good china from the cabinet behind you. I have a pot of Ceylon that will not do in the muck this place serves its beverages in."

Walter did as he was told, returning hastily with three cups and saucers from the cupboard. Something bothered him though. How did Thaddeus know the china was there? His mind had not divulged any further information other than the necessities of existence. He knew his name, held a feeling he knew where he was, and his bodily functions seemed intact. Beyond that, information presented to his brain was scant to non-existent. How did a man, who claimed to have experienced the same thing, know where the fine china was located? It made no sense.

"Can I have those, Wagstaff?" asked Thaddeus, looking at him with impatience. "Or are you going to stand cradling them all night? We will need some side plates too. If we are to have tea and cakes, it will not be taken in the manner of barbarians."

Walter turned at Thaddeus' new request and moved to the cupboard. He carefully selected the matching set of side plates for the cups recently returned, his mind eager not to anger Thaddeus further. That thought stopped his actions again. He was remembering something. Something vivid and recent wanted to be heard, but it was wrapped in fear and doubt. An involuntary shiver returned him to the present, forcing him to hurry over with the plates.

"Very good, Wagstaff." said Thaddeus, upon receipt of the china. "You have even selected the correct pattern. We may make a gentleman of you yet."

Walter watched, as Thaddeus put the plates on the table and made his way into the pantry. A few shouts and hollers later, he was walking back out of the room, pulling the other man by the scruff of his neck.

"Mister Tirney says that he will pour the tea for us. Did you not, Mister Tirney?" said Thaddeus, shoving the man across the room with a snarl.

The man simply nodded, his form held in a cowering manner with his back turned. It was clear he felt the same reservations.

"I will be back with cake presently, gentlemen." said Thaddeus, straightening his white coat and running a hand through his hair. "I expect my tea to be poured and waiting."

As Thaddeus returned to the pantry, the other man bolted into action.

As soon as Thaddeus left, Walter became hypnotised by the way the new man moved. He shuffled, hunched as a question mark, his rough, striking features hidden behind dirt and blood. He often flicked his hair, exposing his eyes to the lamp light of the room and startling him with each stolen glance.

One eye was remarkable enough. It was large and its iris was a crystal blue one could only see in the stained glass of a church. The other was fearsome. It was bloodshot and its pupil was so large no iris was visible. It was at once dazzling and yet freakish to gaze upon the man.

"I heard Thaddeus call you Mister Tirney." said Walter, finally edging around his trepidation, as the strange man continued to bustle, seemingly unproductively, over the stove. "My name is Walter."

The singular lack of response was uncomfortable. Before he could continue with a second attempt at contact, the man snapped round. He quickly arranged the saucers next to empty seats on the table and poured three cups of tea, his movements jagged and irksome. Upon completion of his task, his eyes flicked up and stopped their frenzied dance. Much to Walter's amazement, he raised a finger to his cracked lips and bade him to be silent with a light expulsion of air.

Presently enough, Thaddeus returned to the room and smiled broadly. "The wonder of stern motivation is never lost upon me. Good show Mister Tirney!" he said, with chirpy enthusiasm, as he placed a tray of excellent looking cakes on the table. "I am unhappy to report there is not a single napkin in the pantry fit for such a feast. We will simply have to ensure we eat in a manner that befits our status as free men."

Free men? thought Walter, as he reached across and took a large piece of gateaux. Why would he be anything other?

"Once we are sated, we must try to involve ourselves in our surroundings." said Thaddeus, as he nibbled on a honey covered sponge. "We must determine the reason for our continued entrance into the realm of the unconscious. It would also be prudent to detail in minutia the locale in which we find ourselves."

Mister Tirney nodded silently as he ate his cake.

Walter could tell it was consuming a great deal of Mister Tirney's concentration to not cram the cake into his mouth and devour it whole. Something about Thaddeus was markedly changing how he was acting.

Something was wrong with their companion, and both he and Mister Tirney could feel it. When they set off to explore their surroundings, it would be one of the first things he would seek to clarify.

Chapter 7

Their light repast completed, Thaddeus instructed his two companions to ensure their plates were washed and returned to the cupboard. There would be no return to the animalistic whilst he could ensure it.

Whilst he sipped at his tea, he thought. His brain was still a mess, but even through the haze, it was clear something happened. Some event he could not remember put him in this state. Although he was unsure as to the exact nature of whatever transpired, he was positive that finding out would lead to a revelation about how to restore his memory. It was the most logical assumption.

He slapped Alouicious across the back as he finished putting the last of the plates away. "Ready we are then, gentlemen". He was still confounded as to where the information was coming from. Perhaps his memory was returning on its own. Even if that were true, he experienced a momentary clarity that showed him the location of an office, set to one side of a long corridor, outside the main entrance to the kitchen. "Follow me." he said to his companions, who begrudgingly began to meander out of the room.

He walked briskly and assuredly toward his destination. He stopped outside the door, as a wave of recollection rushed through him. He could remember turning the handle and walking into the office. He was wearing a long jacket, just as he was at present, and pleasingly neat, black leather shoes. The insides of the office glowed with the orange fire of multiple wall sconces, which illuminated the heavy wooden panelling and gave it an air of masculine authority. Lines of books, each a work of art in parchment and leather, lined the walls and an enormous mahogany desk dominated the middle of the room. The fine, decorated edges and plush, green leather top gave it the lustre of majesty, and magnified the overall effect of grandeur pervading the space.

Almost on tenterhooks, he gripped the sturdy iron handle and walked inside. The room was a hollow ghost of his memory. The book lined walls were looted, their contents spilled haphazardly to the floor. The wall sconces were empty, the oil lamps that once filled the metal adornments long since removed, and the mahogany desk ripped and littered with torn pages. Unimpressed, he took note of the objects, carefully logging how they sat in the room.

From the piles of books and their arrangement, it was fair to surmise at least two different people looted the room. Some books strewn haphazardly on the floor, suggesting no thought to the effort. Yet occasionally, some were stacked in neat piles, which suggested a reasoned order to the work.

He moved from the shelves to the wall sconces. He fingered one of the metal rings and placed it in his mouth. The taste was acidic, but not overbearing. The iron had not begun to rust in the heavy sea air, and thus left unattended for no more than a few weeks.

He turned and looked as at his two companions, the dolts afraid to enter. "Come in and make yourselves useful." he said, with a gestural wave of his hand. "I want you to make a neat pile of books for me that have had any of their pages removed. Do you understand?"

The pair nodded and cautiously began to edge into the room.

"I want this task completing quickly so I have more time to study what you uncover. Therefore, I require no dawdling on your parts. Put the undamaged books back on the shelves so I know they have been checked." Hopefully, whoever ransacked the room was too lazy to carry the whole book and maybe they simply tore what they needed from it. It was not a gamble of time he would have taken if he were alone; such was the shortness of chance in its success. Nevertheless, whilst he had assistants, he should put them to use.

The pair quickened their pace, seemingly eager to complete the task set. This pleased him greatly, and he made a mental note to consider their efforts the next time he felt it necessary to hurt one of them.

He turned his focus back to the desk in the centre of the room. Walking over to it, he could see a forced open drawer and papers from it littering the surface. He casually looked one over. It was from something called 'The Royal Outlook Society'. Thaddeus' heart fluttered. A distasteful distraction to his reasoning and one he forced back down within his soul immediately. He could recall the name, but why?

He looked at the other documents, some from companies and some from private individuals. As he removed letter after letter from the table, his eyes were drawn to a lighter piece of wood that became visible after the quantity thinned.

It was a simple piece, perhaps six inches long, but one that fascinated him immensely. His mind simply would not allow him to turn away from it.

He reached out towards it, the feeling in his fingertips reaching a fever pitch. His movements were slow and delicate, as if touching the object was somehow a precarious activity. Somewhere deep in his mind he could feel a surge; a memory perhaps or an emotion of some kind, which struggled and fought against the cage of his ego. He stretched, almost anticipating the contact with the wood, the hairs of his hand rising to meet his growing urgency. Eventually his skin brushed the surface, sending a shockwave of emotion through him. He recognized the object; he knew it and respected it. He gently curled his fingers around the wood and began to pull the object from out of the pile of papers. It slithered, almost as if it wished to crawl free across the desk towards him. The wood he was holding grew longer, until he could begin to see an attachment of metal; like teeth on the face of the slowly curling edge. Slowly, horrifyingly, the shape continued to come out. Put it back, Thaddeus! he heard a woman cry, from the distant, languished realms of his mind. But he could not. His mental fate was now locked once more into its course. He recognized the blade. He recognized the handle. In his mind's eye he could see the doorway. He could feel the wind at his back and the rain in his hair. He could smell the scent of the woman as she yelled out across the corridor of the house. Even though the blade was clean, he could still see the matted flesh stuck in the cast iron teeth of the hand-saw that now hung at his side.

As another wave of black engulfed him, he managed to utter a solitary request: "Forgive me."

Chapter 8

Alouicious Tirney awoke in the room long before his two compatriots began to stir. He was not sure of anything, but was certain there was light in the room. A ball of white, like a wil-o'-the wisp, danced and fizzed in front of his blurry vision and bade him rouse from his slumbers. His skin burned with its presence, and he wished it gone. Closing his eyes from the demon, he willed it away. When eventually he spied a chance to look again, it was no more, and he was alone in the silence.

It took all his powers of control to stop himself exploring his companion's prone forms, as they lay helpless on the floor. Instead, he managed to focus his attention on completing the task Thaddeus set him before they collapsed. It did not take long, and was soon finished.

A pile of seven books sat in front of the desk, each one missing some measure of its bulk through the removal of pages. In the room around him, he replaced all the other undamaged books on the shelves. He organized them based on colour and height and now the rich mahogany walls were decorated with his achievement. He crouched on the table, atop a pile of letters, and gently fondled himself as he appraised his handiwork.

"Mister Tirney!" boomed a voice from behind him. "Do not make me impose upon you the manner of decency... Again!"

He turned to see Thaddeus standing and dusting himself down. He could see the stare of discontent glowering out from his brow and cautiously removed his hand from his britches and moved back to the floor.

"Now, Mister Tirney, where have you put the item I was holding?"

He had no idea what Thaddeus was on about. Then a thought hit him. Just before the last blackout, Thaddeus was hovering over the table. He moved a couple of the letters strewn on its heavy top and then slowly drew his empty hand back from the table. At the time, he thought nothing of it, as he was busy with sorting the books in the room as requested. But now… Was it possible that Thaddeus thought he was removing something from the table? He shrugged and shook his head, moving away from Thaddeus as he did so.

"My hand!" said Thaddeus, moving forward menacingly. "I was holding a saw in my hand!"

"I don't think you were" said Walter, slowly righting himself from the floor. "I was watching what you were doing before you collapsed and I don't remember you having anything in your hand."

"Don't play games with me, imbecile!"

"I'm not. Please!" said Walter, instantly cowering and drawing his arms across his face in protection.

He watched as Thaddeus closed on Walter and grabbed him by the shirt collar. He moved so he was staring the whimpering man only a few inches from his face and then threw him to the ground. Thaddeus then opened his hand and stared at his palm. His scowl dissolved, as he turned it over a few times and inspected it carefully. Shaking his head, he eventually turned and looked round the room, noticing the neatly arranged books on the walls. He smiled at him and then moved to the stack of seven books that were left on the floor.

Alouicious knew what the pile contained. There was an early print of Prognostications by Paracelsus; a tired looking copy of Sir William Hamilton's Lectures on Metaphysics and Logic; a rather distressed and heavily thumbed first edition of On the Origin of Species by Charles Darwin; a leather bound and surely not original copy of Philosophiae Naturalis Principia Mathematica by Sir Isaac Newton; a rare edition of the The Birth of Merlin by Shakespeare; a strange red book that seemed to belong to a group of individuals known as the Rosicrucian's, and a tattered looking journal of some kind. He already noted the pages removed from each of the major works and was pleased to find his mind could somehow return to him the information once present. For the moment he was unsure what that could mean, but was hopeful something would eventually come to him.

As he sat and watched Thaddeus struggle with each book, his spirits lifted, as he realised it was not a gift his compatriots possessed. He bore an advantage. He was unsure why at this moment, but somewhere in the back of his brain, something told him intellectual advantage was to be cherished.

Chapter 9

Thaddeus stared at the books in front of him and flipped backwards and forwards through the pages. He could not make sense of why anyone would remove anything from such a strange collection of books. What were they to do with what was going on? He could not be certain of anything. He was, however, certain he was holding a hand saw before the last flash. Or was he?

Wagstaff was telling the truth in what he said. The idiotic creature was too stupid and too afraid to concoct an effective lie. Therefore, he needed to assume he was not holding a saw, and yet his memories told him he was. He shook his head. Distraction by the meaningless would not assist his efforts. If it was important, his mind would remind him of it when the time was right. He must focus on the here and now.

He turned his gaze back to the books and looked down the spines. The only book that may hold some information was the journal. He picked it from the stack and flicked through its coarse pages. It belonged to a man called O'Reilly and seemed to be notes from a hunting expedition of sorts undertaken in the spring, but without a current timeframe to reference anything by it was guesswork to conclude if the expedition was a recent event. What was of interest was that the journal's last pages were ripped from it; everything from the point at which O'Reilly's first attempt was made to find 'The Society'.

Thaddeus reached into his inside pocket and drew out the letters placed there and looked at the name of the sending party; 'The Royal Outlook Society'. It could be a coincidence, but it could also be important. He put the journal in his front pocket and stood up.

After ensuring there were no other letters of any import, he turned to face his followers. "Shall we continue our search of the building gentlemen?" he said, keeping his voice light and chirpy. "I am sure there is much to learn and potentially only limited time to complete the task in."

His unbalanced search party nodded eagerly and left the room without a word.

As he strode out of the office, he took a moment to appraise the corridor. It would make sense if all the administration offices were located together. He ordered his followers to check the surrounding rooms, as he strode off to get his bearings.

As he surmised, the corridor contained a series of offices and clerks rooms along its length. As he reached the end of the corridor, he found a document storage room and, interest piqued, made his way inside.

The large room was dominated by a series of long, wooden, file racks. With a strange distance of thought, his mind sent him back to his days at university where similar banks of filing lined the walls of the plush library in which he spent many hours. The memories were faded, and faces and textures were difficult to bring back, but a large carved motto 'Dominus Illuminatio Mea' did stand out. The Lord is my light. Even with this revelation, he could not place the location. It would have to wait.

He took the flickering oil lantern hanging in the doorway and started looking down the ranks of notes lining the shelves. Each section headed by a name. It was possible these were patient notes. He walked in between the rows until he found a name that caught his eye. 'A.M. Franks (Test Case 015 - MUR)'. The acronym used at the end of the name was puzzling. It was not an abbreviation he had seen before. Nevertheless, the contents of the documents were more important than the naming convention used on the exterior, so he once more noted the curiosity for later analysis.

The shelf heaved with the weight of paper loading it down. He reached over and snatched a hefty looking, twine wrapped, bunch of hand-written notes and, placing the lantern on a free shelf, opened them. He expected to find his own handwriting inside the folder, but instead found a script he did not recognize. The flowing sweeps and rounded lettering was unmistakably feminine. The script spoke about the person's mental state and the fact no evidence could be found for the trauma's he repeatedly stated were visited upon his person at a young age. When medicinal and herbal remedies failed, the document went on to describe he was responding well to something called 'The Treatment'. Although no information was given as to what this constituted. Frustrated, he replaced the notes in the rack and withdrew another sizable portion. As he read them, he again came across references to the 'The Treatment', but try as he might, he could not seem to find a suitable explanation of what it was.

He put all of the notes back and scanned the rest of the names on the current rack, trying to find another name or title of significance. After a few minutes searching, he located a suitable rack. The name on the shelf read 'G.S. Andrews (Test Case 024 - RAP)'.

The first set of documents was a formal notification of sanity, signed by a person known as Administrator Smithson and was dated the eleventh of March eighteen ninety two. Administrator Smithson's writing was formal and angular, a clear sign of masculinity. The spacing between the words suggested hands that required moving regularly during writing and pointed to a heavier set individual, perhaps even a portly gentleman.

The second set of documents was bound by a heavier piece of card, on which the words 'Treatment – Test Patient 002' had been printed in thick, blue ink. He flung the backing card open and began to pour through the document contents, but to his dismay found all references to the Treatment blacked out. Page after page spoke about the benefits seen in its use, before details pertaining to its exact nature were blotted out.

He held a sheet up to the naked flame of the lamp, hoping to be able to see an imprint of the quill marks through the thick paper. "Dear Lord! Who would beset perspicacity so?" he said, his frustration boiling over.

"Levi!" a woman's voice snapped. "Lower your tone and cage your tongue in front of our guests."

Thaddeus' head snapped round to the voice and he found himself staring out in amazement across a finely laid table. He sat in a picture perfect dining room with a stern faced, yet beautifully presented woman opposite. To his right and left, two other couples sat, all of whom now stared, mouth agape, in his direction. He recognised no one. His mind still spinning, he looked down at his attire and found he was pleasantly well dressed for such an obviously formal event.

"You will have to forgive Levi," the woman continued, in an almost regal accent, "his work can be a terrible strain sometimes. He means no ill."

"It is quite alright, M'Lady." replied one of the male guests. "His work cannot be easy on him, and I for one can easily tolerate the odd misplaced word in return for the handsome salary being involved in this venture will bring!"

The statement was met with a round of guffaws from the guests seated at the table.

Thaddeus did not know what was going on. Only that he was more uncomfortable than he had ever been. "If I may be excused." he said, as he lifted himself gingerly from his chair.

He quickly scanned the room and located what he assumed to be the exit and, nodding to those seated at the table, stepped through.

He found himself in a ludicrously opulent hallway, lined with all manner of exquisite art and finery from all corners of the globe. Leaning against the thick wooden frame of the door, he attempted to make sense of what was going on. Even through the broth his thoughts had become, he had to order his world. He checked his pockets. There was a golden pocket watch and a snuffbox in one and in the other... his mind froze, as he drew the soft, leather bound journal from his pocket and turned it in his hand. He looked around the hallway as a new daze settled over his consciousness. He tried valiantly to keep his composure, as a wave of nausea swept over him. He spied a narrower door and, hoping it would contain an indoor rest room or some manner of servant galley where he could fight off his queasiness without disturbance, he hurried toward it.

He snatched at the handle and flung it open. Almost without pause or recognition, he made his way across the neat kitchen area, jogged over to the beautifully square Belfast sink in the far work surface, and proceeded to vomit. He gagged and struggled for breath, as he fought wave after wave of continued malady, before slumping to the cold, stone floor exhausted.

His mind raced with questions, but no answers came. Was he going insane? He plunged the thought back down into his core. It would not do to bemoan his situation. He should gather his composure and begin to work his way toward an empirically assessed rationale. One would be present; it simply had to be. Logical determination, devoid of emotional clutter, was the only course.

Only a few moments later, a high-pitched whistle coming from the opposite wall spiked his slowly lowering heart rate once more. He carefully looked out over the enormous oaken table dominating the middle of the room and across to where the noise was issuing from. Mesmerised, he staggered to where an old, copper kettle sat atop a gas fired oven. He looked at the kettle. He stared at its intricate handle and down its pitted edges. He picked it from the oven top, its warmth giving chaste feeling to his skin. Lost in a dreamlike deliberation, his eyes scanned downward, following the trail of his thought along the oven's lines.

"Are you alright Doctor Thaddeus?" a voice asked, quietly, from behind him.

He spun to see Walter stood no more than a few feet away, holding a flickering oil lantern in his hand.

"You were just stood facing the doorway is all, Doctor Thaddeus. I thought mayhap you'd had a fright."

He looked around. He was back in the records room, holding an oil lantern in one hand and the journal of O'Reilly in the other. "I'm perfectly disposed, thank you Wagstaff." he lied, breathing hard. "I take it you have a purpose in disturbing me?"

"I do doctor." said Walter, excitedly. "Mister Tirney has found something."

Chapter 10

Walter walked Thaddeus back to the room he and Alouicious were exploring, mentally noting the twitch that seemed to have settled into his companion's otherwise fluid motions. He was not certain, but Thaddeus appeared to be struggling with something, and it was affecting his ability to function.

Thaddeus reminded him of the doctors treating him when he was a young man. He was tall and well built, with a strong chin that propped up a purposefully lustrous moustache. Although probably just into his thirties, his skin was clean; not pitted with the telltale marks of childhood infection. He looked and acted like a well-bred and educated man, but he now knew that was not all he was.

Back when he was a youth, Walter had become insular to the point where he would not even go out of the house. In an attempt to make him a man, his father sent him away to receive treatment for his ailment. He could remember the place well. It was one of the only memories his mind would recover.

It was a dark and foreboding building, built on an austere prominence in the hills surrounding his town. Before his incarceration, he remembered looking up at the building as it loomed over their town. When the storms came, as they often did to the coast, it looked like it was the palace of the devil himself.

He pleaded with his parents not to send him; to not let his malediction become his torture. However, neither his father nor his mother paid him heed; they said he need to be rid of afflictions if he was to progress as a man.

Over the next three years, he was probed, beaten, shocked, bled, dosed, and habitually starved. All this torture meted out by nurses and doctors who seemed to care little about what was wrong with him, and greatly about the devices and methods they would apply to try to cure him.

One treatment they seemed to draw great pleasure from repeating was to place him in a cold bath in the middle of the common room. It was as if they knew what situation would extract the most pain. The other young adults would point and laugh at his listless, shivering form; fuelling his desire to remove himself from their presence. If he even so much as lifted from the base of the bath, nurses would come and drag him around the building; parading his nakedness for all to see. To a boy of his frailty, it was a hideous application of power, and one he slowly had to find a way of dealing with.

He remembered rocking himself to sleep on the firm, coarse bed of his new home. He prayed every day to be released from the hell his life had become, but there was never any answer.

In the end, the constant, unrelenting abuse he endured forced him deeper into himself. It was the only way to find solace. He found refuge in books, most of them scientific in nature, as hospital rules would not allow social literature, and slowly receded from the world. He cut off his ties to his emotions; an automaton by day to endure the suffering, and a student of the page by night to maintain his fleeting grasp on sanity. He could not remember quite how, but one day it was over and he was free. Free enough at least, and possessing enough faculty, to know something dark stirred in his newfound companion.

As they arrived at the small office, Thaddeus composed himself and strode in with an unflustered air. "What have you found, Mister Tirney?"

Alouicious squatted on a chair at a desk in the room, looking every inch a monkey dressed in rags. His strange eye flicked up at the entry of Thaddeus and he quickly moved from the chair and scampered on all fours out of the way, pausing only briefly to motion toward the desk's surface with a crooked arm.

Thaddeus walked over, dusted the chair with his palm, and sat down. There, on the surface, were a collection of letters and a small, golden pocket watch. "So which of these items holds interest, Mister Tirney?" he said, shuffling the assortment.

Alouicious skittered over to the desk, cautiously moved the papers, picked out one, and held it at arm's length. As Thaddeus snatched it from his grasp, he scurried away into the corner of the room.

"A legal correspondence, Mister Tirney? What, pray-tell, would be interesting about this, I wonder?"

Walter knew the answer all too well. As Thaddeus began to scan down the page, he shuffled back toward the door. He knew the response to the words would not be good. As he read on, Thaddeus' demeanour changed. He could see the rage begin to build in his eyes, and at the page's end, his anger rose to the surface and manifested itself with a powerful bash of the desk.

Walter knew the contents of the letter. It was from Walsh and Conroy, a solicitor's. It was addressed to Administrator Smithson and stated, in no uncertain terms, one of his employees was not who he claimed to be and strongly suggested the immediate sectioning of the individual based on the grounds of diminished capacity to act in accordance with the rules of moderate society.

Thaddeus could not be a doctor who worked at the Institute. The letter was regarding him.

Walter watched as Thaddeus sat at the desk, a clenched fist pressed against his pouted lips and the letter trembling slightly in the other. For any normal man, this revelation would be hard enough. However, for a man of Thaddeus' undoubted mental stability, the outcome could not be predicted.

Without warning, Thaddeus stood and advanced on Alouicious, who attempted to scamper round the outskirts of the office toward the door. As he bounded, Thaddeus snapped out a leg and kicked him in the midriff with a mighty boot. The force of the blow sent Alouicious flying through the air and into the book cabinets on the far wall with a howl. He crashed into the wooden frame and slumped to the floor like a wounded animal, loose books and pages showering down from the shelves like rain.

"I will not tolerate these deceptions!" said Thaddeus, bellowing and turning to glare at Walter. "Do you understand me?"

Walter nodded and bowed his head, reflexively preparing himself for an assault.

"Whoever has deposited me in this place has left this information here to make it look as though I should be incarcerated. Maybe they even wished to blame me for what has happened. I am not certain. It should be our first priority to establish what is going on, not to start to blame one another with letters of an obviously forged nature. Now pick up Mister Tirney and go and find something useful to us!"

Walter ran across and warily lifted Alouicious up from the floor. He was badly winded, and a slight trickle of blood from his mouth belied the damage done internally.

Never looking back as he left the small office, Walter turned toward the kitchen. He would take Alouicious somewhere where he could make sure he was fit to continue, before they finished their search.

Chapter 11

Alouicious sat in the kitchen cradling the mug of water Walter had given him and rubbed his side. Three cracked ribs. He knew it, even without looking. He did not know how he knew; just that it was not always the case.

He could remember with fondness his early childhood. He lived in Oxford. His house was grand and his parents were young and successful. His father held a position of some authority in banking. It was a well-paid position, and one that allowed his mother to be free from the stresses or work. Their family were part of the newly emerging middle class and Alouicious was proud of it. They had chambermaids and a cook who resided in the spare rooms of their house. They went on holidays to exotic countries and he went to the very best school money could afford. Life was carefree and easy, and he felt loved and secure.

Then it all changed.

His father was part of a society of sorts. Businessmen would come to the house once a week and meet in his private chambers. They would talk for hours and Alouicious was repeatedly informed they must not be disturbed. Even through this warning, he would hide at the top of the stairs and await the men's arrival. The feeling that what he was doing was somehow wrong and dangerous, only heightening his ambition to repeat the feat, week after week. He would lie, still as a mouse against the plush carpet on the first floor landing, and peer down at the front door as the men arrived. As he grew accustomed to each of their faces, he would take great interest in the arrival of anyone new; as rare as such an event was. Every new faced looked tense and harassed at their arrival, and he assumed this was because they were always late, arriving a good half-hour after the rest of the men.

One individual however, always stood out. He came dressed in garb that would not look out of place on a priest. He was large and his laugh sounded like it came from a French horn. He could tell his father respected the man above all the others. He was the only man his father would answer the door for, personally. He was sure he even saw his father bow slightly as he arrived. It was a mark of respect given to no one else.

Just before the events that changed his life forever, things slowly altered in his idyllic little corner of the world. Arguments, thing that never occurred between his parents, broke out. At first, they were sporadic, but over time, their frequency grew, until they were so regular that if an evening went by without one starting it was an aberration from normality.

His mother's once perfect, beautiful visage became drawn and old. At one time, she would come up to his room every evening after his bath. She would read him a story, her voice soft and soporific, and would tuck him in with a kiss. At the end, it was all she could do to look at him and manage a smile.

His father would spend less and less time in the house, and when he was there, their only conversations would be about his schooling. How was he doing? Was he still top of the class? Was he sure he still wanted to be a chemist? Should he not consider studying to be part of the new fields of oil or electricity? His father repeatedly told him it was in those fields where all the money in science would be made in his life. It was emotionless contact, born only of the need, rather than the want, to do so.

One evening, after a particularly violent row, he was escorted up the stairs by one of the house's maids. By happenstance, he looked back into the hallway and caught a glimpse of his parents. His mother was sobbing and his father was holding her close and stroking her hair. His face was red and his eyes glistened; a clear sign he too was on the verge of shedding a tear. As he stared back at his father, he caught his look and his frown softened. He gazed at him in a way not seen in months and mouthed three words now etched into his mind forever, as he kissed his mother on the head; 'I love you'.

Confused, the maid hurried him into his room and began to remove strips of oak flooring from the side of his bed. To his amazement, inside the cavity exposed, a plate of food and a blanket were already laid out.

"You have to get in here and stay here, Master Tirney." the old maid said. "You have to stay quiet, no matter what you hear and you have to promise me for your mother that you'll be brave."

He opened his mouth to question the request, as the sound of someone knocking at the front door echoed into the room.

"You have to be quick, Master Tirney." the maid said, grabbing his arm and forcing him into the small space. "Please do as your mother asks. Do not leave here under any circumstances." She pushed him into the recess and began to cover him with the removed planks. Once the boards were in place, he could hear something, perhaps a rug of some kind, dragged over the top of where he lay.

Only a few moments later, he was alone in the dark confines of the space. He could only assume this was what being buried must be like.

He heard the front door open. He heard men shouting. He heard his mother scream. Then he heard three loud bangs.

Shivering and panicked, he waited for anything else. Every now and again, he heard more bangs and more shouting, but eventually everything went still; the screaming replaced by muffled chat, too quiet to be audible through the thick floorboards.

It was difficult to pick out, but he was sure someone was searching, room by room. Eventually, his fears were realised when the heavy clump of sturdy boots on wood closed on the door to his room. The oak creaked under the careful steps. He wanted to cry, but he would not; not for his mother's sake. The sounds came into the room. He could hear whomever it was kneel down above him, presumably checking under the bed for his presence. He could smell them. He could pick out the scent of cheap tobacco clinging to their rain soaked garments. He could almost taste it in their breath, as it drifted between the gaps of the boards. Nevertheless, he remained silent.

Whoever it was, they trashed his room. Emptying wardrobes and sending draws clattering across the floor, before another figure came into the room.

"Any sign of the boy?" the new figure asked, in a low, measured tone.

"None." the figure in the boots responded. "He's not here. They must have been warned we were coming."

"Then we check the houses of their next of kin. We go to everyone they know if we have to."

The figures left the room. Once more, he heard the front door open and close, and the house adopted a silence it perhaps may never have experienced before.

Terrified, he nibbled at the food left for him, before nervous exhaustion claimed him into nightmare-filled sleep.

The following morning, he was not sure when, thirst drove him to movement. Silence had been his solitary companion in the floor for hours, and taking the risk, he pushed the boards out from above him. The scene in his house was one of total devastation. He ran from bedroom to bedroom, looking for anyone, but all he found was smashed furniture and emptied cupboards. There was no avoiding it; he would have to go down.

He stood at the top of the stairs and looked out toward the door. It was closed. He could not hear anything in the house. Pushing aside his trepidation at what he might find, he slowly began to creep downward. Only a few nerve jangling steps into his descent, his gaze fell upon the scene that would change him forever. There, lain sprawled across the floor of the hallway, surrounded by a pool of blood and gore, were his parents.

Ignoring everything, he ran to the foot of the stairs. His mother's limp form lay face down in the ooze with his father atop her. His father's arm still wrapped around his mother in vain protection.

He fell to his knees in the mire. The squidgy, ochre juices squirmed through his woollen trousers and reddened his skin, as he looked at his parent's lifeless forms.

One bullet had torn his mother's face in twain and the sight of it made him recoil and gag. A pair of large, encrusted holes in his father's suit jacket showed where the bullets that killed him exited his torso.

He clasped the material of his father's suit and squeezed as hard as his soul would allow, howling out into the vacant house. He dropped his head onto his father's back and threw his arms over the morbid pile, ignorant of the smell of decay already festering there, and sobbed.

He could not remember how long it was before a hand, delicate and emotive, placed itself against his shoulder. He bolted up at the contact, faltering as he tried to stand, and landed on his backside. Still panicked, he attempted to crawl away from the hulking man standing to his side.

"You do not need to fear me, Master Tirney." said the figure. "My name is Thomas O'Reilly. Your father arranged for me to collect you."

He looked up and caught the soft expression of the man. His broad shoulders and weathered face bore the marks of military training and violence, but his expression belied no intent.

"I was hoping I would catch you before your eyes fell upon this, mayhap. But, I am afraid in that duty I have failed. Please, come with me so that I do not fail in another."

Alouicious did not move. He sat, frozen in place and stared at the man before him, his mind in total disarray.

"Please, Master Tirney. We have little time. I need to get you somewhere safe. It is my promise to your father." said O'Reilly, slowly inching forward and extending a hand. "Your father and mother loved you very dearly, Master Tirney. There is nothing that you, nor I, nor God himself can do to change what happened. All I can do now is make sure the love they bestowed upon you, and what they had to do because of that love, is not in vain."

Alouicious looked out at his parents again and then looked back at O'Reilly, cautiously extending a hand to meet his.

With that action, O'Reilly reached forward and picked him up as if he was a feather, putting an arm round him and carrying him like a rugby ball. "You must do as I ask, Master Tirney from now until you are safe. Come, we must make haste."

As O'Reilly jogged effortlessly out of the hallway and towards the back door, Alouicious took one last look at his parents. Love, pain, and hope left behind, as the remainder of his soul was dragged from his home.

"Are you trying to ignore me, Mister Tirney?" said Walter, still holding a cake out in front of him.

Alouicious came back from his daze, snapped out a hand, clutching a couple of slices in his grasp, and yanking them from the tray. He greedily consumed his food, gulping down the last lingering drops of his water as he did so, still trying to push the pain of his memory back from whence it came.

"So you were ignoring me? That's good. I thought you were having a problem."

Walter was like an open book. Alouicious could tell something terrible happened to the man and yet, just for fleeting seconds, he could see the dirty hand of hate in his eyes. In deference to his situation, he shrugged, unsure the palliative motion would hold his companion's eagerness for actual response long.

"You took something from the desk, did you not?" asked Walter, sitting down at the other end of the table. "I noticed two items on it when we first entered the room and when I returned, there was but one."

He stopped his repast and looked Walter in the eye. He knew. Shrugging once more, he reached into his pocket, withdrew a snuffbox, and placed it on the table.

Walter seemed discomforted by the cake now smeared over its surface, but soon found the nerve to pick the object up.

The box itself was an odd-looking item. Made from porcelain, its edges were inlaid with gold, and ivory animals adorned its surface.

Walter studied the object for a moment before he held it to his ear and shook it.

Alouicious already knew what the snuffbox contained, but he found Walter's attempt to decipher its contents amusing. Involuntarily, and much to the obvious disgust of Walter, he began to smile.

"Alright." Walter snapped, turning the box in his hand to open the delicate lid. "I did not know you knew what it contained."

Alouicious watched as Walter opened the box and bemused, studied its meagre contents. He sighed, drawing a stern look from his companion.

"It's powder. All this contains is a white powder."

Alouicious' mind was lost in thought at the puzzlement Walter was experiencing. It's cocaine Walter. It's used as an analgesic. People suspect it is not as good for you as modern medicine would have us believe. They say it is addictive. But what was the point? He sighed again. That was not even relevant.

"This would be much easier to understand if you said something once in a while, Mister Tirney." said Walter, the demon in his stare returning.

Alouicious shook his head and reached over the table. He extended a warped finger and pointed inside the lid. Almost instantly, he knew Walter understood.

There, etched in fine lettering, was a dedication.

To our darling boy 'Alouicious'
We will always love you

Chapter 12

Thaddeus waited for the two men to exit the room before he turned back to the desk. As soon as they were out of sight, his hand trembling, he reached out to the golden pocket watch and picked it up. He did not want to make a scene when they were in the room, but it was exactly the same watch he saw in his waking dream. Involuntarily, he reached into his jacket to make sure it was not there. It was not.

The pocket watch was weighty. It had to be solid gold. It was probably worth a fortune. He turned it over in his hands, remarking of the fine detailing running around its edges. Unsure of what to do for the best, he fingered the delicate clasp and the lid flipped open.

The interior of the watch was even grander than the exterior. Its mechanism beset with jewels. Rubies glistened through the glass façade in the clockwork. Diamonds sat precariously on the tips of the hands. Each number on its dial created from emeralds and everything layered in gold. It was an astounding work.

He looked at the inside panel of the lid and noticed an inscription. Bringing the lantern closer, he could pick out the subtle script.

To LAW
For everything that you mean to me

He recognised the inscription, but it made no sense. What did it mean? "Who, in the name of the all that is holy, is Law!" he shouted, his frustration boiling over again.

"You are asking me!" a female voice said, to his side. "It is I who should be inquiring who would have given you such a fine gift!"

He turned to the sound and once more found himself in an unfamiliar place. He sat in a neat drawing room, next to roaring fire. His chair upholstered in the finest velvet and soft to the touch. Books lined vast shelves, encasing the room from floor to ceiling, and there, directly in his view, was the woman he was betrothed to; Jennifer Grahams. She was dressed in a flowing, brightly patterned dress and her ginger hair was down; allowed to stream around her slender, aristocratic neck. She stared, puzzled and alarmed, awaiting a response.

"I… I…" stammered Thaddeus, unable to comprehend what was happening.

"Oh, do not bother yourself." said Jennifer, aghast. "I try Thaddeus, I really try. But you make it so difficult sometimes."

Thaddeus composed himself as quickly as he could, reaching out for her with his hand. "Please do not think of me so, Jennifer." he said, uttering the only things his mind wanted to say. "I love you."

"I think that is a highly inappropriate response, Doctor Thaddeus." said a deep, masculine voice.

Thaddeus shook his head and stared. The scene had changed again. Now he was standing in a majestic room. On the far wall, pictures of the stars twinkled against a blue background, surrounded by shapes and symbols he could barely recognise. To his left and right, long rows of benches pointed toward him. Each row crammed with men wearing strange purple and red sashes, who gasped in unison at his comment.

In front of him was a lectern. On it sat a hefty, open tome and behind it stood a burley, equally strangely attired man. The man's face warped in shock, his hand slowly retracting. He was sure the man was Administrator Smithson.

He lowered his head in disbelief and noticed one of his neat, silken, trouser legs was hitched up to his knee; exposing his stocking suspenders to all. Suddenly, and without reason, he knew where he was. "Majoris lepus septim arrus." he said, not knowing where the strange language was coming from. "Pilus mortimi ex acratis es tempi."

The man stopped what he was doing and looked at him. He glowered, showing his teeth and moved from behind the lectern. "Your little display impresses no-one." he hissed, getting as close to Thaddeus as he could, and speaking so that no-one else could hear. "If it were not for your undoubted expertise, I would have you expelled from the society immediately. Think yourself lucky you have the abilities you do, doctor." he said, stepping back and cracking into a smile. "Cajous Thaddeus imparti exultas!" he shouted, raising his hands to everyone in the room.

At the words, which somehow he knew meant 'In Thaddeus we trust', the congregation stood and cheered, their applause filling the space.

The sound rattled through him like an earthquake. It dislodged his emotion from its carefully entrenched sanctum and sent it pouring forth into his consciousness. "I do not require or accept your adulation!" he screamed, his exasperation at fever pitch, as he lifted his head and dared the heavens to swallow him whole.

His only response was silence. He lowered his eyes and found he was back in the room where he found the pocket watch. Wagstaff and Mister Tirney looking worriedly at him from the open doorway.

He waited for a moment, unsure of when or what the present was anymore, before he spoke again. "Have you located anything of peculiar circumstance for my inspection?" The two men just stood and stared. Mister Tirney at least having the respect to divert his gaze. "Then I may presuppose you have a great deal of work ahead of you." At the words, the two men slowly backed out of the room and continued across the corridor.

He slumped back into the chair by the desk and put his head in his hands. Controlling his emotions was always something he prided himself on. Now, here, in this most capricious of predicaments, his most treasured intellectual ally was slowly eroding. He must find out what was happening and soon, before he succumbed to whatever manner of confusion beset him.

As he sat and thought, he began to feel a strange buzzing in his head and across his skin. He sat up and intuitively knew another blackout was on its way. His continued contemplation would no doubt have to wait.

Chapter 13

Walter woke up on the cold, stone floor of the corridor to the strangest of feelings. It was as if something was crawling around his ear. He opened an eye, the hazy, dimly lit space taking time to resolve into focus. There was a shadowy form in front of him. He closed his eyes once more and then reopened them, hoping that the action would clear his fuddle. It did.

Squatting on the ground next to him was Alouicious. As he began to move, the man huffed, pulling up his britches and stepping away.

Panic and anger ran through him. He did not want to know what Alouicious was attempting to do. He sat up and spat into his hand, trying to wipe away any residue left about his face by his companion's inappropriate behaviour. "You're an animal, Mister Tirney!" he yelled, eliciting a light yelp from Alouicious. "Get on with you!"

Alouicious did not baulk at the order and trotted off down the corridor on all fours like a dog. Good for him. Walter was not a violent person, but there were limits.

He stood up and checked himself over for any more signs of Alouicious' activity, but found none. Happy to have stopped the actions before they escalated, he took stock of his surroundings

He sat a long way down one end of the corridor. From the end near the kitchen, especially with only a limited amount of light available, it was impossible to see how far it ran. Now, only a few strides from the other end, he could see the corridor terminated with a door.

Thaddeus ordered them not to look for the inconsequential, and although he still wished to know more about his overbearing companion, he would take it as an opportunity to do some exploration of his own. If Thaddeus did not want irrelevance, then looking in more offices would not be to their advantage. He would go through this door.

He strode over and tried the handle. It opened with a light click and a cool breeze rushed round his feet. It lapped high enough to flicker the precarious flame of his lamp and he instinctively wrapped a hand round the flue to protect it, cutting out its radiance.

When he removed his hand, the brightness seemed to fall into the space and his eyes struggled to make out shapes. Slowly, transiently, forms began to resolve in the dark passageway beyond.

He could see the corridor continued for about ten feet before it turned into a set of stone steps, descending into the black. Carefully, he took a couple of strides, to judge how far down they went.

The air breezed up the stairs and flapped at the cloth of his trousers, as he leaned forward and peered down. A shimmer of shapes greeted his view, as the lantern struggled with the breeze, and its faltering light danced twisted shapes across the high ceiling. Everything seemed to be moving under the cascading glow. The walls shimmered with orange and the floor seemed to crawl. But there, just at the end of the flight, was a ball or orb of some kind. It swayed lazily as it drifted out of sight, illuminating the corridor in an almost holy glow.

He rubbed his eyes, not sure of what he was seeing, as somewhere out in the depths, a low groan sounded. It drifted on the breeze and only added to his dilemma. The noise was sonorous and stood the small hairs on the back of his neck to attention, firing his apprehension. He strained as

56

the noise intensity grew, leaning forward and attempting to localise his lantern's light on its source.

Before he could react, a grey shape, howling like a banshee, snarled up the stairs and crashed into his sternum. The impact was so heavy, the lantern flew out of his grasp and down the stairs, and its fragile glass casing shattered as it tumbled off into the inky darkness. His head snapped back as his feet left the floor and he slammed into the ground, the back of his skull making cruel contact with hard stone.

Dazed, his limbs struggled to put up any resistance to the assault that followed, as he felt blow after blow land about his chest and face. The figure, whoever it was, was unrelenting. He could feel their nails, sharp like knives, digging trails of flesh from him with every swipe. Beaten and stunned, his mind finally gave up the struggle and he drifted off into a sea of black.

When he awoke, he was surprised to find himself on a soft duvet in a small bedroom. Looking around quizzically, and checking his torso for the injuries he felt sure he received, he was astonished to find he was uninjured. He was even more amazed to realise he recognised where he was. It was his childhood home.

He stepped out of the bed and across to the simple window in the room. Flinging back the curtains, he looked outside and breathed in the salty air. It was good to be home. He gazed at the mosaic sky above; a clear sky with fluffy white clouds. A homely sky, if ever there was one.

In the street below, children ran and played, each one a blur of motion in uniform. Uniform? He turned and scanned his room. There, sat atop the ottoman bridging the gap at the end of his bed was his; neat, tidy, and ready to wear.

He remembered this day somehow. It was Monday.

Monday mornings were not his favourite time and his cacophonic yawn reflected this. At this point in his childhood, if that was really what this was, he had not yet settled at his new school and could not, for the life of him, determine why his father suggested it in the first place.

Suddenly, an over-zealous cuff about the head brought him to his senses. "You'll be late again Salty. Better move your pathetic rear, 'cos if I be late because of you again, I will blacken your other eye!"

This voice was one he recognized and despised. It was his brother, John. Big John, as he was known in school. He was a renowned bully and tormentor who took an almost zealous pleasure from giving and receiving pain, particularly from those of a weaker disposition.

"Leave him be, Johnny. I have told you before, pick on someone your own size!" said his mother, as she appeared on the landing through the open door. "And get yourselves washed and out the door in the next ten minutes, you're setting a bad impression already. You were late twice last week."

"Salty Walty, you're such a prat. A tiny, scrawny runt at that." said John, almost in song. "Why are you such a weed? An embarrassment is what you are!"

Walter could not understand why, but he started to get dressed, ignoring the barrage of abuse. He was familiar with it. So, flinging his clothes on as fast as he could, he hastily buckled his shoes and darted out of the room.

He and John were still chewing porridge, as they hurried down the cobbled street towards their school. As they approached, the sign 'St. Theresa's Catholic School for Boys' greeted them by iron gates.

As he remembered it, most boys at the school held board and lodgings within the grounds. To them, it was more like their permanent home than a place of education. However, Misses Wagstaff heard rumblings about unorthodox practices in the school and a rumour spread that one boy died in unexplained circumstances. Based on this, she ensured their new dwellings would be in earshot of the school. Their father was not happy with this choice, as he felt the boys' pranks and squabbles around the house interrupted his work. Nevertheless, the decision was made.

Running as fast as he could, he was first through the open gate and could see another boy closing the entrance door behind him. They hurried down the corridor to the main assembly room where the morning register was already being called.

Being last on the register had its advantages; they might just make it in time. Met with several stern glares from the sisters at the side of the hall, the Wagstaff brothers sat down quietly on the floor towards the back.

Catholic schools held a reputation of being strict and over-bearing, and none more so than schools run by Irish nuns. The family's roots were in Ireland, in Enniskerry near Dublin, but due to their Father's work commitments, they spent most of their childhood in the north of England.

"Thomas, Conroy!" said the stoic faced Sister Rose.

Sister Rose was a large and powerful looking woman. Her hair held in a large bun and her hips over-sized, forcing her to wobble as she walked. A mole on the side of her face, sprouted thick hairs, and her eyes, even for a woman of only forty years or so, were surrounded by lines and furrows. She was a wicked looking testament to the power of god.

"Present Maam" a voice whimpered.

"Thomas, Delaney!" A silent pause ensued. "Delaney Thomas, are you present? Delaney Thomas, answer me boy!" A second silence indicated that Delaney was either not present, had been struck deaf, or was on a mission to meet his maker. Either way, Sister Rose was not impressed, and summoned over Sister Molloy and whispered something in her ear indicating she must find the errant child immediately. A severe punishment would be the cure to his tardiness, as in all cases.

When their time came, Walter was nervous. He did not know what was going on. He had to act in character, but it was so long ago he was not sure he could remember quite how and this showed in his warbled response to the register in comparison to John's almost military retort.

A moment later, all the calm and relief gained by passing this first test was instantly shattered, as John espied an opportunity of mirth and, leaning to one side to clear an exit from his buttocks, sounded his horn.

Sister Rose stared at her audience in disbelief. Some of the boys sniggered whilst others hung their heads to avoid the eye contact that could become a catalyst for disaster.

"Who is responsible!" said Sister Rose. "Now, answer me or you will all suffer, I swear to bloody Jesus that you will be sorry for your sins!"

One of the boys turned and gave a look toward he and his brother, and several heads followed suit; simulating a finger of blame. John stared hard into the boy, who was bent on baring witness; his bloodshot eyes telling full-well what he would do if the boy spoke up.

However, one boy was not willing to suffer for someone else's silence and raised his hand. "Maam. It was Walter Wagstaff, Maam."

Walter's mind raced and his face went pale, as another boy seconded the false accusation.

"Stand up boy and own up for your sins." said John, as he whacked him across the back.

All the neighbouring boys were now giggling. Even those who knew the truth backed the verdict. Guilty by association.

Walter knew what was coming. The thought of it terrified him. Sister Rose needed no further evidence. She saw it as important to deliver punishment as a deterrent. Making an example, the primary objective. Whether he was truly guilty was incidental. However, there was something else.

Now he was older, he could assess more readily the looks on people's faces when they thought. When he was young, Sister Roses' stare seemed like nothing more than rage. Now he had chance to witness it again, he saw it for what it was. It was lust.

He began to cry. Hideous memories flooded back to him, as Sister Rose stood and made her way over. She grabbed his arm and began dragging him toward the private offices at the back of the hall.

The memories came in showers. From now on, once this first seal was broken, this would be his torture for even the most trivial of transgressions. And all the while, John, perfect mother's-boy John, sat and laughed.

Even though the events were something he knew he endured himself, his heart went out to the boy he was. This should never happen to a fourteen year old.

Sister Rose looked anxious, as if sceptical about what she was about to take part in, as she threw him onto the rug before the stone fireplace in the office.

He looked around the room. He could remember the poker being used on his back, of hot candle wax being poured over his scars, of the horrible contacts of flesh he was forced into, and the cessation of his innocence. It was his private pain. He was too meek and embarrassed to tell anyone about it.

Sister Rose walked to the small desk at the side of the room and picked up the wooden paddle laying there. She sat in her chair, smiled a wicked smile, and opened her legs. With a light tap of the paddle against her thigh, she began to hitch up her petticoat.

Waiting for the vengeance of the cloth to be exacted upon his form, Walter closed his eyes and began to scream.

Chapter 14

Alouicious shook Walter for all he was worth, but the sobbing simply would not abate.

When he heard the crash of the lantern, he made his way back out into the corridor and saw Walter on the floor. He writhed as if being attacked, but there was no one present. As he approached, the wriggling stopped and for a few minutes, Walter simply lay motionless. Half curled into a ball with one arm pointing skyward. Unsure of what to do, he nudged and prodded him, his constant eagerness urging him to do more. Nevertheless, he resisted.

When, out of nowhere, Walter began to howl like a wounded animal and coil himself up like a rope, he began to rock him. When the howl turned to sobbing, his shaking became more and more fevered. However, it was no use.

Tired from the effort and frustrated of not making more of the circumstances, he let him go and sat on the floor by his side. Before, finally, a deep voice snapped him out of his confusion.

"What is wrong with the wretch now?" asked Thaddeus, as he drew up behind him.

Not for the first time, he shrugged a response.

"Well, you must have seen something, Mister Tirney. What happened?"

He turned and looked Thaddeus over. His once demanding, powerful persona was losing its edge and his words seemed less sure. Understanding Thaddeus was also struggling to retain control, he shrugged again; the fear of reprisal once held for inaction, diminishing with every passing moment.

"What worth are you to me, Mister Tirney?" asked Thaddeus, as he knelt down and inspected Walter.

He did not respond. He sat and thought about what was happening and how he just wanted to roam the vacant halls to continue his explorations. His companions were dolts. Neither one possessed any real fire in their thoughts. They were inconsequential. He should leave.

"And what, pray-tell, are you thinking about?" asked Thaddeus, turning. "Stop your idling and make haste to the kitchen and bring me a mug of water. Wagstaff is in shock."

He looked at Thaddeus again. He had two choices: assist or use this as an excuse to leave. If it were not for Walter, he would take the second option.

Something about Walter's affliction reminded him of his own. It may be too late to help himself, but maybe it was not too late for Walter. Picking himself up with a huff, he hurried off to the kitchen to retrieve what was requested.

When he returned, Walter was sat against the wall in the corridor, his head in his hands. Thaddeus squatted by his side, one arm pressed against his shoulder. He scrambled over and handed Walter the mug, eliciting a pleasing smile as payment.

"Thanks Alouicious. I'm not sure what happened there. I thought I was somewhere else."

"You've been like that all day, Wagstaff." said Thaddeus, rising to his feet. "Now, should we see what is actually down these stairs? Rather than spectres and ghosts."

Walter finished the mug of water and tried to stand, but his emotions had purged his muscles of energy and he could barely manage to lean against the wall.

"It appears I will be assisting Wagstaff for the time being, Mister Tirney." said Thaddeus, grasping Walter tightly round the waist and heaving him to his feet. "That would make you our forward scout. There was a spare lantern in the room I was just in. You should retrieve it."

Alouicious looked at the pair and judged the suggestion sensible at least. After a quick detour to retrieve the lantern and light it from the one Thaddeus carried, he made his way over to the doorway.

The air was thick with the smell of the lamp oil coating the stairs. As he tentatively made his way downward, he moved as many of the shards of glass from out of the way as he could, lest Walter cut himself.

The stairs descended down for at least a hundred feet. Every twenty feet or so, another sconce would be on a wall and he took care to light them as he went, to illuminate their progress.

When he reached the corridor stretching outward from the base of the stairs, he looked back. Thaddeus and Walter were making slow but measured progress. They would be at the bottom presently. The time gap gave him enough spare moments of free discovery. He held his breath and listened. He could hear nothing but the light hiss of the breeze drifting through the corridor. That was a shame. Exploration was much more fun with the living. Arbitrarily, he selected one of the three doors highlighted in the glow of his lantern and scurried to it.

The door was heavy set, with large iron hinges and sturdy metal rivets running through its construction. It was re-enforced. Curiosity piqued, he clawed at the handle, and the door creaked and groaned open.

A blinding flash of blue light and a gurgled howl later, Thaddeus and Walter watched from half way up the stairs as Alouicious' lantern flickered and went out.

Chapter 15

Thaddeus placed Walter carefully down on the steps and grabbed his lantern with his spare hand. "You will have to stay here, Wagstaff. I will go and see what has happened to Mister Tirney." The look on Walter's face to the comment said everything. He was terrified of the thought of being left alone. "I do not have time to give you salient argument about why this must be as it is, Wagstaff. Control yourself and your fear. I shall return presently."

Leaving Walter on the steps, he strode downward and quickly reached the bottom. In front of him was a long, straight corridor. On the floor, only ten feet ahead, lay Mister Tirney's lantern. It was on its side and no longer lit, but otherwise seemed undamaged. Just ahead of that, was an open door.

As he walked toward it and more of the doorway came into view, it became apparent there were feet protruding from the room beyond. Feeling his heart race as he approached, he could tell they unmistakably belonged to Mister Tirney. Increasing his pace to a jog, he was horrified to watch the feet slide into the room and door slam shut. Almost at a sprint, and oblivious to the dangers of his situation, he charged at the door and flung it open, barrelling into the room beyond.

"Surprise!" yelled a group of high-pitched voices, as he entered the fiercely lit space.

He skidded to a halt on the surprisingly shiny floor, his eyes struggling to adjust to the sudden change in brightness. Raising a hand to block out the majority of the glare disrupting his vision, he could make out the vague shapes of twenty or more people stood in an arc in front of him.

As his vision slowly returned to normal, he started to pick out his surroundings. He stood on a polished, parquet floor in a massive library space. Many thousands of tomes lined heavy, oaken shelves, interspaced at even intervals between enormous, arch-topped, windows dominating the wall opposite. On the wall to his right, carved into a marble plaque and hung above a gigantic fireplace, was a motto on a blue crest: 'Dominus Illuminatio Mea'.

His heart was pounding so hard he was sure it would be audible to everyone within earshot. He scanned the crowd of faces surrounding him. Intermingled between the numerous young people were the odd aged and wizened one. All were clapping and cheering. Above their heads, painted across what looked like a bed sheet, were the words 'Congratulations Thaddeus'.

He knew where he was. It was Oxford, his university.

"Three cheers for *Doctor* Levi Thaddeus!" one of the older men cried. "Hip Hip!"

"Hooray!" responded the gathered throng.

"Hip Hip!"

"Hooray!"

"Hip Hip!"

"Hoorah." said Thaddeus, meekly.

Yet more clapping and the revealing of a table laden down with an array of foods and sweets, dissolved the directed appreciation into the background murmur of chatter.

"Do not be so unbecoming of your achievements, Mister Thaddeus." one of the elders of the group said, as he made his way over.

The man wall tall and sported a long, grey beard, which hung over the top of his hand-knitted, green woollen jumper. His face was warm and inviting, and he held himself with an authority and grace not usually ascribed to someone as elderly. It was his housemaster, Professor Haviland.

"Are you alright, Levi? You look peculiarly distracted this fine evensong."

"I… I am…" he stammered, confounded by his predicament.

"Cat got your tongue? Well I never. For someone who has worked so hard and for so long to make good the benediction of their aptitude, you certainly do not seem comfortable with the fruits of your undertakings."

"I… I…" he tried, but the words would simply not come out.

"Oh my! Drink, my boy, and make merry. For by tomorrow's fleeting dawn, your voyage at our fine didactic facility will be at its end. It has been a pleasure to mould you into the man you have become. Make me proud, Levi."

He watched as his professor left to join the crowd. Perhaps he was right. A drink and some food may assist.

He made his way through the masses, most of whom he transitorily found association with in his crumbling memory, and over to the table. After selecting a slice of game pie, one of quiche, and a drink of cloudy lemonade, he tried to find a quiet corner in which to sit and think.

He sat alone for no more than a few moments before a young and smartly dressed youth joined him. The boy was no more than twenty-three and had long, flowing brown locks and perfect skin. His suit was immaculate and he reeked of French cologne. It was Cornelius Smithson, his supposed best friend.

"Are you packed and ready, Thaddeus?" asked Cornelius, smiling politely.

"For what?"

"For what indeed! For the rest of your existence,
Thaddeus! For the move to the country and your chance to
get into the wider favours of my father!"

He remembered now. All the way through university, he
had but one goal, to study science, become a doctor and get a
job with… His heart stopped. Tossing his plate to one side,
he frantically rummaged through his jacket pockets, looking
for the letters removed from the office.

"What has got into you today, Thaddeus? First, you turn
away Mary Whittingham, the Viscount Whittingham's
daughter I'll add, and one of the most deliriously entrancing
creatures ever to have been crafted by God's good hand.
Which could only been seen as blindness and not complete
insanity unless you were not aware, and you are, that you
could retire right now on the dowry her father would give
you if you accept her advances. Then you act as if you did
not even know where you were five minutes ago, and now
this. I think achievement has gone to your head."

He stopped scrambling through his pockets, leant over,
and grabbed Cornelius by his overly expensive lapels.
Snarling, he pulled him so they were facing each other,
eyeball to eyeball. "Tell me what is going on here!"

"Unhand me, you oaf!" a woman yelled, as a slap landed
squarely across his cheek.

The blow caught him off guard and he reflexively brought
a hand up to his stinging cheek. He looked around, unsure
of where the woman had come from and found he was
outside in a lush and serene park. The wind billowed lightly
across the freshly cut grass at his feet and the sweet scent of
summer flowers filled his nostrils.

The vision before him was serene. Mary Whittingham
stood silhouetted by the early morning sun. Her lustrous,
blonde hair tied loosely underneath her bonnet and her
faultless, white gown swaying gently in the breeze. She was

beautiful. If angels could cry tears of joy at their feats, they would upon gazing at her countenance.

He looked her in those perfect, wide, immersive eyes and saw the look of fear filling them. He wanted to hold her. He wanted to tell her he was sorry. He wanted her to know he had no choice.

Before he could utter a word, she spun and walked away.

He knew why she was angry. He remembered the day well. It was the morning before the surprise party. He brought her to the park to tell her they could no longer be together. He must do something first, and once it was complete, he would find her and they would live in peace and happiness.

When he told her, she cried. He could not remember why. She said she did not want him to follow the work he needed to complete. She said she needed him by her side. She said they should go away together, forget everything, and live somewhere else. However, he could not.

He could not remember if he ever got the chance to fulfil his promise, but as he could remember being engaged to Jennifer, it was no feat of presumption to assume it was not the case.

This was as close to true happiness as he ever got. It was a twisted and sick torment to make him relive it. He closed his eyes and wept, holding his hands over his ears to drown out the noise of his tears, as his emotions finally found a chink in the armour of his control and spilled over into everything.

With his eyes held shut, he never noticed the ball of blue fire as it drifted down the long, underground corridor. He never noticed it bob and sway as it flashed and crackled off the surface of everything it touched. And he never saw it spark out and strike him in the back; slamming him face first into the wall of the room and fall unconscious on top of the crumpled form of Alouicious.

Chapter 16

Walter sat terrified on the steps. He pulled his knees to his chest and snared them close with his arms. He comforted himself, as he once had before, by rocking on the cold, harsh stone.

There were two flashes. Two screams in the dark. Two sets of moans. Now silence.

He could not go down. He would not.

Hours passed, only god knowing how many, before he raised his head from its resting place between his arms and noticed the oil sconces in the wall were all but spent. Of the five lining the steps, only two still flickered and they too were not long from dissipating into stillness.

Alarmed, he looked up to the corridor above. It was pitch black. He looked down to the corridor below. It too dipped in inky stillness. He was out of options.

He wracked his mind. Did he go after his new friends and into the teeth of the monsters his mind told him were patrolling the deep of this place, or did he scurry like a rat to the surface? He had to make a choice.

He was cold and hungry. He needed the safety of his companions. Nevertheless, they could be dead. The images of the people seen on his journey would not let him be.

Gathering his courage into a ball, he held it to his breast and took a long calming lungful of air. He had to go down and help his friends. Death was everywhere, and he needed to get over his fear of it. Standing on trembling limbs, he slowly made his way down the steps.

He could feel anxiety flowing through him. It heated his blood and caused his skin to writhe. It was an awful sensation.

The light breeze blowing up the stairs, gusted passed his legs and tingled hairs, sending shivers of unpalatable sensations running through him. He stood, pressed against the wall at the foot of the flight, not daring to take the last step onto the corridor.

It was dark. Horrors lurked in every shadow and he could not shake the sensation someone was watching him. He strained against the failing light, hoping against hope to pick out anything he could recognise.

"Alouicious? Doctor Thaddeus?" he called out, timidly. "Alouicious?" his voice was like a child's, edgy with emotion.

When no response was forthcoming, he strained again into the corridor. There was something on the floor. Was it a lantern? He could not be certain. No, surely he could see a lantern. He needed that lantern, but what if it were broken. What if some demon of the depths held it on a piece of string, waiting to snare him as soon as he touched it?

He perch on the last step, one foot dangling toward the corridor's surface. If he could just get his mind to accept he needed the lantern, he would be fine. Yet, it would not let him go.

The light around him was getting darker by the moment. He could barely see anything. Looking back up the stairs, he saw another sconce now spent. Just one remained. Its pitiful flame barely lighting the rim of the bowl in which it sat. His time was out.

Screaming as loud as he could to scare away the monsters, he ran across to the lantern and picked it up. Without pause, he ran back to the stairs and up them, his heart pounding like timpani. Scrambling as he reached the delicate flame in the sconce, he opened the side of the lantern and pulled the wick to the fire. It spluttered, over-soaked in oil, and nearly doused it. With little time left, he put the wick in his mouth and tried to suck off the excess. The taste was foul. Now terrified and nauseous, he held the wick out once more.

Nothing.

The tiny, orange glow was burning his fingers, but the lantern would not light. He could smell his flesh searing and could feel the pain, but he drew the wick closer.

"Please!" he begged. "Please light."

With a joy that flowed throughout his entire body, he watch as the small wick flickered and caught. Nimbly, he wound it down to a sensible level and shut the cover. Slowly, as the oil heated and caught, the light increased. His world was now an oasis of brilliance in the black of night.

Leaning against the steps and breathing hard, he relaxed, allowing a giggle to escape at his achievements. He had done it. He had done it by himself. He was a hero. Now all that remained was to save his friends.

Gathering his newfound composure, he made his way to the foot of the stairs and looked down the corridor. Where once there were monsters, there was but stone.

Just ahead of where the lantern once was, an open door lay. He strode confidently towards it. No demon or spectre would stop him. As he turned and looked inside the room, he could see the forms of his friends piled atop one another. They were not moving.

Before he could act, a buzzing sound, like a distant swarm of bees, erupted in the corridor. As he turned toward the sound, he could see a ball of light, bluish and dancing, in the distance. Fingers of twisted fire leapt from it, as it passed the numerous doors lining the corridor. With each contact, fizzed crackles spat from the doors as response.

Almost as if it sensed his presence, the ball began to race toward him, as bolts of light arced over everything.

With only seconds remaining, he ran into the room and slammed the door shut. He backed away from the heavy frame and nearly stumbled over his friends, as his fear pushed him to the back wall.

Instantly, white tendrils spat between the bolts on the door and popped as they skirted the handle and hinges. The room lit up, as if the sun itself was present with him, and he drew an arm up to protect his face, fearing the end.

Then it was over. The sound passed and he was alone.

He stood and stared for a few minutes, fearing the ball's return. However, there was no repeat. Slowly, still with one eye on the door, he knelt down and checked his friends. From his reading, he knew where it was possible to check the heart still beat, and reaching round to both men's wrists was reassured to find this pulse was clear and strong on both.

He moved them from atop one another and placed them in positions of comfort against the back wall, checking as best he could for injuries. He assumed a similar position himself and relaxed. All he could do now was wait.

Chapter 17

Alouicious awoke in the back of a cart, entirely covered by a tattered cloth. He peered out from behind the sheet and could see the infinite, twinkling void of the heavens far above. He sat up and looked around. The cart travelled along a dusty track, pulled by a single horse and rider. As he stared, the man turned and smiled.

"I thought you'd be out for the entire trip, Master Tirney." said O'Reilly, his voice strong and reassuring. "Three days you've been out. Three solid, no less! Never in all my days have I seen anything like it."

He looked down at himself and back up at O'Reilly. He could vaguely remember this. It was the journey he took after the death of his parents, the journey to his new life.

"I know this has been tough on you, Master Tirney. But, you need to keep your strength up and keep being brave. There's some food by your side and water in the back of the cart if you want it. We're nearly there now though. I can smell the sea."

He lifted his head and breathed in. The ozone-laden air wafted into his nostrils and reminded him of holidays taken with his parents. His parents. He sniffled. It would not do to go over this again. Finding respite in action, he reached over and began to eat the sweet breads and fruits O'Reilly mentioned.

The track descended sharply and before long they were pulling up to the side of a quiet town, nestled between two rocky bluffs by the sea's edge. Soon after, they were slowing to a halt by a small cottage sat at the town's periphery.

O'Reilly jumped from the horse and stretched his limbs, before turning and placing a hand against his shoulder. "You just stay put for a moment, Master Tirney. I'll go and see if these good people are awake."

He watched, transfixed, as O'Reilly walked toward the door to the cottage and knocked, awaiting his response. A light sprung to life in an upstairs room, travelling through the house, before the door opened.

The woman who appeared was young and comely. She smiled at the realisation it was O'Reilly who broke her slumbers. He could not make out the conversation, but from the hugs and other familiar contacts the pair were making, a family bond would appear a sensible conclusion.

After a few moments discussion, O'Reilly and the woman came walking over.

"Master Tirney, this is Elizabeth, my younger sister."

"It is a pleasure to make your acquaintance." said Elizabeth, with a tender smile.

"Maam." he responded, with a respectful nod.

"You will be staying here for a while, Master Tirney. Elizabeth and her husband will be taking care of you."

Alouicious could remember how he felt at this moment. Everything he knew had been taken away and now O'Reilly, his only remaining friend, was leaving too.

"Don't look so glum, Master Tirney. I promised your mother and father I would look over you. I will be back to see you soon."

"There's nothing to fear here." said Elizabeth, reaching out a hand and stroking his cheek.

"Now, before I go there's one other thing, Master Tirney." said O'Reilly, a seriousness coming over his face. "You can never tell anyone what happened, do you hear? Whilst you are a guest in this place, you are Elizabeth's son and not a Tirney no more. Just like when you decided you wanted calling Alouicious and not the name your parents blessed you with. It will be our game, our secret. If you play it well enough, the next time I see you I may have a present for you."

He did not want calling anything else. He was a Tirney. He was proud to be a Tirney. And his father said if he wanted them to call him Alouicious it was his right. It was not fair. "No fair, I say! No fair!" he shouted.

"Don't be so." said Elizabeth, clasping him up in an embrace. "You can choose any name you wish. All you have to do is say and it will be so. My brother tells me you are a well-read and intelligent young man, so there must be someone who you would like to be named after. Come. We'll go inside and get you some warm food and a good rest. In the morning you can tell me all about yourself and we shall pick."

He put up no resistance, as she lifted him from the cart and, pausing only to thank O'Reilly, walked into the house from the cold. As they crossed the threshold to his new life, he closed his eyes and began to weep.

It was the day he said goodbye to who he was, and one of the last memories of his life until now.

"Are you alright, Mister Tirney?" asked a voice from the black.

He snapped his eyes open to the visage of Walter crouching next to him, a worried look on his face.

He raised a hand and wiped away the tears from his cheeks, smudging the grime lingering there. Attempting to compose himself, he nodded to Walter and looked around. He sat in the room seen before his world descended into black. To his side, Thaddeus lay unconscious, a large bruise forming over one eye.

"There is a ball of fire that roams these corridors, Mister Tirney." said Walter. "The door protects us from it."

A ball of fire? What was Walter talking about? Was he still dreaming? Ignoring the clawing hand trying to keep him back, he made his way to the door and opened it. Without thought or fear, he peered into the darkness. All he could see was an empty corridor.

He moved back, turning his attentions to Thaddeus. The man may be a bully and ignorant of his emotions, but he was powerful. If they were to find out what was going on, his abilities would be required.

Chapter 18

Thaddeus found himself sat in a chair in a drawing room. Around the thick, mahogany table, four other men nursed glasses of scotch and smoked long, rich cigars. How did he get here?

He scanned the faces in the room. There was Administrator Smithson, a man who he only knew as the Marquis, a doctor called Malcolm Evesham and a financier by the name of Reginald Fatharingham.

It was a meeting of the society. Something in his mind told him it was important to be here. Unflinching, he decided to wait and see what transpired.

"I simply cannot allow us to take the risk of attempting this when there is so much going on around us." said Doctor Evesham.

"Malcolm, you are a bore. If we became distracted every time the local constabulary came knocking, not one of us would get anything done." said Fatharingham.

"I agree, Malcolm. I understand your concerns, but there would be little reason for them to go to the Institute. A school has burnt down. Nothing more. Marquis? Your thoughts please." Administrator Smithson said, swigging his scotch and leaning back.

The Marquis sat, unmoved by the comments around him, drumming his well-manicured fingers together in thought. "This venture could make us a fortune. I have already invested heavily in this, too heavily to continue to get little or no return. If Doctor Thaddeus says we are ready to proceed, then I say we proceed. To hell with the law."

"And what of Sister Rose? I suppose her connection to the school and then to us will be ignored?" said Doctor Evesham, obviously worried about the consequences. "As soon as they find out she was involved with bringing Thaddeus our test subjects..."

"Enough!" bellowed Administrator Smithson, slamming his empty glass down on the table. "If people are suspicious, it is even more reason for us to step up our preparations so we can complete before we are exposed. Doctor Thaddeus?" he said, turning to face him. "Are you certain we are ready for the demonstration you promised us?"

Thaddeus knew what he said next, but could not place why. Why was he involved in this? Unless he could figure that out, he would respond as he knew he had. "I am indeed."

"Indeed what?" asked Walter.

Thaddeus turned and looked to his side. He was in the room he followed Alouicious into. He sat on the cold floor with both of the men leaning over him. It was distasteful to look at them so close. "Back away from my person." he said, as low and measured as he could. Once they shuffled back, he stood up and dusted himself down, feeling the large, tender mound on his forehead. "What is going on?"

"I found you on the floor." Walter said, surprisingly cheerily. "I saved the lantern and saved you both." He held the lantern up as if to show off his accomplishments.

He snatched it from Walter's grasp and sighed. "I suppose I should offer you some measure of thanks, Wagstaff?" he asked. Without giving any, he walked to the door.

"Be careful. The ball of fire that knocked you out may still be roaming around."

"What are you babbling about now, Wagstaff? You will no doubt be telling me you have also recently gained the ability to see fairies." He opened the door and looked out along the corridor. It was empty and quiet. "You are still our scout, Mister Tirney. On you get." he said, pointing to the other lantern on the floor.

Alouicious grabbed the lantern and lit it from his with eager exuberance. He scampered out of the room like a freed chimp and disappeared into the black, Walter trudging along behind, his ego deflated.

Cursory glances into the rooms lining the corridor revealed nothing, each one as bland as the next. The only item of note, another lantern to give Walter, taken so each now carried a glowing haven.

Nearly twenty rooms and sometime later, they reached the end of the corridor; the terminus marked by three iron doors. One located in the end, and two either side. Each one plated and riveted by the finest metalwork, and none possessing a handle or any other means of opening.

He stepped forward, placed a hand against the one at the direct end of the corridor, and pushed. It gave slightly at the contact and he let it shut once more. "Judging from the layout we have seen, it makes sense this one will take us on beyond this corridor to another corridor or room. The ones to our sides are perhaps just variants of the empty storage rooms we have seen already. Mister Tirney, you will take the door to our left, and Wagstaff you will take the right. You will come and join me beyond this door when you have ascertained I am correct."

Neither of his companions seemed too delighted being split up in this manner, but he knew time was wasting and their oil short. Their progress required an essence of urgency if they were to complete their search.

As the men heaved through their respective doors, he returned his attention to his own. Planting his foot next to it and applying weight through his shoulder, the door eked and whined open.

The room beyond was a massive dome about one hundred feet wide, ringed on its outer edge by a series of iron bars. In addition, dominating the centre was a sight that filled him with both joy and terror.

As he stood and stared at the three metal orbs, which stretched in a column from floor to ceiling, his head began to tingle.

"Not now!" he yelled.

But it was too late.

Chapter 19

Walter pushed through his door, holding his lantern above his head to fill the space beyond.

"You do not have to raise your hand to ask me a question, you know." a voice said, with mirth.

He could not believe his eyes. He stood on the deck of a boat out at sea, the light sound of gulls trapped in the sea breeze billowing round his face. In front of him, a young, red-haired man was winding rope round a mooring point. He looked familiar, yet not. "Who are you?" he asked.

The man turned and peered strangely at him. "Seriously there, boy? Again?" he said, looking Walter over. "Are you sure y'are fit for this?"

Fit for what? Where was he? Had he ever had this conversation, or was this something new? "I am sorry." he said, trying to buy himself time to think. "I have trouble with my memory sometimes, is all."

"My father told me what happened to you in that place. If he were still here, he would give you hug and say sorry. I, on the other hand, after hearin' what came by you there, do not feel that would be doin' either of us a sweet Jesus of a favour now, would it?"

Father? He would recognise his own brother, surely. "John?" he asked.

"Who in name of Mother Mary is John now, I wonder?" the man laughed. "You need to focus on what you have on the horizon there, boy. This has taken too long and cost too much for you to lose your way when it counts." The man walked back from tying the rope and playfully ruffled

Walter's hair. "I hear y'are a quick study. Maybe you could spend your time reading up on seamanship. You ne're know lad, it may come in useful. Either that or you can go below and knock me up a plate o'food. I have a hunger on us that could kill."

Glad for the opportunity to figure out what was happening, Walter walked to the back of the small boat and descended the stairs to the galley. He swung the doors open and strode inside to find something to take the man on deck. Instantly, he was greeted by the sensation of burning. Fire surrounded him and scorched his skin. Smoke filled his lungs and he turned and ran back, fleeing from the pain.

"Whoa there, brother" a familiar voice said, as arms wrapped themselves around his waist. "What in the blazes did you think you were doing, you nearly ran back in there!"

He looked up and caught the face of his brother, John, staring back at him. A large grin spread wide across his face. However, it was not the John he remembered. He was older, perhaps into his thirties. He turned and looked back. He was outside. In the still night around him, the school that had sent his life into turmoil boiled into the night. Flames licked from the roof and the air was filled with the crackle of wood and sounds of shattering glass.

"It is a wondrous thing, revenge." said John, letting him go.

He stood transfixed on his brother, watching the red and amber glow wash across his face. This was not the man he remembered. His words were warm and sincere. It made him smile.

"Get going you insufferable skank!" said John, shoving him away from the building. "The locals will be along soon to see what is happening and you have work to do."

"John, I…" he tried, the words not coming as he wished.

"Oh, go on with you, Salty, will you? You're gonna make me cry." said John, as he reached over and hugged him, the tenderness and emotion of the contact catching him off guard. "I know you never wanted an apology, but I have to give it. I only wanted to toughen you up, you know? I never meant for anything to happen. Jesus be damned if you needed anything else like that in your life! Mother and father are the same. If they had known what was going on they would have saved you from it, but…"

He watched a stray tear roll down his brother's face as he spoke, and subdued his response to it. All he ever wanted was a brother to live with and learn from. Until now, he never realised he had one.

"Oh, now look what you made me go and do. Get on with you! Get on with you and get it done, Salty. Be rid of it all for good."

Memories, suppressed and forgotten, washed over him and finally he understood. He closed his eyes and laughed. Years of pain, doubt and torment fading away, as he bellowed out his release.

When he opened his eyes, he was back beyond the iron door. There, strapped to the solitary chair in the room was Sister Rose. On the floor around her was a limpid pool of blood. As he turned to head back and tell the others he knew what was happening, he paused to spit on her; the expelled globule landing squarely on the open wound marking where her head once was.

Chapter 20

Alouicious heaved the door open, cursing his bent form for not allowing him more leverage. As the door sprung back into place, he peered at the strange contraption sat in the centre of the small room beyond.

Cables, black and coarse, ran from a hole in the wall to a metal box stood upright at the room's heart. The box was waist high and had an angled top pointed toward the door. In the middle was a solitary lever; an inverted Y of metal with a wooden handle extending between two sets of metallic grips.

He knew what this was. He was sure. He walked over and carefully extended an arm. Fingers tingling with excitement, he wrapped them round the shaft of the handle and pulled.

"Give it back, Alouicios." said a voice.

Blinking hard, he recoiled in shock from the face of someone not a stride's length in front of him. However, it was not a face to spark fear. The face was pleasing and full of love. It was his mother. He sat outside in one of the parks lining the outskirts of their family home. This was an old memory, a good memory.

A surge of emotion ran through him and he leapt forward and hugged her with all his might; the image of her fallen form witnessed before, urging the response and heightening his desire to make contact.

"Whoa there, Alouicious. You'll squeeze the life from me!" his mother said, laughing as she fell back against the picnic blanket they sat on, as she playfully wrestled with him.

He looked at her, a tear of unbridled joy dribbling down his cheek, as he giggled. He was happy. He could not remember the last time he felt so alive.

"Now give me the box back, Alouicious. If you damage it, I cannot give you it later."

He stopped what he was doing and looked down at his hand. There, clutched between his fingers was a white snuffbox.

"Come on now. I know you like the box, and you can have it one day, but you have to earn it. It can be your eighteenth birthday present, if you keep up your studies."

His focus fell on the box. He flipped it in his hands and deftly opened the perfect, ivory lid. It was empty. But he already knew that. It was always empty.

"Don't be breaking it now, Alouicious. That's your inheritance that is. Treat it with respect."

He carefully closed the lid and handed it back to his mother with a broad smile. "I look forward to earning it."

"That's my boy, Alouicious!" his mother chirped, wrapping him up in another hug. "Now come on, these strawberry tarts won't go eating themselves!"

He played for as long as he could in the sunshine with his mother; overjoyed to be with her again. They ate the cakes she baked, they drank the cloudy lemonade she hand-made, and they talked until the sun was almost setting.

As the last draining hues of evening settled over the trees on the edge of the park, he was laid in his mother's arms. She was stroking his hair and humming him a melody, lovingly punctuated by light kisses to his brow.

"I love you, mummy." he said, turning to face her and reaching out toward her face.

"Please stop! I will do anything you ask, you know I will!" a woman screamed, her ginger hair tangled in his grasp and her clothes torn like rags, revealing her womanhood.

The scene had changed again. He was in the kitchen of a small cottage. A woman, one he knew well, was trying to pull herself away from him.

He hated her. He hated what she was, whom she came from, and what she stood for.

Without pause for consequence and with an undiminished pride, he reached out with his spare hand to the stove, picked up the copper kettle sat there, and bludgeoned her over the back of the head with it. Boiling water and blood sprayed out as soon as the object made contact. With each successive blow, her beautiful face and flowing gown merged into a fetid mush of red. He did not stop his assault; he would not. Not until he was sure her skull was ground to powder.

Then it was done.

Lifting his arms over his head in a triumphant V, he growled out his success to the heavens, as the battered kettle dropped from his grasp and fell to the floor.

When he returned his eyes to the horizontal, he was back in the room with the metal box. But he was no longer hunched. He stood straight and tall, as proud as he had ever been.

As he stepped outside the room, he saw Walter making his way from the room opposite. He smiled, a reciprocal and knowing look returning as he did. Not understanding where the voice came from, but suddenly recognising it, he spoke for the first time in many years. "I am ready."

Walter nodded and turned toward the last door. They would go to Thaddeus together.

Chapter 21

Thaddeus stood before the strange globes and clutched his head. The pain was incredible, but no blackout came to save him. A buzzing, like swarms of wasps trapped in his skull, rattled his teeth and blurred his vision. For a split second, just on the outskirts of his consciousness, he could hear a voice. Then, with a mighty whoosh of relaxation, everything stopped.

He scanned round, lowering his hands back to his side. He still stood in the same room, but it was not the same time. He knew when it was. This was it. He remembered. After all the pain and suffering of his other memories, this one he would enjoy and savour. It was his greatest triumph.

Stood between the cages circling the room and facing the orbs, an arc of strangely attired men chatted, red and purple sashes worn by all.

"It is a truly wondrous machine, Thaddeus." said Administrator Smithson, as he came and stood by his side. "You say it is powered by a petroleum generator, but utilises electricity to accomplish its feats?"

He smiled. "Yes it does." It did indeed. A German engineer called Gottlieb Daimler kindly allowed him to modify a design patented the year before. Instead of driving wheels, he modified it to turn belts of hessian and leather against one another. The resultant pull generated a charge. He remembered his conversations with Harold Brown in the United States about how to convert the charge to usable current. Four months into their discussions, Brown let slip he was working on a design for Thomas Edison that would fit his needs perfectly. It had not taken him as long as he thought to extract the specifics of the device.

"And you can really use this to retrieve any information you desire from inside a man's mind?"

"The images we extract will appear on the globes in the centre of the room." said Thaddeus, brimming with pride at what he was about to bear witness to again.

"You know what this means, Thaddeus?" said Administrator Smithson, grabbing him by the arm and grinning. "We can get anything we want from anyone. Our order will become an unstoppable force! We will mould how the world evolves."

Evolve? Do not lessen a great work by ascribing its utmost subtlety to your own lust for power, he thought. "We will all surely go down in history for this." he said, forcing a smile.

Administrator Smithson left him, after an irritating pat on the back, and wandered into the throng, as another man sidled up.

"I knew you'd make my father proud." said Cornelius, standing shoulder to shoulder with him. "I told him you were a genius."

"I know." he said, not drawing his attention from the globes.

"After your demonstration, you'll probably be elected to the council of elders for this. Spare a thought for me as you climb your way to the top."

"Of course, Cornelius." he said, almost laughing. "How could I ever forget the impact you had upon my life?"

"Thank you, Thaddeus." said Cornelius, shaking him exuberantly by the hand. "I will not you let you regret anything."

Do not fret Cornelius, he thought. I regret nothing.

He looked round the room. He recognised everyone. They were all here. Every member of the so called 'Royal Outlook

Society', who based themselves on the order of the Rosicrucian's in all bar name, stood awaiting their chance to see one of history's greatest moments. Adminstrator Smithson and his son Cornelius, the Marquis, Doctor Evesham, Fatharingham, and all the rest. Every single member had accepted the opportunity to be part of his grand showcase. It filled him with pride to see them all here.

It took him years to get into the society. He knew, when he arrived at university, that if he were to become part of their order he would have to excel. That is what he did. He held a singular focus, and it served him well.

He sought out Cornelius because of his undoubted ability to get him the chance to contact his father. It had worked. One day he was graduating, the next day, the end of everything he planned was suddenly within sight.

He was elated when the society bought the Institute for him to produce his masterpiece in. It was a fitting location.

He knew that to reach his goal he would have to do things he would find difficult to deal with, so he locked his emotions away. He drove them deep within his soul and ploughed onward. He would only set them free once he was sure his task was complete.

The large door stood behind him creaked open and a man in a leather trench coat leaned into the room. "Your test subject is ready, Doctor Thaddeus." he said, his shock of ginger hair glowing like fire in the lantern light of the room.

He knew him. His face drew a smile that brimmed with happiness. It was the late Thomas O'Reilly's son, Seamus.

Thaddeus turned to the group and raised his hands. "Gentlemen, if I may have your attention." he said loudly, as the chatter diminished to respectful silence. "We are ready. If you would all like to form into a line facing the orbs, I shall make final preparations and we shall begin."

As the group turned excitedly to face the orbs, he made his way out of the room. As he travelled to the corridor beyond, he caught himself from laughter. It was so perfect. Only an idiot would not notice the door held no handles when they were ushered into the room. Only a greater idiot would not notice the door sprung to force itself back, to almost hermetic perfection, into its niche when left to close. And only someone who was an interminable moron, whose only focus was greed and power, would not notice the door was therefore impossible to open from the inside.

As Seamus allowed the door to close, he smiled and gave him a hug. "It is good to see you again!"

"It is pleasing to see you too, O'Reilly." he said, returning the embrace. "Are all your tasks complete?"

"The woman is being strapped into the chair by John presently, and their ship has been grounded in the harbour, just as you asked. There'll ne're be a soul outside of these walls who will ever know what went on."

"I owe a debt I can never repay you, or your family."

"Oh, get going with you. I just be finishing what was started."

He nodded and shook him by the hand, before turning and going through the door to his left.

The simple room contained just one thing, a strange, mechanical chair. As he entered the room, John Wagstaff was wetting a sponge and placing it underneath an iron skullcap on a terrified woman's head.

"Good evening, Sister Rose. Are we sitting comfortably?" he said, with menace. The woman was strapped down and gagged, unable to respond with anything but a muffled yelp and a frantic struggle for freedom. "Mister Edison will be most upset if you damage his prototype, Sister Rose. I would suggest you try to remain calm and still." he said, striking the woman hard across the face and taking the hacksaw being offered by John. "We would not want you coming to harm before you know what I have in store for you." Sister Rose's head sagged down into her bosom and she wept. Good. She deserved to weep. They all did. "When I was testing I had this chair at just the right setting to do this properly," he said, reaching into his pocket and withdrawing a snuffbox as he couched before her, "I would give those condemned to my treatments some of this, to ease their passing. Even though, as you well know because you brought them to me, they were all convicted murderers and rapists." He turned the box round so that she could see the white powder held inside, before he snapped it shut. "You, however, will be the first and last to see its full potential with your eyes open."

Leaving the woman to howl, he motioned to John, and the pair exited to where Seamus was waiting patiently.

"This is as far as I will allow either of you to go." he said, brimming with love for the two men stood in front of him. "You must leave this place and get as far away as you can."

"That is not the deal we made." said Seamus, striding forward. "You are coming with us."

He turned and grinned broadly to the pair of men. There were his friends, his kin. However, their journey with him was at an end. "No I am not. You have done enough and I still have tasks to complete, even after this. My destiny lies along a different path to yours now. I thank you both for your every kindness. I could not have done this without you. I am grateful to you from the very depths of my soul for the opportunity you have given me."

John leapt forward and hugged him. The grip was strong and powerful and he could feel the man's chest heaving as he tried to restrain his emotions.

He motioned to Seamus who grabbed John and began to drag him off down the corridor. He knew they possessed little time to make good their escape from this place.

As the men slowly disappeared from sight, he readied himself and went into the third room. The lever sat on the metal table and dared him to pull it. As he reached out toward it, he contemplated his genius.

The device was designed to run off alternating current, but after he read about the horrible death of the elephant they tested the direct current method on, that was the one he chose.

He laughed, as he pulled the lever and the steady whir of the motor started. In only a few moments, millions of volts of electricity would build up in the globes. When the room's air could no longer hold back the charge, lightning bolts would sweep from them to the bars, which were nothing more than collection rods, and destroy anything non-metallic stood in their path. His machine did not look into people's minds; it ended them. In addition, when the bolts hit the rods, massive surges of current would force through the chair Sister Rose sat in.

Her end would be swifter than some of those trapped in the room, but it would be no less brutal. The current would not alternate. It would blast its way through her system. Her blood would vaporise, her extremities would explode, and her internal organs would boil. Moreover, all of it would take minutes, not seconds.

Another delightful consequence of pulling the lever was that all the rooms on all the levels of the institute would unlock. The inmates of this place would now be free to exact their vengeance on their hosts.

He waited for a few minutes, taping the hacksaw against his leg in a rhythmic fashion and whistling a melody he last heard many moons ago, before the first crackle of electricity and the muted screams began. It was time.

Still whistling, he crossed the corridor, now filled with the delirious sounds of death from the room beyond, and entered the one where Sister Rose sat. The sight was truly gruesome.

Her hair flayed outward in all directions, blood frothing from around the cloth in her mouth and out of her nostrils. One of her eyes had boiled out of its socket, bursting over her cheek, and her fingers had swelled dramatically. Yet, still she screamed and wriggled.

He turned the hacksaw in his hand and, wondering if the sensation would be seen as pain or relief to her now, began to saw at the flesh of her neck. He marvelled at Brown's insistence the saw should have a wooden handle. It did its job well; removing any chance the continued current would jump to him.

With each new vein cut, steaming blood hissed and spat out. It splattered his pristine coat and dampened his hair. After struggling for a while with the hard bone of the neck, the head lolled sideways and fell to the floor. Grabbing the gruesome mass by its hair, he left and made his way back up toward his office.

The halls of the Institute were filled with the sounds of mayhem. As he strode toward his sanctuary, a young female orderly, the one who he used to prepare his patient notes, screamed for help from a side room when she saw him. A pair of male inmates, both of whom he knew repeatedly brutalised their own wives, were holding her down and lustfully tearing her clothing off.

As he turned to face her, the saw in one hand and the severed head of Sister Rose swinging in the other, the macabre visage elicited a horror filled look in her eyes. "I am way beyond helping any of you." he said, as he continued on down the corridor.

All the staff in the Institute were employees of the order, handpicked by the elders. Each bore a burning desire to advance through its ranks. They were all the very worst kind of scum. He felt no pity for anything that happened to them.

Once he was in his office, he put the head and the saw down on his table and reached over toward his bookcase. Flipping through his books, he removed any pages that could lead people into determining what really happened here and, more importantly, who else was involved.

He removed the sections on revenge from Paracelsus' discourse and notes on how to outwit those of an illogical disposition from Sir William's work. He ripped out swathes of Charles Darwin's concepts on animals, and yet more from the mathematical notions for engineering from Sir Isaac's masterpiece, before extracting his adaptation of a plan from the stories of the Bard. Finally, he turned his attention to the last two books. With glee, he shredded the pages detailing how he needed to act so he fitted like a glove into the Royal Outlook Society from their brethren's manuscript, and all details of Thomas O'Reilly's quest to locate every single one of the membership.

He looked in his drawers and laughed. Administrator Smithson's request he deal with all correspondences regarding the Institute had worked out well. He took the letter sent from the solicitor's and lit it with his lantern, no one would ever know.

With his tasks complete, he strode from the Institute. The inmates ignored him as they continued their villainy on those poor souls remaining. They could see the animal unleashed within him. He was one of them.

As he strode out of the main door, beyond a hall porter beset by maniacs, he turned and rammed Sister Rose's head on the spiked railings circling the building. "Watch what you have done, good sister. Watch the horror you beset in your town." he said, pecking her on the cheek.

The wind howled down the narrow valley and he struggled on the bleak stone steps that led to the harbour and the road.

It was late into the night by the time he arrived at his house. This would be his final act. During O'Reilly's investigation, he found that the man he knew as the Marquis did not have an heir, but he did have a solitary child, sired out of wedlock. Although she could never take his place at the head of the order, he feared she would one day discover her heritage. He could not allow it.

He opened the door, the storm still raging at his back, as she appeared in the hallway. Her time had come.

"I am home, Jennifer." he said, as she cowered in the dimly lit space.

Not awaiting a response, he walked inside and grabbed her arm. Her skin was soft and tingled to his touch.

There was no doubting her beauty, but that was not why he was betrothed to her. He did it so she would find it easier to accept when he forced himself upon her. When he humbled her in every manner his Lord allowed. In their time together, he had his way with her in the most foul and wicked manner a man could, and the bitch enjoyed every moment. Tonight would be different. Tonight, he would thank Sister Rose for her education.

Standing, gasping in his kitchen after he was done, he walked out into the neat living room and sat down. No doubt, the constabulary would be visiting him soon. Nevertheless, he did not care. It was finally over.

Then he was back. Behind him, the metal door opened and his two companions came into the room. He recognised them for who they were and was happy to see them.

They caught the look in his eyes and came over, wrapping him up in their arms.

"It's over, is it not?" said Walter, a tear in his eye.

"It is." he said.

"I never thought I would see this day." said Alouicious, his voice strong and powerful.

"There was always hope." he said.

As he stood and hugged his strange companions, they looked up at him with beaming joy, and slowly dissolved into the background.

Wiping a tear of remembrance, he reached into his pocket, withdrew the solid gold pocket watch, and flipped in open. 'To LAW', the inscription read. It was his name. He was Levi Alouicious Walter Tirney. His new name was Thaddeus.

He was Alouicious, the boy whose family was killed by the Royal Outlook Society and was rescued from the house by his mother's brother, O'Reilly. When they died, his foster parents were the Wagstaff's. There, he had chosen Walter as his new first name. In their house, he plotted. In addition, when he left to go to university to begin that plan, he had returned to his unused, original name, as an homage to his parent's wishes, but chosen an apt new name to go alongside it; he became Levi Thaddeus.

All his life he sought revenge on those that killed his family and he had done so, ensuring the people who tormented him along the way, were judged for their sins. He broke himself into pieces to accomplish it, just as O'Reilly asked. Now it was over, and he was whole again.

As he stood and watched, the Institute faded before his eyes. Clutching the pocket watch tight and remembering the serenity of the woman who gave it to him, he wondered if it was his time to be judged.

Chapter 22

Doctor Levi Thaddeus' eyes fluttered and rolled. He could control no part of his being. Images, twisted and blurred, danced in his field of vision. His skin was on fire. It felt as though he was burning at the stake.

Just on the vague periphery of his hearing, he could hear a whirring noise. He thought he recognised it, but the spark of perception would not turn his insight to detail.

He tried to gain composure, even through the daggers he felt sure were being plunged into his skeleton, and concentrated hard on his vision. If he could see, he could understand.

Haphazardly, almost as if the ability was lost to him somehow, fleeting visualisations and forms emerged from the haze. He was sitting. He was inside. The room was white. There was a wall in front of him. The wall had a large window. Through the window were people. They were looking at him.

Then the smell came. It was rancid. He was surrounded by the stench of death. He remembered it from his time during dissection classes. The aroma came from inside a living thing.

He wanted to gag. He wanted to move. However, his predicament meant he could do neither. Perhaps if he could grab the attention of someone through the window, they could help him. He had to focus. He had to, just for a second of time, find the will to resolve a solitary person.

The faces swirled and twisted across his view. There were many, perhaps forty individuals. They were all dressed well.

He scanned from left to right, the occasional face finding resolution before dissolving back to vague colour. He recognised no one. He tried again, redoubling his efforts to remain calm as the pain forced panic in his deeds. Then he saw her.

Mary Whittingham sat in the middle of the crowd; an angel in white, in a sea of devils. She was crying. A handkerchief, trembling as it was held, nestled over her mouth, and her face was at once ashen and flushed. How he loved her. Looking down at the small bump in the cloth near her abdomen, he suddenly realised where he was.

When he told her that day he must complete what he started, she was upset. Not because she did not understand, he had told her everything, but because she was pregnant. That was why he was here.

His original plan had him leave; escape with O'Reilly's son and his brother and find Mary, to have the life fate stole from him. However, the more he thought about it, the more it bothered him.

His life with Mary would always be lived with one eye turned backward. He could never be sure if someday, no matter when, his name would come up as the perpetrator. It did not matter how good the plan was, someday, someone might figure it all out. He could not risk his child ever having to live through that. It would ruin them, just as fate once ruined him.

Therefore, he sat and waited in his house by the sea. Jennifer's smashed body lying in the kitchen. He would go down for his sins. He would make the sacrifice.

The constabulary eventually arrived and found him in the house. All he told them was he was guilty. The abilities he gained as a youth, in keeping the darkest of secrets from the prying eyes of anyone, meant no matter how forcibly they asked, he told them nothing more. It was fitting. The people who killed his parents were above the law, and he made it his business to slaughter them all. The police would never, and most probably could never, touch any of them. It was only right he should be punished for his crimes.

He rolled his eyes down to his arms. He was strapped into a chair. This too was fitting.

At his movement, a voice shouted out with terrified anguish. "He's still alive. Oh dear Lord, he's still alive!"

In his mind, he broke into laughter. It took him over forty attempts to get the settings right for his chair. It did not surprise him they were struggling with theirs. It was probable, knowing the laws surrounding such things, this failing would mean the death knell for its usage in such ways.

He looked back at Mary. She pressed against the glass, hands beating the pane, as officers attempted to restrain her. He put everything still remaining him into a single, heartfelt gaze. He hoped it would be enough. She caught his stare and stopped her rebellion, allowing the men to escort her back. She smiled as she was forced back into her seat. She understood. This was all for her and her child.

"Quickly now." another voice said. "Replace the cowl and start it up again! Leave it on longer if you have to this time. I do not care. Just do it quickly!"

He turned to the voice and there, stood by a wall, was a man dressed in black. His hand wavered by a lever; an inverted Y of metal with a wooden handle. Next to the lever was a single sign of caution. He laughed again. Alternating current!

He modified the chair's original design to be an instrument of pain as well as death, but curiously, it became his treatment. Somehow, it scrambled his brain enough to put him back together. It had allowed him to gaze upon the woman he loved through the eyes of a solitary entity.

Edison's great instrument of death had cured him of his self-inflicted malady.

As the hood was replaced over his head and re-secured, his world finally fell back to black. Although these men thought they meted out their judgement upon him, he knew the real judgement was yet to come. He was ready to face it. His God was a vengeful God, surely he would understand.

Then he heard the lever creak, as the man in black pulled it down. It was over.

Bang.

Part Two

DISSAPEARANCE

Chapter 1

Bang.

Joshua Thaddeus fell from his precarious perch on his sofa, smashing his temple into the edge of his coffee table. The half-consumed bottle of gin sat there rattled with the impact and toppled over, glugging the pungent liquid onto his living room carpet.

Startled into consciousness and in pain from the unsympathetic contact, he rubbed his brow and looked at his watch. It was half past ten. He was late again. Righting the bottle with a shaking hand, he staggered across to his bathroom to get himself ready for his therapy session.

Staring into the mirror, his gaze was met by a repulsive scene. During his sleep, drool mixed with the residue of the evening before and formed a brown crust that trailed across his cheek and coated his teeth. He must stop smoking.

He was only just into his thirties and yet, as he washed away the detritus of another evening of heavy drinking, his bloodshot eyes, and sagging skin reminded him of a man twice his age. Even though he could remember vaguely returning to his house before midnight, he looked and felt as though he had not slept at all; the shame of drunkards.

Almost ready, he combed his hair, plucking out the grey already sprouting along his otherwise proud, light-brown fringe, and applied some cologne. The smell of it would hopefully mask at least some of the stench lingering from the night before and save him the constant questioning that came with his visits to Doctor Sallinger. Grabbing a jacket and putting on his teashades, he stepped from his apartment into the bright sunlight of the Arizona day.

He lived in Phoenix. A bustling city made grand by the expansions of industry and the war. The recent invention of air-conditioning made it possible for people to come here in their throngs and the work generated during the war brought wealth and prosperity to the area.

When he left to join the fight just four years ago, the population was no more than fifty thousand. When he returned, only eighteen months ago, it had doubled, and it showed no signs of slowing. The streets heaved with cars and noise as he made his way across town, but at least the walking was easy.

He liked the smoothness of Phoenix. Everywhere was flat as a pan. Yet, if you enjoyed the angular and loved inclines, you were surrounded by mountains. Its location bore something for all tastes. For that reason alone, he disliked Europe. Everything was rolling; nothing was flat.

When he was posted to France, his sergeant told him not to become distracted by the scenery. That was easy. It may just have been because people were shooting at him and most of it was on fire, but he never really saw the splendour others did. All he saw were endless hills. They filled everything. Just when you got to the top of one, you would find yourself surrounded by more. It was torture. Trudge up, trudge down - day and night - constant - unending - unrelenting humps of mud that filled everything. It was gross monotony. It was no wonder Hitler wanted it removed from the face of the earth. By the end of the war, he was sure that was what the Third Reich was doing there. They were going to level it and turn it into a giant car park, or maybe an airport. He could understand that. Not that Germany was any better. Thousands upon thousands of shattered stone houses and yet more hills. 'The Black Forest is a wonderful place' someone once said. When he got there, it was lined with busted tanks and smelt of diesel fires and rotting corpses. Wonderful was a word it had long since forgotten. It was a dump.

He had not joined the war effort to fight an enemy; his job was to fight his own. Before the war, he was a Federal Marshall. He was a law bringer, in a city that still bore some memory of the Wild West. It was a vocation that brought him great pleasure and satisfaction. When America joined the war, he was drafted as a military detective. At first, the position seemed pointless, but as he soon found out there were far more deaths caused amongst the ranks than anyone could ever have suspected. It was an inevitability of the draft. Eventually you would bring in a killer. A person who would not look out of place in a war, and sometimes they would not limit their bloodlust to the enemy. That was his role; to root out and find these men. To bring to justice those who transgressed moral society, in a war that had ironically left that society, and the pleasantries of formal civility, far behind.

At first, he did well. His 'hit ratio' as it was deemed, was exemplary. Then, as the war took them further into the bowels of the enemy, things began to sour. A series of murders remained unsolved and, as the armies of the Allies and Russia marched on Berlin, the sequence eventually claimed his partner.

After the war ended, things really nose-dived. Unable to cope with his failure, he succumbed to his feelings and dissolved into self-pity; allowing his longstanding battle with the demons of drink to consume him. Now, back home and out of work due to his condition, he was sinking fast. His only hope of finding his way out was his therapist; and all she ever did was complain at his lack of will power.

As he turned the corner of Washington and South Central, narrowly avoiding a speeding Desoto, he looked up at the sandy building and sighed. He was going to be in serious trouble for being this late.

Chapter 2

Doctor Alison Sallinger's office was on the third floor of the county municipal building in downtown Phoenix. It was a small office, sat in an old building.

As Joshua walked through the neat reception and into the small waiting area, the unmistakeable aroma of cigar smoke wafted round and made him feel ill. He was in no state to be reminded of his transgressions.

Ignoring taking a seat, he walked across to Doctor Salinger's door and knocked, peering round the frame to see if she was at her desk. She was. In addition, she looked as though she was in a bad mood.

Alison Sallinger was in her mid-thirties and was always immaculately dressed. She had long hair, but wore it in a curled bob on the back of her head, exposing her delicately arcing neck. She was a woman of fashion and her corsets, many of which he could only assume were incredibly painful to wear, forced her frame into a perfect hourglass. Her skin was flawless, white like porcelain, and her lips were always bathed in rouge; counterpointing the azure depths of her eyes. Her soft features bore no menace, but when put alongside her exquisite tailoring and thin spectacles, she held an air of authority and grace difficult to ignore.

"You are late once again, Joshua." she said, not taking her eyes from her desk.

"I'm sorry." he replied, shuffling into the room and attempting not to flop into the chair provided. "Busy morning."

"I am surprised you make the mornings, sometimes. Heavy night?"

Involuntarily, he sniffed at the air. Did he really smell that bad?

"Your aroma is such that I could discern your approach when you were stood outside, Joshua." she said, almost reading his mind and looking up, sternly. "Do you feel it appropriate to waste my time?"

"I…" It was pointless. There was no excuse. "Sorry."

"The military pays me to help you. Do you want that help?"

"Yes, maam."

"Then please do not disappoint me again, or I may be forced to renege on our agreement."

He did not want the sessions to end. They were helpful and he greatly enjoyed being in her presence. He would try harder to stop his personal issues causing problems.

"So, as we do have some small measure of time left to us today," she said, looking up at the carriage clock sat on the mantelpiece in the room and moving to the door to close it, "do you want to tell me what it was that drove you into the arms of intoxication last night?"

As soon as the door closed, the background noise of the world outside disappeared. As he looked down and rubbed his hands together, gathering his thoughts, the rhythmic ticking of the clock gave his actions a feeling of countdown.

He remembered well what he was thinking about the night before. It was the first murder in the sequence. The first time he and his partner saw the handiwork of their opponent. The day his world began to unravel. He sighed. He told Alison, as she requested being called, this story on many occasions, but never gave her the detail. Perhaps, this time, telling her everything would help her understand, and he forget.

-

It was late in forty-four when his assigned division, the fourth armoured, made their way into Chambrey.

At that point in its history, Chambrey was nothing more than a bunch of crumbling ruins sat around a bullet-hole ridden church. A disused train station, extravagantly referred to as the 'Gare Imperial', sat to one edge of the commune and three roads, each more potholed than the last, were the only thoroughfare. At one point, it held a population around two-hundred. When they arrived, there could not have been more than twenty people who remained.

Combat Command B, or CCB as it was known, was sent to Chambrey to fortify the position and halt enemy incursions. It was to be a defensive site. He wondered if it was originally thought to be of strategic value due to its railway. However, after close inspection of the track and the realisation all the sleepers and every available inch of steel runner was deployed around the town in the form of makeshift roadblocks and fortifications, that reason became quickly mute. The railway was gone.

CCB was commanded by the irrepressible lieutenant-colonel Creighton Abrams; a young, aspiring military type, of which the term 'breaking the mould' was often used. He made it clear on many occasions he did not like Joshua being with his unit. "You presence here causes a disruption to focus and to morale. And more than that, I just plain don't like you." he once told him. The feeling was mutual. He would like nothing more than to leave.

He and his partner were only assigned to the battalion to get to the bottom of a series of accidents that looked too suspicious to be unrelated, or not hold something darker. In the end, after an exhaustive four week assessment, that was exactly what they turned out to be; accidents. All caused by diesel contaminated gasoline. They were only with CCB until something new came up.

After assisting make good a defensive perimeter, they were given a holdout in the train station and asked politely to "stay the fuck out of everyone's way". That suited him fine. It did not, unfortunately, suit his partner.

Humphrey Galloway joined the war effort from Boston. He was the son of Harrison Galloway, who held a position of some sway in the area. When drafted, his father ensured his influence counted and got him the least combat intensive role available: military detective.

Humphrey was a pup, barely into his twenties. Tall, brash and handsome, and spottable at some distance as the rich kid he was. He spent most of his life before the draft in education; partying his life away. The war however, robbed him of his mirth. The youthful exuberance he displayed when first assigned to be his partner, a distant and shattered memory. Now he was an automaton. He lived to work. It was his way of dealing with the situation he found himself in. He could not blame the kid. Humphrey's escape was focussing on what he must do. His escape was alcohol, even then, so he did not have to focus on anything.

It was the second evening when the call came. A young private called Frank Jones came running into their small room and woke them. It was no more than half five in the morning.

He was up drinking wine until the small hours, much to Humphrey's disgust, and could remember slurring a whiny response before he was summarily dragged from his sleeping position and forced to get dressed.

Still nursing his head, he walked out of the train station and toward the periphery of the village, as Humphrey proceeded to question the private about why they were so rudely awoken if it were not life threatening.

"Colonel Abrams said if you were to stay at his convenience, you should make yourselves useful, sir." said Private Jones, as formally as he could muster.

"And how exactly is waking us up before sunrise useful, Jones?"

"Colonel Abrams wishes you to take a look at something that has happened to one of the villagers, sir."

"Does he, now? I assume Forrester has better things to attend to this evening, does he?"

"He has already assessed the situation. It is his opinion, it does not call for a medical officer, sir."

He stopped Humphrey before he could ask any more pointless questions. It was obvious Jones was ordered not to discuss anything with them. There was nothing to gain from continuing the conversation. Besides, the respite in noise would help his hangover settle.

The group marched in silence down toward the low, stone wall encompassing the main collection of buildings and across a shell blasted field toward a pair of crumbling barns at the base of the small tor the commune sat upon. Even from distance, it was clear torches were lit in one of them, and a serene, amber glow blanketed the muddy scrub surrounding the structures.

When they arrived, they were greeted by a distressed looking Lieutenant Forrester.

Forrester was a young, talented medic and organiser, but he was a worrier. As the group stopped before him, he finished his frantic pacing and came over, rubbing his hands. It was clear he was panicked.

"Please tell me you haven't been drinking." said Forrester, getting up close and then taking a step back with the pungent odour suddenly surrounding him.

"I'm not going to lie to you, Forrester. So, what's going on?"

"Good god, man! Pull yourself together, will you? One of the villagers is dead."

"It may have missed your attention, but half the fucking country is dead!" said Humphrey, stepping in and surprising everyone in earshot. "Maybe if you gave us something to do other than just sit around, we wouldn't have the need to amuse ourselves in other ways."

Humphrey was a fine kid. He always stored an excuse away somewhere, just in case it was needed. This morning, as the smell of bad wine drifted on the breeze around them, he was glad it was a good one.

"Just get your assess in there and tell me what happened." said Forrester, pointing toward the barn and shaking his head. "Abrams will have my head if we don't get to the bottom of this."

As the men walked purposefully forward, Forrester started his march back up to the fortifications.

"I owe you another one."

"Please stop putting me in these situations." said Humphrey, as he held the barn door open. "Your wilful longing to destroy yourself bothers me as much as it does everyone else. The pity is that I have to live with it."

He nodded. There was little he could say. He would try. Nevertheless, he had before.

The inside of the barn was strewn with the spotted remains of the harvest. A few, straggling bails sat in one corner and the remains of a farming village no longer wishing to farm lay rotting around the edges.

But there, spread-eagled across the centre of the room, was the body of a woman. She was young, only just into her late teens, with her auburn hair splayed out across the floor. She was wearing a long, white coat of some kind, perhaps a milkmaid's garment or nurse's outfit, but those scant coverings were ripped, exposing the series of scratch marks covering her face, neck and torso.

"What in the name of god happened here?" said Humphrey, moving close to the body and kneeling down.

He studied the woman. Her face was pitted and broken, and a large gash crossed her bottom lip. He studied the mark; it was not surrounded by as much blood as it should be. He looked closely at the scars covering her body and found once again, the blood that should have pumped from the wounds was not present. Moving his attention to the legs, he noticed about half way up the inside of her right thigh, a tell-tale patch of purple blotches. Reaching out a hand to gauge the size, he sighed; a man's hand - no doubt.

Humphrey leant over, noticing the expression that wracked his face. "What have you got?"

He stood and looked around the floor. "Something's wrong here. This guy's a menace."

"So it's a man we are looking for?"

"If a woman did this, it would most likely be brutal or clinical. Female killers either want to see their victims die, or want to be somewhere else when it happens. Women commit crimes of passion; explosive outbursts that cause harm to the living. Alternatively, they poison people. They don't stick around to scratch corpses."

"So what can we tell about the killer?"

He looked into Humphrey's expectant eyes. This was his escape. Watching him work and learning from him, gave Humphrey his respite. Saved from the horror of war by attempting to fix horrors within it; it was strange.

Nevertheless, after sparing his blushes with the lieutenant earlier, he owed him this much. "Ok. You give it a shot and then I'll see how close you get."

"Alright." said Humphrey, returning to a crouch and looking the woman over. "He's a man. Moreover, judging from the hand marks around the thighs, he's probably a well-built man. His hands are manicured too, because the scratch marks on the sternum are in even stripes of four; so no missing or chewed nails. He's got to be comfortable with death up close too, to have stayed after he killed her. Therefore, he's a fighter; maybe frontline infantry? And he has an eye for the beautiful, because she's actually quite appealing."

He hated to admit it, but that was pretty good. It missed some major points, but the basics were there. He knelt down alongside him and smiled. "Really good, Humphrey. But what else do you see?" Humphrey looked for a while, but turned and shrugged. To him there was nothing else. "OK, so here's what I've got. The trauma she suffered to the face and body are indicative of rape, but the marks were made after her death. The heart wasn't pumping when her lip was bust and neither was it pumping when she was scratched." He reached over, lifted one of her slender arms, and held it up. "She still holds faint warmth above the ambient, so she probably died in the last four to six hours. In addition, from the lack of abrasions to her arms, we can assume she died in a manner that did not require forcing upon her. And there is no residue in the nails to posit any possibility she died during a struggle. Yet, none of those are my greatest concern."

Humphrey was smiling; the enjoyment he got from watching him work palpable. "So what is?" he said, with barely restrained eagerness.

"Can't you tell what's missing?"

Humphrey looked back at the body, puzzled. "I'm not sure; jewellery?"

He rose to his feet and started to gaze around the barn. "No Humphrey, nothing as mundane as jewellery. What should be present at every murder scene?"

"A murder weapon?"

"Almost. Think about it this way; what would you say killed her?"

Humphrey stared at the body and began to check every surface of her fallen form for a giveaway mark. "I actually can't tell."

"Look at her face, Humphrey. Notice the reddened eyes and the bluish lips and tongue?"

"I do. But she's dead. She's supposed to be blue."

"Not that blue, Humphrey. The signs you see are the clear indications of asphyxiation."

"But she's got no marks around her neck. There's no way she's been strangled."

"And now you can see my concern." he said, rubbing his chin and making his way back out into the darkness.

"What concern, Joshua?" said Humphrey, jogging after him.

"That woman was probably asphyxiated during her sleep; maybe with her own pillow. And then she was brought here."

"Good grief!"

"That's not all though." he said, staring out into the night sky and lighting a cigarette. "How many women do you know who wear something like that to bed? Not one, I'd wager. Therefore, she was killed, and then dressed like that. Then she was carried through the village, brought down here, then raped, bitten and scratched; all whilst she was still warm."

"Who would do such a thing?"

That one question scared him more than any other. The only sort of person who would even begin to think of doing something like that was a planner; a dyed in the wool psychopath. A man with a clear understanding of what he was doing, how he wanted it done, and the brains to back up his needs. What was more worrying, and what he would not tell Humphrey, was there was something darker. Whoever did this wanted the body to be found; otherwise, it would have been dumped in field after they were finished and not left in plain sight. This man, their new foe, wanted people to see what he had done. And even more unnervingly, he probably wanted to be hunted for his crimes.

With CCB on the hillsides all around and more men passing through the village daily with supplies, there were thousands of suspects. This could take time. And as with all psychopaths, especially ones looking to be chased, time was one thing that was never on your side.

-

Alison sat behind her desk in stunned silence at his story's end. Perhaps he gave too much information this time. "I'm sorry if my candour on the subject caught you off guard. I meant no offence."

Alison did not respond. Mouth still agape, she reached over, picked up her sturdy Bakelite telephone, and tossed him the copy of the Arizona Republic sat on her desk.

As he stared in horror at the front page, he barely noticed her connection request.

"Police Sergeant Houghton's office, please."

Chapter 3

Police Sergeant Houghton was a gruff older gent, whose glass panelled office sat at the back of the west section of the city-county building on South Second Avenue.

Back before the draft, Joshua met the man a couple of times when investigating organised crimes in the city. Back then, he was just a cop on the beat. After the youth was stripped out of the department to fight the war, he was promoted. There was no other way it would ever have occurred. The man was a dolt. Sat across the desk from him, as he lit another cigarette and stared lustfully at Alison, he was sure it was a position of power he found greatly satisfying.

"You finally handing this guy over to the proper authorities, Miss Sallinger? About time." said Houghton, leaning back on his chair and taking another drag. "He's a menace to everyone he comes in contact with."

"I'm not here to incarcerate him. I'm here because I feel certain Mister Thaddeus can assist you in your enquiries."

"Him?" said Houghton, coughing a laugh. "How do you figure that? He can hardly help himself. Look at him, for Christ's sake!"

"His current woe is under my regulation, Sergeant." said Alison, curtly. "His knowledge could be of real benefit to your investigations."

"I wouldn't trust his word if it was written down, signed in triplicate, and rubber stamped by the president himself. I can smell his lies from here."

"Mister Thaddeus is currently recovering from psychological trauma sustained during the war, Sergeant. That does not, in my professional opinion, mean his other mental faculties, including his memory, are in any way affected."

Houghton baulked another laugh and leant forward, clasping his nicotine stained fingers together. "I'd be surprised if he can remember his own name, most days. How do you know anything that guy says is true?"

"Your name is Conroy George Houghton." said Joshua, his tolerance for the way the oaf was talking to Alison at an end. "Your Arizona State badge number is one eight nine two. You were born in Massachusetts, but your father, Frank Thomas Houghton Junior, moved here to work construction on the sewerage system for the city. Your mother, Henrietta Marlene Cleary, was born in Wales and moved to America sometime in the late eighteen eighties. You are a keen angler and you used to like riding and hockey, but I can see those pastimes are now a fading memory to your waistline. From a professional point of view, I recall you were once cited a ticket for parking a squad car illegally at a traffic junction to buy donuts; overturned as I remember in May of thirty-eight on a technicality. There are other things I could try to recall, but I think that's the salient parts of your police profile covered."

"Do you need anything else, Sergeant?" asked Alison, a glint of happiness in her normally serious eyes.

Houghton almost snarled, as he vigorously stubbed his smoke out in the glass ashtray on his desk. "And what makes you think this circus freak show could assist us in any way? No matter how good his darn memory is."

"Because Mister Thaddeus has just told me a story that matches, in almost precise detail, a murder that happened in our town last night." She tossed Houghton the morning edition and waited for his response.

"How could you know anything about this?"

"Because I've seen this before." he said, leaning forward and pointing to the front page picture of a dead woman dressed in a nurse's outfit. "She's not a nurse, is she?"

"How the hell do you know that?" said Houghton, leaning away from Joshua and lighting another smoke.

"She was asphyxiated and taken to the warehouse where you found her body too, wasn't she?"

"I don't know where you're getting this information, but that's protected police knowledge. We haven't even released those details to the press yet. Who's your mole? It's bloody Saunders, isn't it? Little runt fuck. I'll have his badge for this."

"Believe me, Sergeant." said Alison, with soft, calming elegance. "Mister Thaddeus was as surprised as you are to find out he could be of assistance. I saw his reaction to seeing the headline and have been with him all the way here. He has spoken to none of your officers in that time. He knows because he has seen murders like these before."

Houghton exhaled heavily, one eyebrow raised expectantly. "Where?"

"That's a story I can tell you en route, Sergeant."

"En route to where, exactly?"

"To the crime scene. I need to see the body, if you don't mind."

Chapter 4

It was all Joshua could do to contain his excitement. His nemesis was here, in Phoenix. Not only would he get chance to avenge his partner, he would get chance to finish the game. This was exactly what he needed. If he could finally solve this, he could put his life back in order. He was sure of it.

As they drove across town, he recounted the story he gave to Alison earlier; Houghton startled by the similarities the two stories contained.

"So this sick bastard is part of the military?"

"I always suspected as much, but I never got to the truth. The war ended before I nailed him."

"You do know that I'm taking a hell of a risk allowing you to do this, Thaddeus."

"I know, Sergeant. However, all I can offer in thanks is the knowledge I will not fail again. You have my word."

"If the chief gets wind of this, I'm finished. But if you can solve it… hmm."

He knew what Houghton was thinking. If he solved this, then he could steal the glory and would get yet another promotion he was not worthy of. That was fine. He wanted no spotlight for anything he did; just the chance for redemption. The man was making an educated gamble. It could be the first intelligent move he ever made.

The squad car pulled up at a battered warehouse on the outskirts of New Town. The milling throngs of police, paramedics, and press alike, swarmed around the makeshift barriers leading to the rusty, iron doors of the dilapidated structure.

As Houghton led them into the heart of the structure, he paused and turned to Alison. "I think you should wait here. It's not a pleasant sight."

Alison nodded and stood in the cascading light drawing between the gaps in the doors. She looked like an angel.

Snapping his focus back to the job in hand, Joshua questioned what was already known. "What is the approximate time of death?"

"Between midnight and four, as far as anyone can tell. It's difficult because the body has been moved."

"Witnesses?"

"None. No one saw or heard anything. This entire area is unused. They're going to knock it down soon; part of the expansion programme. Due to start on Monday."

The middle of nowhere, but somewhere. A place where the body would no-doubt be found quickly by construction workers. That would make sense. "So, what do we know about the victim?"

"Mary-Anne Matherson. Twenty-eight. Mother of two, but separated from her husband Andrew Matherson; he lives in Florida. We're currently trying to get hold of him. She worked as personal assistant to Guy Michenbahn, one of the bigwigs over at Valley Bank. Are you not going to write any of this down?"

"Don't need to. Anything else?"

"That's about it. I'm sure you can pick up what you need for the attendants and from inspecting the corpse for yourself." said Houghton, stopping and grabbing his arm. "I want to make it perfectly clear that if you lose control or let me down I'll throw you in the slammer and destroy the fucking key. You get me? I remember you were once pretty darn good at your job. Let's see if that's still the case, shall we?"

"Sure." he said, shaking himself loose from the sharp grip and striding over to the woman. "If I find anything, I'll let you know."

"You'll do more than that Thaddeus. I want an update, every morning - my office - nine sharp - both you and Sallinger. If you miss it, you break our agreement and I'll make sure she pays for your mistakes."

"Great. Should I wear a suit?"

"Don't worry about clothing, Thaddeus. I'm assigning Detective Walker to work with you. He'll make sure you're dressed accordingly."

"I don't do partners anymore."

"Oh, tough break, Thaddeus." said Houghton, sarcastically, as he smiled and left. "Because you don't have a fucking choice in the matter."

He did not want a partner. Tracking people like this was treacherous and this guy was more dangerous than anyone he ever trailed. However, Houghton had him by the throat, and he knew it. If he really wanted to make good what went wrong, he was just going to have to live with the insufferable cretin's request.

He turned, grumbling under his breath, and made his way to the body. He needed to focus.

The woman was probably in her late thirties, judging by the slight lines and crow's feet around her eyes, but her skin was tight and soft like a woman much younger. Her long, auburn curls were flayed out around her head, and the nurse's outfit she wore was ripped and torn. Scratch marks lined her chest and once again, the peculiar pattern of blotches was present on her left thigh. The woman had been asphyxiated and her arms and fingers showed no evidence of struggle.

As he completed his scan, a pair of sturdy, black leather, police-issue boots appeared in his peripheral vision. The boots were neat and immaculately clean. As his looked up, he noticed the trousers hung above the boots were also in a state of near perfection; the delicate seem running from hip to toe, ironed into the fabric with almost military precision. With trepidation, he looked up into the face of the man stood by his side.

The man was in his early twenties. He stood to attention, as if nailed to an invisible board and was groomed within an inch of his existence. His blond hair, spiked like a brush, greased with so much lacquer it was probably a fire hazard. In addition, his beaming smile displayed rows of gleaming, pristine white teeth. Damn; a young, aspiring rookie. That was all he needed. "I take it you're Detective Walker?"

"I am, sir." said Walker, extending a rigid, formal hand to shake.

He ignored it and turned back to the body. "Tell me what you see."

"Er… It's a woman…" said Walker, shakily; the sound of paper from a notepad adding to the silence. "Her name is…"

"I didn't ask you to tell me things I already know. I asked you to tell me what you see."

"A murdered woman, sir."

This could be torture. "Is there anything else that stands out, or is that it?"

Walker knelt down next to the body and began to probe the woman with the end of his pen. After three minutes of poking and prodding, a couple of which were spent taking notes, he turned with a smile. "The woman was killed by asphyxiation. More than probably a couple of hours before she was brought here, as pooling marks can be seen on her back and right side, suggesting movement after death. The man who killed her was probably about her height, judging from the location of the hand mark on her thigh, and is probably right handed because of how he has grabbed her. We can also assume the individual is neat and well groomed, because the scratch marks are indicative of a person who takes time to manicure themselves."

Shit. The kid was annoying and smart. Perhaps torture would be the better option. "Anything else?"

"Only that I would assume the location the body was deposited and the manner in which it was done, means something."

"Explain."

"The body is in a warehouse due for demolition. To most people that would suggest the perpetrator would like the evidence of his crime disposed of with the bulldozers due here. Then, why leave the body in the middle of this warehouse, on the floor? I think the location is important somehow. Also, the body has not been dumped. It's arranged. The hair, the arms even the rips on the clothing, they are not random. It is almost as if it was staged for some reason."

He rose to his feet and started scanning the building. Could it be the location was important? "What is this place?"

"The warehouse belonged to J.H. Longstone. It used to be a storehouse for farming machinery."

He froze, an uneasy feeling taking root in his thoughts. "Say again."

"Farming equipment, sir. And was occasionally rented over the summer, when the machinery was out in the field, to store…"

"Hay." he said, interrupting and walking back toward Alison.

"Yes, sir. Hay and grain." said Walker, following behind. "How is that important?"

"France. It's not another in the sequence, it's a replica of the first." he said, jogging toward the doors.

"What first? What about France?" said Walker, struggling to keep pace.

He arrived at Alison and grabbed her by the shoulder. She looked at him, half startled by the contact and half by the look that drew tight across his brow. "The guy who did this isn't just in Phoenix out of some twisted coincidence." he said, panting hard. "I knew there was something I was missing all those years!"

"Clam down, Joshua." said Alison, grabbing his hand and attempting to soothe his panic. "What is it?"

"I don't know why yet, but this place has been set up as it is to entice one person to look; and one alone. There's not a single other individual here who could possibly understand the meaning of this and the perpetrator only has one reason for doing it. This guy's not after his victims for some reason I can't fathom; he's after me. He's always been after me."

Chapter 5

"If this lunatic is after you, then why not just kill you in your sleep? Hell, you probably wouldn't even fucking notice most days, Thaddeus." said Houghton, angrily, from the far side of his desk.

"I can't explain that. All I can tell you is there's only one reason why he can possibly be doing what he's doing. And that's because he is after me in some way."

"What's so special about you? Torturing a coward drunkard is not the most challenging pastime I've ever heard. Shit! This guy's more insane than I thought."

"Could it be one of the guys you put away before the war?" asked Walker, taking notes. "You worked as a Federal Marshall, you must have sent down some real vagabonds in your time."

Vagabonds? What sort of person used a word like vagabonds when talking about killers? "Knock yourself out, Detective." he said, rubbing his aching forehead. "Eighty-three men across seven counties. Plus, they must have been in North East France in late forty-four and then in Central Germany in forty-five. Also, you might want to correlate that against those who profile as killers and any of their known associates who match against all those criteria. But hey, it's not my idea. You go for it, sunshine."

Walker continued to take notes, clearly unperturbed by the scale of the task.

"If you want, I can get you information on any psychological testing done on the men before they stood trial. It may help." said Alison.

"Thanks. I'll get a list of the men together and pass it on."

"Oh, will you now, Detective?" said Houghton, almost snarling. "You think we can spare the time to do that kind of work, do you?"

"If it helps the case sir, then…"

Houghton banged a clenched fist against the desk and stubbed out another smoke. "May I remind you that we have a psychopath on the loose in this town? It may have escaped your notice, but a woman has lost her life. We don't have time to do a fucking state-wide analysis of anything! I want you out on the street gathering evidence and then I want an arrest. Clear?"

"Yes sir." said Walker, lowering his head into his notepad.

"And you two… If you think his idea is good then, rather than laughing at it, you fucking work on it! Got me? It's your fucking shit anyhow, Thaddeus. Grow some balls, grab a fucking shovel, and start clearing it up for Christ's sake!"

"On that subject," he said, leaning forward and motioning to Alison he was not going to make a scene, "you know this is just the beginning, don't you? I mean, there were seven deaths in total in France and Germany; if you include Humphrey's."

"Oh, what now, Thaddeus!" said Houghton, almost exhausted with frustration, as he flopped back in his chair.

"We're dealing with a psychopath here. This guy is not going to stop until his plan is complete."

"And what plan is that?"

"Like I said, I don't know."

"Then how in the name of holy hell do you expect me to understand what the fuck you are on about?"

"I mean if he's doing this as part of a plan and if that plan now involves replicating the first murder, here in Phoenix, then logically…"

"The second murder will also be replicated." said Walker, suddenly understanding.

Houghton lit another cigarette and put his head in his hands. "Are you telling me, this guy, this psychopath who carved a trail of blood across Western Europe in his quest to fuck you up, is now here in my town and he's going to do it all again?"

"I think you have to assume the worst."

"Fuck me!" said Houghton, with an expressive sigh. "I should shoot you in the fucking head right now. Maybe he'd stop if he knew you were dead."

"That may not do you any good, Sergeant." said Alison, interjecting, "You have to assume the man is probably fundamentally deranged. Once his plan is complete, whatever that is, he will most likely find another target and make another, equally deranged plan. He will only stop when he is forced to. You have to find him."

"Wrong." said Houghton, standing and hitching his pants underneath his bulbous gut. "You three have to stop him. I'm going to have a word with the mayor and get you assigned to the detail full-time, Doctor Sallinger. Everything else in your life is put on hold until this thing is over."

"You cannot do that!" said Alison.

"Watch me. As of now, you three are all working on this. You don't breathe, eat or sleep without reporting it. Anything you need, anything you want, anything at-fucking-all, it comes through me. I'm not letting this place get turned into a morgue on my watch. And if you fail to find this guy Thaddeus, I will personally hang you by the balls from the tallest street light I can find and let the Mexican kids use you as a fucking piñata!"

Chapter 6

An excruciating hour of histrionics later, they were sat in a small office, tucked away in one corner of the station. Houghton agreed to allocate twelve men to assist and informed the mayor he was leading the investigation. Even though, in reality, he was probably only going to be in his office, surrounded by anxiety driven smog.

"He really does have a language barrier to overcome." said Alison, arms crossed over her chest in disgust.

"It's just his way. He's not got the mental capacity to cope with much and when he's pushed, profanity is his only outlet."

"That may be so, but it would not surprise me if soon, all we can get out of him is cussing."

"True enough." he said, chuckling. "Well, Detective Walker, what's the plan?"

Walker shrugged his shoulders, tapping his pen against his pouted lips. "We have to start somewhere. Did you have a suspect list when you tracked this guy the first time?"

"I did, of a fashion; that was my first thought too. I could do with finding out who from the events before is here in Phoenix or its environs."

"If you can get me a copy of that list, I'll have the guys search the local records and contact the Office of Strategic Services to correlate it. We can do the same for those you locked up before the war."

"I will give you the contact names for the psychological profilers we sometimes use in the FBI. I know it is a long shot, but one of the names may bring back a match." said Alison, already scribbling on a notepad in her lap.

"Then let's get to it."

For the next three hours, until well into the evening, the three made notes and started the process of collecting the data required to understand the range of people they could be dealing with.

Even though they were under pressure, Joshua simply could not feel it. Alison's presence was distracting. He could not stop staring at her. It was all he could do to stay focussed on his work.

By the time the alarm in the station went off to signal the end of the current shift, he was tired and hungry. However, most worryingly of all, he was almost sober. He looked at his watch; it was seven. If this was any other day, he would have been drinking for at least eight hours by now. The queasy, uneasy feeling in his gut at the lack of alcohol in his system, reminded him of what he had allowed himself to become. It was feeling he wanted rid of as quickly as possible. "Could anyone else use some food?" he asked, almost expecting his response.

"Sure." said Alison. "I know a quiet little place that serves Spanish food. I will pick up the tab on this one."

"Oh, don't worry about the tab." said Walker, packing away his extensive notes. "As long as we spend some of the time talking about the case, we're cleared for reasonable expenses. After the ear torture Houghton put me through this morning, I'm willing to test the waters; if you are?"

Alison smiled, and after grabbing his jacket from the back of his seat, he followed the pair out into the evening.

Dos Amigos restaurant was a quaint establishment perched on the quieter end of downtown. It was run by a mixed family of Mexican and Spaniards and served something called 'Tapas'; small bowls of heavily spiced, exotic dishes and stuffed olives. The group sat at a table, underneath a fluttering canopy on the outside of the building, and were soon chatting over a bottle of Chianti.

Joshua was struggling not to gulp at his wine as the group talked, but he refused to succumb to his demons whilst Alison was around. In response to his restraint, her mood seemed lifted.

When Walker stood from the table to use the facilities, she leant over and smiled. "You are doing very well."

"I actually thought you would ban me from drinking at all."

"Why would I do that? I need to know how you cope with alcohol in order to help. I can see you're struggling from time to time, but the fact you are conscious of your struggle tells me a great deal. There may be hope for you yet, Joshua."

Her playful tone and elegant smile was more intoxicating than any amount of liquor. In order to experience it, he was willing to make a small sacrifice of his desires. "Do you not have anyone waiting at home?" he said, suddenly wanting to know more about her.

"Not anymore." she said, thumbing her glass and sitting back in her chair. "My work means I am out for long hours. I was with a man a while ago, but I just could not find enough time to make the relationship a worthwhile proposition to him. So he left."

"A worthwhile proposition? I don't think I'd want to be in a relationship where the ideal was classified as that. It was probably best it ended."

"Oh." said Alison, deflated.

Shit. He must think before opening his mouth in future. "So, is there anything interesting that happened in the life of Doctor Alison Sallinger? You must have a few stories to tell." he said, trying desperately to find another topic.

"I could not disclose the content of my sessions with anyone, even if I wanted to. Doctor patient confidentiality prevents it."

"I see."

"Although my grandfather did work with Freud, the renowned Austrian neurologist, for a while. That's where I get my passion for it, I suppose. And your family?"

"Oh, dear lord!" he said, strangely willing to share any facts with her, even outside their sessions. "My grandfather was a monster. One of the only men put to the chair in English history. He killed everyone in the institute where he worked. Reading up on his life is probably where I get my passion for crime."

"I had no idea your roots were in England. How did your family come to be in America? Were they persecuted because of his actions?"

"Not at all. My grandmother was the Viscount Whittingham's daughter. She bore two children by him, my father, and his brother. My uncle took over the estate after my great grandfather's passing and my father was effectively ostracised when it happened. They were twins, and there was a lot of rivalry. He came to America with me in the twenties to work on the railroads as an engineer; he'd done it during the war, you see. Whilst he was here, the crash came and we were left destitute. My family's recent history is not a good one."

"The crash affected everyone. How did your mother and father manage?"

"My mother died giving birth to me, it was just my father that tried to deal with it. Then he died in a railroad accident in thirty-three. I funded all my education, and most of my life since, with the insurance pay-out."

"I'm sorry. I always assumed your problems were caused by the war. You held a good job and were well respected

133

before it started. I assumed your past was of little relevance to what was bothering you. I see now I could have been mistaken."

"Please don't analyse me." he said, clasping her hand and almost begging her with his sullen eyes. "Not tonight."

She nodded, grabbing the bottle from the table and topping up both their glasses. "Then we drink to the future; to making amends and setting new goals."

As they clinked glasses and shared a respectful gaze, Walker returned to the table. "What are we toasting?"

"Our health and our success."

"Count me in!" said Walker, raising his glass and laughing. "If we crack this and Houghton moves on, I could be the youngest Sergeant in station history!"

"Wouldn't that be a thing." Joshua said, restraining a giggle. "Do you have first name, detective?"

"John."

"How come everyone calls you Walker?"

"Because of letterheads."

"Letterheads?"

"Mister John Walker? Mister J Walker? Jaywalker... Get it? I did the first time and the millionth. Walker is easier for everyone."

"Oh dear. Children have no sense of boundary. They can be very hurtful." said Alison, sympathetically.

"Children? My training instructor called me Jaywalker. My childhood moniker was Wally."

"Then here's to Walker." said Joshua, as he light-heartedly raised his glass again. "The biggest Wally I know!"

The group chatted, drank, and ate with an air of frivolity for the next two hours. As the sun set over the mountains and they dispersed to make their way home, Joshua felt true relaxation, for once in as long as he could remember.

Chapter 7

The next morning, still awaiting the return of information from their assistants, they sat around the desk in their office.

Alison dressed more casually than usual. Her habitually, tightly restrained hair allowed to flow around the soft curves of her shoulders. With nothing else to focus on, Joshua was finding it hard not to stare at her.

"So, if our killer is following a pattern, it might be prudent to go through what happened after you found the first body in Chambrey. It may give us some inkling as to what to expect." said Alison, breaking the silence.

"That's logical." said Walker, twisting his chair to face him.

As he looked over their expectant faces, he gave an involuntary shudder. Reflecting on the past did just one thing; it made him want to drink. He pushed down his longing to fall into himself and calmed his fear. They were right. The information could be vital.

-

It was December in forty-four by the time the investigation of the death in Chambrey took him to the commune of Xanrey. It was a tiny place; a collection of run-down buildings straddling yet another hill in the shadow of a small church. Even so, the sheer amount of men and armour deployed around the settlement showed its strategic importance.

When the fortification of the position at Chambrey began, most of the men now here were assisting the work. Any one of them could be who they were after, and there were four-thousand of them.

Humphrey suggested they limited their search to just the lieutenants and above to begin with. That way, not only would the pool be smaller, they may gain insights into the superior's thoughts on their men, before they were interviewed. It was a simple tactic, but a decent one.

Setting up their base of operations in the tiny manse at the back of the church, they quickly started interviewing as many of the officers as they could. It quickly became apparent the units making up the battalion were very closely knit. No one would speak ill of anyone else. However, as the men soon found out, that tactic was not as wise as first it appeared.

One evening, after taking a break from the constant notation, they were brought a bottle of local wine and left to chat. The room had no windows and so a flickering oil tin, half-used for light and half for warmth, provided the space the feeling of a campfire.

Humphrey refused to imbibe alcohol as usual, so he consumed the wine himself. It tasted awful; a mixture of vinegar and rotting fruit. Definitely no vintage. Nevertheless, as the minutes turned to hours, he finished the two-pint bottle with little effort. It had been a good two weeks since his last drink and his system eagerly processed the foul substance like nectar. By the time Humphrey tolerated as much of his slurring as he could, the light was extinguished, the bottle empty and the disturbing disquiet of wartime darkness settled in.

It was four in the morning when their door crashed open. Even at the noise, Joshua remained out cold and snoring.

"Get up!" screamed a voice, piercing his slumbers, as a boot dug into his ribcage. "C'mon you sacks of shit! Get up and get dressed."

Rushed and tired, his movements were neither fluid nor helpful, as he crashed around attempting to put his pants on.

"For god's sake! Do I need to assist you?" said the stern looking private.

"A little space and some light might help."

"I'll see what I can do, shall I? Oh, wait, that's right, I and the rest of the battalion would prefer not to get shelled by giving the enemy something to pinpoint in the dark. So, I thank you for your helpful suggestion, but think I'll ignore it. Hurry-the-fuck-up!"

Scrambling out of the room, carrying one boot in his hand and a sock in his mouth, he attempted to tuck in his shirt, as they crossed the floor of the church and marched outside.

"Is it far?" he said, hopping along behind and trying to pull the now damp sock up.

"Does it matter?"

"Could do. If it's far then I need to put my boots on. If it's not, I give up the exercise and go barefoot."

The private stopped and glowered at him; his muscular jaw line and busted teeth clearly showing a man not disinclined to close, personal combat. "Hurry up! It's on the other side of the village."

"It's a commune." said Humphrey, arriving at Joshua's side and steadying him whilst he tugged his laces tight. "Not a village."

"Well fuck me. I couldn't care less if it was a fucking latrine. I need to get you somewhere as soon as I can, and that's where we're going. So get ready for a little jog gentlemen, because I never break my word to a superior officer."

He tried to respond, but the private was already making tracks across the ground in front of them. He did not do jogging. It upset his balance; what little of it remained.

"Come on, Joshua. If we get this guy really mad, he will probably beat us both within an inch of our lives." said Humphrey, grabbing his arm and dragging him along the narrow street.

Five torturous minutes later, panting and sweating heavily, he arrived at a series of camouflage tents, set off the brow of the hill. The tents were large and heavy. They clearly belonged to hierarchy.

"Don't tell me…" he tried, through gulps of strained air, "that we're going to get the hard word before we start."

"Looks like it."

He looked at Humphrey and then back at himself. Humphrey looked like a man who had taken an age over getting ready and did not seem in the least flustered by their exertions. He, on the other hand, looked like a police sketch artist's interpretation of a tramp after a marathon. "Shit." he said, trying to straighten his shirt and neaten his hair.

"Shit indeed gentlemen." said a powerful voice, as an immaculately dressed man strode from the tent in front of them. "I'm Colonel Howe. And I have brought you here to figure out what has happened in my tent." The man was tall and proud. His puffed out chest, and excruciatingly well-kept moustache, gave him the air of a civil war re-enactor.

"In your tent, colonel?" said Humphrey.

"That is correct." said Howe, walking purposefully around the men and looking them over. "You are here to investigate the murder in Chambrey, are you not?"

"We are, colonel."

"Then I assume you and your disgusting colleague can take a look at something else whilst you are here."

"We can, colonel."

"This way then."

The tent was large. A simple oil lamp lit up the space and a fly-netted hammock, stretched between four poles to make a makeshift bed, lay in the centre of the room. Sat just by the side was a bulky, expensive looking trunk. Laid naked on his back atop it was a man; his face heavily brutalised and a solitary eye hung loosely from a smashed socket.

"I woke up to the stench and found him just laying here." said Howe, pressing a handkerchief against his mouth and nose. "I have no idea who it is and neither do my men. It's difficult to tell when he has no clothes on and his face is in that kind of state."

Joshua walked over to the body and studied it. Although the face was smashed, the eye was cut from its socket, clinically. Taking note of the quantity of blood coating the face and drooling to the floor, he carefully opened the mouth and checked inside. "His tongue's been removed too."

Humphrey stood by his side and gazed in horror at the display. "This is pretty grim, even for a war."

"It is."

"How do we go about identifying the body? Should I organise a search for his clothes?"

"Whoever did this would have destroyed them. They went to the trouble of stripping him and leaving him in a presumably heavily guarded tent, so they'll have brains enough to have dumped the clothing in a fire or buried them around the commune somewhere. I mean, who'd notice a patch of fresh mud around here? Besides, we don't need to. I know who this is and I know who did it to him."

-

"So who did do it?" asked Walker, clearly uncomfortable.

"It was the guy from Chambrey. There was no doubt."

"How did you rationalise that?" asked Alison, shaking her head. "Is some of the story missing?"

"No. I had everything I needed to make that determination right there in the tent. I knew who it was, so it was only logical."

"So who was it?"

"It was Lieutenant Forrester; the medic who found the body in Chambrey. He lost an earlobe when he was younger. I noticed the scarring when we first met. When I saw the body and noticed it again, I knew it was him. We confirmed his identity through dental records."

"So, he was killed because he was in Chambrey at the time of the other murder? And what was he doing in Xanrey?"

"We found out he was in Xanrey to assist with cases of Nile fever reported in the troops there. Some of them had just returned from Egypt, after assisting with the desert campaign. They brought it back with them and Abrams didn't want an outbreak. As for why he was murdered, I'm not sure. My original thought was he must have seen or noticed something in Chambrey. That would explain why he was in the state he was. Blinded and muted to show he could no longer speak about what he'd seen, perhaps. Now I know our guy's after me though, that doesn't make much sense."

"Maybe it does." said Alison, leaning forward and tapping on her notebook. "Did you ever consider Forrester might know something more because he was a medic? Who performed the military autopsy of the woman in Chambrey?"

"That would have been Forrester. However, the remaining family did not want her cutting up. They asked for her to be left intact for burial. Therefore, I assume Forrester simply looked over the body and nothing more. If he did make any notes of the investigation, they were not present in his things; we checked."

"You also said he was the first person on the scene." said Walker.

"Why would that be relevant? Your suggestion implies that our killer's modus operandi somehow includes that as a driver; which it doesn't."

"It's not relevant to the first murder, but it could be helpful now."

"Oh no." said Alison, dawning horror crossing her face. "We need to warn Sergeant Houghton."

"About what?"

"Our killer is duplicating everything from the first time, right? So, that means in order to make the repetition as analogous as possible, the finder of the first body here in Phoenix…"

"Is now in mortal danger." said Joshua, suddenly realising the link and grabbing his jacket from the back of his chair. "Nice thought Walker. Let's go."

Chapter 8

The three plus Sergeant Houghton sat in a squad car outside the house of the man who first found the body in the warehouse; Trent Cockerill.

The man worked as security for the site. He found the body in the early morning whilst evacuating squatters from the building in preparation for the demolition. He was a nobody. His record had a few misdemeanours, but nothing Alison thought could point him out as a perpetrator.

"How do you want to do this?" asked Houghton, leaning out of the side of the car and dragging on his fifth cigarette of the journey.

"I don't want to do this at all. This is your show remember sergeant?"

"Go fuck yourself Thaddeus!" said Houghton, leaning over the front seat and opening the passenger door. "This is your game now. You go tell this guy some lunatic is going to chop him up because he fucking hates you. I'll be right here."

He sighed, as he prised himself from his seat and tucked his shirt into his trousers. As he removed the teashades from his pocket to block out the low glare of the morning sun, Alison and Walker joined him on the sidewalk.

"I can do this, if you want sir?" asked Walker, the brightly polished buttons of his police-issue jacket glaring fiercely as he straightened himself out.

"It's ok. I'm used to this."

"I forget you once worked in law enforcement. Sorry."

"Don't feel bad." he said, as he made his way up toward the busted screen door. "I do too, sometimes."

After three knocks, Trent Cockerill arrived wearing only a pair of briefs and carrying a bowl of cereal. "You want something?" he asked, eyeing the strange ensemble before him.

"I'm Joshua Thaddeus, and this is Detective Walker and Doctor Sallinger. We're here to speak to you about the body you found at the Longstone warehouse."

"I've already given a statement at the scene and I spoke to the guy who came to my house yesterday evening to check up on me. What do you want now?"

"A few moments of your time will do."

"Ok. But be quick, I'm needed back on site in an hour." he said, ushering them inside and wiping milk off of his chin. "My foreman says if I'm not back at work by this afternoon I can go find another job."

Cockerill's house was a mess. Washing was piled in the sink and the smell of rotting vegetation emanated from the trash and filled the cramped abode. As they walked through the kitchen into the equally depressing living area, Alison caught his look and shook her head. The guy they were looking for was tidy and orderly. If he was ever on it, Cockerill was now definitely off their suspect list.

"So what is it that you wanted to know?" Cockerill asked, scooping dirty laundry off a mangy couch and motioning for them to sit.

"I am happy to stand." said Alison, tentatively trying to find a patch of clean carpet to occupy, as the men sat down.

"We need to speak to you about the warehouse, Mister Cockerill."

"What about it?"

"Not the specifics of the event Mister Cockerill, but perhaps your involvement hitherto and beyond."

Cockerill placed his bowl on the table and glared, leaning forward. "I'm a suspect, am I?"

"Not a suspect sir, no. We believe the individual who committed the atrocity is following a pattern."

"What sort of pattern?"

"One that could see you as his next target."

Cockerill laughed and relaxed back into his seat. "I thought you were about to tell me something I should be worried about."

"You should be worried."

"I don't have the time to be worried about a guy who picks on women! I've seen men who do that, my pop used to. They're all cowards. Besides, I have a four year old kid and an ex-wife who say I have to be in work soon." said Cockerill, as he stood and pointed toward the door. "All you need to know is I have a job and a gun. If your guy comes here, it's him that needs to be worried."

"I really do not think you understand, Mister Cockerill. This is no ordinary man." said Alison, almost pleading.

"Neither am I. And I'm tired of being talked to by people about this. I found a body and reported it. I've done my duty, now please get the hell off my property, and let me do my job; if I've still got one."

"Mister Cockerill…"

"NOW!" shouted Cockerill, stepping forward menacingly. "Your welcome is over. Exit my house before I show you why this guy would be a fool to come here!"

Without a warrant to be there and with nothing further to say, they made their way quickly back to the door, as Cockerill slammed it shut and locked it behind them.

"That went well." said Walker, cracking a smirk and folding his notepad into his pocket. "What should we do next? Try to convince sarge to lose weight?"

"Oh, Christ no! I don't know about you two, but I could do with a drink."

"It is only just eleven in the morning, Joshua." said Alison, startled.

"The bars are open at this time, aren't they? Or have licensing hours changed from yesterday?"

"No drinking during the day!"

"I'm joking. If I really wanted a drink, do you think I'd be stupid enough to invite my councillor along?"

"It would not surprise me."

As he walked back to the car, his attention was caught by a figure stood next to a tree on the opposite side of the road. It was a man, maybe early thirties, wearing a brown, military issue outfit and a strange purple and red sash over his shoulders. His head was lowered and he was smoking. He was so out of place in the area. As he stared, the man lifted his head, stubbing the cigarette out on the sidewalk and smiling. It was difficult to tell at this distance, but he was sure he recognised him. Bolting to a jog, he ran toward the kerb, as a speeding Greyhound flashed passed his vision and halted his progress. When the vehicle left his view, he stared back to where the man was standing. He was gone.

"Holy smoke man! What's up with you?" said Walker, arriving at his side panting. "Just because you are not allowed alcohol does not mean you should be throwing yourself under a bus!"

"Where did he go?"

"What are you talking about? Where did who go?"

"The man who was stood on the opposite side of the road. Where is he?"

"I didn't see anyone, Thaddeus. Then again, I wasn't really looking."

Alison ran over and grabbed his arm. "Not funny, Joshua!"

"What?" he said, still too distracted to engage her look of disgust.

"Not funny at all. Get a grip of yourself."

"What? Didn't you see him?"

"See whom, Joshua?"

"The guy. The military guy stood underneath that tree."

"Why would I be looking at a tree?"

"You couldn't miss him. He was wearing military clothing, standard issue combat slacks, and jacket. Purple sash. Over there!" he said, pointing to the location.

"I don't know. I didn't see anything, Joshua. I was more worried about you."

"Shit." he said, turning and jogging back to the squad car. When he arrived, Houghton was sitting in the driver's seat, snoring loudly with the window down. "Sergeant Houghton?"

Houghton choked himself awake and coughed loudly, peering up into the bright light and squinting through his sleep. "What the fuck do you want, Thaddeus?"

"We need to get a couple of cars assigned to monitoring Cockerill; round the clock surveillance."

"You think he's our guy?"

"No. However, I think our guy is here. I think I saw him over there just a few moments ago. He was out in broad daylight, watching his house. The guy's here."

"Where is he now?" said Houghton, snapping his head around.

"Vanished. My sightline was occupied for a moment and he must have used it as cover and taken off."

"Great fucking work, Thaddeus! First lead; fuck all to show for it. I'm not really surprised."

"There was nothing I could do. I…"

"Save it. If you'd been on your fucking game, I wouldn't have to be assigning men from the field to watch a guy who

I didn't need to. As it is, that's exactly what I'm going to have to do." said Houghton, lighting a smoke and starting the car's engine. "Looks like you three have first watch until I can get a detail over here." With that, he sped off down the street.

"Where's he going?" asked Walker.

"For a rant and a drink, I would think."

"What are we supposed to do now?"

"It looks like you'll be on guard outside Cockerill's house for a while." said Joshua, placing his teashades back on and grinning, as he walked to the curb and lay back against the grass verge. "And I'm going to catch some rays."

Chapter 9

"Are you absolutely certain that was what he was wearing?" asked Walker, looking puzzled at his notes, as the group sat around the table in their office.

"I only got to see him for a few seconds, but that's what I remember."

"And this sash, is there anything else you can tell me about it, other than its colour?"

"Purple and red; slung around the shoulder and left to dangle down his lapels like a priest's."

"Anything else?"

"What do you want from me? I only saw it for a moment."

"Detail is everything."

Walker was right. Detail was everything. He closed his eyes and replayed the fuzzy memory in his head. "Pointed at the ends - Seemed in gold - Had a tassel as a finish, perhaps."

Walker started drawing on his notepad and held it out for him to look at. "Like this?"

"Almost exactly. That's uncanny."

"What is it, Walker?" asked Alison.

"It makes no sense."

"What doesn't make any sense, Walker?"

"I know this type of sash. I've been to gatherings where everyone wears them. If I'm not mistaken, it's Masonic."

"You have experience of Masonic meetings?"

"All us Yalies come in contact with it at some point. There's no avoiding it."

"You're a Yale man?"

"My father is a work colleague of Robert Yerkes. Not only is he rich, he's influential. If we were all given the choice, who wouldn't want to go?"

"You went to Yale. Your father is a close friend of the renowned psychobiologist Robert Yerkes and you are in with the masons. All of that accepted, what the hell are you doing in Phoenix working as a lowly desk detective?" asked Alison, a look of pure amazement drawing across her faultless face.

"I was given two choices at eighteen; take a decent, but not substantial, wedge of money and go do what I wanted, or be taken into the folds of the company and live like a king, but be at the constant beck and call of my father and his cronies. I decided the former."

"So you paid your own way through Yale?"

"Oh, hell no! I said decent wedge of cash, not a mountain! The Yalies still owed Yerkes after his behavioural sciences endeavours folded. I was given a place free, to do as I wished. I chose law."

"You have a Yale Law degree?"

"I do."

"And you don't want to be on the list of richest people in the world with a qualification like that, because…?"

"Law bores me. Whereas, investigations into the psychological maladies that cause people to break laws; now there's a topic that excites me. So where better to study? Phoenix Arizona; where the Wild West meets the modern day!"

"Are you moonlighting for city advertising too?" Joshua asked, breaking into laughter.

Alison could not help but join in, clearly hurting Walker's feelings and making her cover her mouth.

"I know it is not as glamorous as the life I could have led, but I'm happy. And to me, that's all that matters."

"Here here!" said Joshua, trying hard to repress his giggles. "It's a fine motive, Walker. I hope moving to Phoenix has panned out for you how you wanted."

"Until this case, I have to admit to more than a little boredom. It's not quite the den of inequity the brochure promised."

"It is, Walker. Believe me. You just have to dig deep enough. Phoenix has some serious problems to overcome. With your undoubted ability around, I'm sure they'll get there." His words seemed to soothe Walker, eliciting a smile and a blush. "So who would wear a sash like this?"

"I am not certain. We should go to the library. Lilly should be able to help."

"And who's Lilly?"

"Lilly Musgrave. She's been the librarian for years. Masonic heritage is a pastime of hers."

"And how do you know that?"

"Because we converse regularly. Us Yalies have to stick together, you know."

"There's more of you around here?"

"Phoenix is carpeted in the finest green, Thaddeus. We're here to stay." Walker said, as he motioned for them to follow and strode out of the office.

"Great." he said, offering Alison an arm and following behind. "A library on a weeknight; I wonder if there's going to be a test."

Still giggling, the pair made their way after Walker and out of the station.

By the time they were approaching the Library, it was almost five. He did not want to say it, but he was gagging for a drink. Even with the wine the previous evening, his body was in withdrawal. It needed alcohol. He needed alcohol. He did not want to disappoint Alison; they were getting on so well. Therefore, there was only one thing to do.

Once their meeting with Lilly was done, he resolved to find a way to ostracise himself and then he would be free to quench his thirst.

Chapter 10

Lilly Musgrave was a short woman. Her greying, bluish hair was curly and her tortoise shell glasses were oversized. She was meticulously organised. After only a few minutes discussion, they sat around a small table in the back of the library with a selection of books laid out on the table.

"I would have to say it was English in origin." said Lilly, thumbing through a heavy textbook. "The symbolism points to a Victorian society; perhaps it is a diminutive of one of the older orders." She flipped from page to page, staring at the drawing of the sash and back to the book. "It's the iconography on the left lapel that has me confused. It should be on the right."

"It was on the right as I looked at him. That means it was on his left."

"Cross symbolism is rare in Masonic tradition." she said, tapping the side of her glasses and pursing her lips in thought. "But there were so many orders founded during the Victorian era in England, it is sometimes difficult to pinpoint an exact one. The British have a long-standing fascination with Egypt that started during the reign of Queen Victoria. Thousands of new societies sprung up during the nineteenth century; each one claiming to have deciphered something new from one archaeological discovery or another." She closed one book and opened another, even older one. "My best course may be to see if the symbol matches anything that I know." She ran a finger over the heavy pages, scanning for signs of a symbol resembling the one drawn. "Ah. Here we are. Your man was wearing a modification of the Rosy Croix, twenty first order. I think what you saw as a circle was a rose."

"Rosy Croix?" asked Alison, peering at the page.

"A Rosicrucian symbol, my dear. A branch of Freemasonry that first emerged during the early seventeenth century in Germany."

"Rosicrucian? Are you absolutely certain of that?"

"I am. You're probably looking for a sect of them though. As I said, there will be hundreds. But if you stick with the Rosicrucian's as your starting point, you will find the right one eventually."

"What's your thought, Thaddeus?" asked Walker.

"I don't need to look. I know what order he's from. He's a member of the Royal Outlook Society."

"The Royal Outlook Society is no more, dear." said Lilly, closing her book. "They were exterminated to a man around the turn of the century. If I remember rightly, they were murdered by a single man. Whose name was…" Her speech slowed, as she looked up and stared.

"I know. My grandfather. Shit!"

"Thaddeus, please." snapped Alison.

"Are you saying that you are being hunted by this society because of what your grandfather did?" asked Walker. "Why not just kill you?"

"Hardships are seen as rites in many Rosicrucian orders." said Lilley. "It could be possible they are putting you through this to test your worthiness for something. Has any other member of your family been approached by these men?"

"My uncle doesn't even acknowledge my existence, so I would never find out anything from him. In addition, my father died in a railway accident a few years back. So, there's no way I could…" A knot formed in his stomach at the thought. His father. It surely could not be true.

"What is wrong, Joshua?" asked Alison, leaning over and clasping his trembling hand.

"I always thought there was something suspicious about my father's death. The facts just did not add up. I…" he slumped his head into his hands and tried to quell the tears forcing their way to the surface.

"Are you thinking he was murdered?" asked Walker. "That this guy killed him?"

"It would make sense. Trials and punishments are a common Masonic practise. They are thought to clear the soul." said Lilly.

"Joshua." said Alison, squeezing his hand tightly. "We have no way of knowing if that is true. It is supposition only."

He tugged his hand from her grip and stood up, drawing in a long, calming lungful of air. "I need some time to think."

"Thaddeus, you need to stay focussed on this." said Walker.

"What I need detective, is to find this guy and make him pay." he said, snapping his retort. "And to do that, I need to think." He turned without engaging another look and marched back out into the evening.

He strode down the sidewalk away from the building, his mind still swimming with pained thoughts. Behind him, he could hear Alison calling after him to stop, but he would not listen. He needed to be alone. He needed time to assess what was happening and what he could do to prevent it.

As he turned the corner and made his way through the bustling downtown, his mind raced. He would sit and think somewhere fitting. All he needed now was a drink to drown his sorrows whilst he thought.

Chapter 11

The waxing moon cast ethereal shadows across the surface of the fishing hole, as Joshua tended a quart of vodka. He sat on a simple jetty that clasped the edge of the pond and glugged another warming mouthful of intoxication; splashing the still waters with his toes.

He could remember coming here with his father. The hole was bigger back then; the farms that lay around the edge of the Estrella Mountain Park having used the valuable desert resource almost to extinction. It was the price of expansion.

His father's eyes flashed with pride when he caught his first fish. He remembered the joy of those brief moments better than anything else in his world. His father told him to keep a memento of the occasion and he had; his first hook. He placed it in a box. It was still kept in a desk drawer in his apartment with his life's other accumulated artefacts. He vowed to protect it forever. It had been many years since he gazed upon it. How he wished the cherished item was with him now.

He never expected his life to turn out this way. He could remember his father, his once proud features drawn by the pressures of life, falling ever further from him, the market crash taking away his soul and depositing it on the departing ship of his dreams. He wanted to be able to go back to those days, as his father struggled to make enough money for them to survive, and tell him it was ok. He wanted to say he was a child, and all he needed was his father by his side. But he could not. His father was gone.

The accident happened on a Thursday. It was such a basic failure in safety it was seen as a tragedy. A switch, one that should have diverted rolling stock to a different line, was not engaged. And the four thirteen made no distinction as it travelled. His father stood no chance. Rolled over and bust in two like a doll. His pieces swept aside the track like flotsam.

He could remember the cops turning up at his school. He sat and wondered as his education was paused whilst they talked to his teacher. He could see the face of his friend, James Lipkin, as he turned and joked about how the teacher was to be hauled away, his exuberance evaporating when they came for him instead. His world fell apart that day.

Until that moment, he never once missed his mother. There, as the school nurse comforted his sobbing form and social services arrived to take him away, he could not think of anyone else that could help.

He gulped another bitter mouthful and sighed. It could all now be linked. Did they cause the preeclampsia that claimed his mother and nearly claimed him? Perhaps they planned to kill his mother before he was born to punish his father. That would mean they knew they failed. Moreover, that would mean maybe they were the ones who altered the signal that diverted the train.

Michael Giardino, who worked with his father, testified he was sure the signal and switch were both correctly set before work started on the tracks. The cops could find no trace of tampering. However, paying them all off would not take much.

He finished the first bottle and tossed it into the pond, as he drew another quart from his pocket. He must try to understand. Who would want him to suffer this? Who could he have met that would even know of his past?

He thought back to the third murder in the chain. Perhaps there would be something in its detail to help him decipher his situation.

-

It was forty-five. The defensive line along the border of France held strong throughout the early winter and soon CCB was on the offensive. After ploughing a trail through Belgium, they found themselves assisting the besieged one hundred and first airborne in the principality of Bastonge. After three weeks of heavy fighting, CCB dispersed across Luxembourg, and he found himself in the small commune of Villers-la-Bonne-Eau.

Colonel Howe was in constant contact, driving them to get results as soon as possible. However, their leads were non-existent. Two boxes of observations and six thousand interviews over five months had unearthed nothing. At least the murders had stopped.

Humphrey's assertion this was because they were close to the truth made sense. Therefore, during the brief respite in the fighting, they set up camp and started trawling through the notes collected.

As the evidence was collated and referenced, a list of potential candidates slowly began to resolve. And, after an exhaustive requisition process, Colonel Howe agreed for the men to be brought before them again for more questioning.

Two days later, and more reams of notes taken, they sat in their tent arguing over the details.

"I'm telling you Humphrey," he said, shaking a set of notes, "Private Jones is definitely not telling us something. His story is not corroborated once. Not by anyone we've interviewed."

"But that doesn't mean he's guilty. You saw the man when he came to get us on the first night. He's an order boy; a grunt. He doesn't remember facts because he's not told to."

"That's a cheap excuse and you know it. There's no evidence, but there's definitely something there."

"So what do you want to do about it?" asked Humphrey, raising his voice in frustration. "We've interviewed the guy three times and we still don't have anything to go on."

"There has to be something."

"There isn't! Ok? We have nada - zip - nothing. We've been on this for months and all we've got is the knowledge someone is out there. Hell, the guy could be dead for all we know. Gerry could have saved us the trouble."

Humphrey was right. They guy could be dead. Maybe that was why there had been no further murders. He was tired, out of options and bothered. He reached over into his pack, withdrew the last of the bottles of wine he managed to steal on their journey, and uncorked it, glugging the sour liquid with gusto.

"Oh, that's right Thaddeus, you fucking asshole! You dissolve back into pity. I'll go sort this by myself."

He watched as Humphrey stormed out of the tent into the daylight. He would not be chasing after him or challenging his assessment. He was an asshole, no doubt. Nevertheless, he needed his drink. He cherished it.

Soon, it was late evening. A stiff breeze billowing around the tent roused him. As his vision cleared, he looked up to see Humphrey standing in the entrance, his head in his hands and the late evening sun silhouetting his sagging form.

"It's definitely not Jones."

"How do you know?" he asked, straightening up and buttoning his shirt.

"Because he's dead. MPs found his body about an hour ago."

"Where?" he asked, pulling on his boots.

"In the officer's mess. You might want to take a look."

The scramble to the mess was awkward; Humphrey's look of disgust as he shambled across the broken ground belying his feelings about his state and only heightening his irksome manner.

When they arrived, the neat tent was crawling with personnel. Colonel Howe was barking orders to the men to ensure the site was restricted to all but a privileged few.

The scene inside was bizarre. Jones sat at a table, sprawled across a neatly arranged place setting. He was wearing a full doctor's outfit, including a carefully draped stethoscope. There did not seem to be a single mark on him, but it was difficult to tell whether this assessment was true of his face, as it was submerged in a bowl of soup.

"We haven't moved the body since we found him." said Humphrey, running a hand through his hair.

He checked his wrist. He was still warm. Two to four hours at the most. He checked his nails and his arms. No cuts, no abrasions; nothing. He checked the back of his head and his hair line; still nothing. "I'm going to have to lift the head out of the soup to check his face."

"I'll call Mortimer over."

Alan Mortimer was the new CMO. He was short and podgy, nothing like a military man. He was drafted from New Hampshire where he worked as a surgeon. It was obvious it was not a situation he enjoyed.

"Are you ok with us moving the body to check the face?" he asked.

"Go ahead. I've completed my preliminary assessment and there's nothing to indicate a cause of death. I thought I had better wait until you arrived to continue." said Mortimer, shrugging his shoulders.

He grabbed Jones by his lab coat and pulled him into a sitting position. Although his face was covered in the thick mixture, there appeared to be no injuries hidden. His eyes were not reddened and his lips, although blue, did not bear the deep hints of asphyxiation. "Has anyone got any rubbing alcohol?" Humphrey crossed his arms over his chest and glared at him. "It's not for me. I need to check something."

Mortimer waddled over to the back of the mess, returned with a glass bottle, and handed it to him.

"Do you have any toluene salts?"

"Why would I have those?"

"I don't know. Do you? Any orcin derivative should do."

Mortimer huffed as he left the mess. "I will go and see, but I'm not sure how this is going to help."

"What's going on?" asked Humphrey, kneeling at his side. "Alcohol and a hallucinogen; It's not happy hour."

"Don't start. I know what I'm doing."

Mortimer arrived five minutes later with three stopper-topped vials. He carefully selected the one he needed and removed two teaspoons from the table. He half-filled one with some soup, a few drops of alcohol, and a sprinkle of the salts, and placed the other spoon over the top. Holding the two together, he took his Zippo from his pocket and lit it underneath the arrangement.

"Do you want me to get you a pipe, Thaddeus?" asked Mortimer, bemused by what was going on. "Or perhaps a syringe?"

He ignored the man, watching as the concoction bubbled and hissed. A few minutes later, once all activity ceased, he carefully uncoupled the stack to look at the residue. There, surrounding blackened remnants was a fine, yellow powder.

"What is that stuff?" asked Humphrey, leaning close.

"It's a chlorate. The soup is probably loaded with chloral hydrate." he said, standing and making his way over to Howe. "You need to ensure everyone who has eaten in the mess is monitored for signs of listlessness or hysteria, colonel."

"And why would that be?" asked Howe, glaring down his nose.

"Because someone may have poisoned the food with a sedative, colonel. Jones could be the first of many. The drug affects people in different ways. I cannot predict how others may react to it."

Howe did not respond. He frantically started handing out orders and pointing to the tents around the mess.

"What do we do now?" asked Humphrey.

"This gives us an advantage. Chloral hydrate is rare, especially in a war zone. Check with Mortimer to see if he has any in stores, and who had access. I'll see if there is anything in the local area some could be made from. Our guy's made his first mistake. He's limited the field of opportunity on this one. We need to make the information count."

As he turned to begin his search, he stopped in his tracks. He stood, in silent awe at the scene unfolding around him, as man after man began to wilt; tumbling to the floor like discarded puppets.

-

He downed the last of his second quart and tried to stand, but his head was fuddled and he slumped back to the soft earth. He must get to the station and warn people. He knew why and how the killer was picking his targets; he should have seen it before.

Righting only for a moment, he was struck by a wave of nausea and vomited, collapsing to the ground in a stupor.

Chapter 12

It was late morning before Joshua managed to reach the station. Muddied from head to toe from a night spent in the open, his head would not stop pounding. However, he would not be going home for a change of clothing, he needed to tell people what was going on.

He staggered through the unusually busy station and into the small office, leaning against the doorframe for support and panting hard. "I know what's going on." In response, Alison and Walker simply stared at him, glum, almost shocked, expressions hung from their faces. "I know I look a mess, but that's not important right now. You need to listen to me."

Walker shook his head. "I'm not sure there's any point, Thaddeus." he said, absently tapping his pen against the desk, his face ashen. "I'm not sure what we're doing is helping."

"Seriously?" he asked, shocked by the response. "I know I may have let myself down last night, but…"

"Last night," snapped Alison, head in hands, "is irrelevant! Today counts Joshua, and you are in no state to help anyone."

"What the hell are you talking about?"

"Has no-one talked to you on your way in this morning?" asked Walker, making his way over. "You don't know what's happened, do you?"

Alison looked up and caught his look of confusion. "Have you honestly not heard?"

"Heard what? What is happening?"

"Paul Rollins was found in Sergeant Houghton's office this morning." said Walker, holding back tears. "His body was left in the same manner as you described Forrester's."

"What? Left here? In the station?"

"Draped over Houghton's desk like a doll. Naked as the day he was born."

"Fuck!" he said, turning and leaving. "I hope they haven't cleared the body away yet."

"I wouldn't do that, Thaddeus. Houghton wants your blood." said Walker, grabbing him by the arm.

"He can have it. As soon as I get this son of a bitch, he can have the lot." he said, shrugging Walker off and pushing through the crowding masses outside the small office.

As soon as he got through the bulk, he could see the table. Officer Paul Rollins adorned on its surface for all to see. His face turned toward the room and blood congealed around an empty socket. Houghton stood outside, pacing. As he drew close, Houghton saw him and came straight over.

"You're a fucking dead man, Thaddeus! A dead man!" Two officers stepped from the crowd and restrained Houghton, as he struggled to get close. "Wrong fucking idea! It wasn't the first person on the scene, it was the first officer you lame assed fucker!"

He quickly stepped round the snarling sergeant and ducked into the room where two medical attendants and a photographer were assessing the scene. "Is his tongue missing?"

One of the medics turned, a look of total disgust on his face. "Yep, it's gone. Just like you hopefully."

"This isn't my fault."

"Isn't your fault?" said the man, almost screaming. "Half the force was out protecting a guy on your say so! The building was practically empty last night because of you.

163

That allowed your guy to come in here unopposed and kill an officer in our own station. Of course it's your fault. Now get the fuck out of my crime scene."

He slowly trudged back out of the room, hideously aware of the shooting looks of anger coming from the massed ranks outside. He made his way over to the small kitchenette as Houghton dispersed the crowd. As he stood and queued for a coffee, Walker and Alison came and joined him in line.

"Nobody has done anything but stare at this all morning, Thaddeus." said Walker, reaching over and filling his mug with boiling water from the steel urn. "Your name is mud around here."

"Nothing's changed much then."

"Don't joke about this, Joshua." said Alison. "The men are about five minutes from forming a lynch mob."

"Great. Let me know if they want any assistance with the knots." He walked back into the main office and slumped down at a desk, cradling his coffee.

"You said you knew what was happening." said Walker, as he sat next to him. "You better pray you're right this time."

"I am right; absolutely right. But it only helps, it won't solve anything."

"What won't?"

"Our killer's not repeating what happened in France. Both France and now here are repeats of what happened in the Institute."

"The institute?"

"Where my grandfather slaughtered all those people. Whoever is doing this is seeking revenge for what he did. That's the Masonic link. But more than that, he's replicating the victims' manner of death. I remember from researching it myself."

"So we are looking for someone with ties to those killed at the Institute and to the masons?" asked Alison. "That could severely reduce our potential field of enquiry."

"It should. But it leaves us little time."

"How so?"

"The last act was the use of electricity. He mass executed the whole order in a sealed chamber; fried them like animals."

"How did that play out during the war?" asked Walker.

"It didn't. Our guy never got chance because the war ended. He probably ran out of time. I don't think he'll want to make the same mistake again."

"So what do we do?"

"You start by getting me another coffee and then we hit the books. We'll go back to my original list and round up every last one of them if we have to. If it's one of those people, there's no way they can hurt anyone else if they're locked up." he said, as he gulped the last vestiges and handed the mug over. "More sugar this time though. That one was really sour." As Walker made his way to the kitchenette, another thought resolved and he charged after him, grasping the mug and staring into it.

"It's empty, Thaddeus. My lord you have some issues!"

"Not as many as the rest of us." he said, shaking his head and looking at the fine, yellow powder lining the high water mark in the mug. He turned to the room, hands in the air. "Everyone, put your drinks down." The room turned as one and glared at him. "Fucking do it! The water's been…"

But it was too late. He could see the drool coming from the men around him, as one by one they slumped down onto the tables. He could feel his own head beginning to swim, as he tried to steady himself against the faltering Walker. He staggered, desperate to stay conscious as he made his way to Alison. He stumbled onward, as Walker collapsed behind him, Alison already wilting onto the table. Around him, the echoed thuds of the fallen rang in his ears, as he caught a glimpse of someone making their way through the array of downed officers. It was him, his adversary. As his strength gave and he began to tumble toward the floor, he was sure he saw the man wave, a look of total glee encompassing his face.

Chapter 13

It was mid-March in forty-five, before CCB made its way into Germany. Travelling at pace across the cratered remains of innumerate towns, they followed the trail of destruction ploughed by the British Royal Air Force, as it bombed out everything in their path.

By the start of April, after nights of heavy fighting, they came to rest in the town of Cruezburg in the heart of Nazi Germany. This was to be their resting point before they followed what remained of the Panzer Divisions as they fled toward Czechoslovakia.

The crippled remains of the town were a mess. Corpses, too many to number of animal, combatant and civilian, were piled up around the ruins of a once beautiful core of buildings. Bullet holes, giving structures the air of Swiss cheese, riddled everything.

No one had spoken to them in months, many of the men still in shock from the bizarre occurrences in Belgium. It was an eerie counterpoint to their work.

During their trek across Germany, Humphrey reduced the list to just four possibilities. Now the current operation was over, it was time to prepare for one last round of interviews.

Clutching the handwritten paper to his chest, he made his way down the slight incline to the tent of Colonel Howe. His appearance was neat and organised and his breath was fresh, no alcohol imbibed in weeks.

Colonel Howe sat in a chair, out in the spring sunshine, a table of maps and notes concentrating his focus.

"Good afternoon, Colonel." he said, saluting and standing to attention.

"What is it today, Thaddeus?" asked Howe, not taking his eyes from the notes. "I hope you have something worthwhile to give me. I grow tired of asking for results that are not forthcoming."

"I have a final list of requisitions for attendance at interviews. Our man must be one of these. It is also requested their personal possessions be brought to us for inspection."

Howe took the sheet offered and poured over the details. "I will arrange what you have asked. I will also ask Ardley to correlate your findings with his own."

"Ardley sir?"

"Sergeant Ardley, third core. I thought it would be prudent to get someone sober to look at your evidence. He has drawn up a list of his own. It would be interesting to see if the two match."

"I really don't think that it is a valuable use of time to…"

"Whilst ever this is still my battalion, and I believe it is, I will do all the thinking Thaddeus. You should focus what little effort you put into staying awake on gathering evidence. Dismissed."

He walked away from the tent in quiet contemplation. The last thing he and Humphrey needed was to be considered as no longer required in their roles. Knowing what everyone thought of them, it would mean front line infantry duty for sure. They must make sure they nailed their man soon.

"Do you have any idea what Ardley might have found?" asked Humphrey, as they prepared for the arrival of the men.

"Not a clue. But I suspect it's not much." he said, as he arranged the simple table so it faced the entrance of their tent. "We have been over and over this evidence for months. If we can't find anything concrete, I'm sure he can't."

"But what if he does?"

"Don't worry, Humphrey. We'll get there first. I know we will."

One by one, they grilled the four men about the fine details of each of the murders, each man having the opportunity to commit the vile acts. By the time the interviews were complete, a smile spread far across his face, the list now one man long.

"He had opportunity and access. He's the only one from the list who it can be."

"It looks that way Humphrey." he said, re-reading Private York's record. "To be honest I'm a little surprised. He's got a glowing career profile."

"In with the hierarchy, full access, perfect military history; it's almost too good a cover to not be just that."

"OK then. You take our evidence to Howe and sell him on it. I'll start searching his things for something physical to link him to the crimes."

He took the duffel pack, spread its filling out across the tent, and began to sift, as Humphrey made his way outside. The contents were meagre. A handwritten journal caught the eye and was put to one side, as soiled clothing was checked for blood spatter. Klim cans, many of which contained coins from various countries travelled through, jingled as they were emptied out in search of a killer's memorabilia. Then, as a sturdy pair of marchers was put to one side, a rattle made him stop. He reached inside the stinking footwear and removed a quart of thick, creamy coloured liquid, stored in an unmarked bottle. Careful not to put his fingerprints on the cap, he unscrewed the lid with a handkerchief and smelt the contents. Aniseed. Just to make sure, he poured a blob onto his index finger and licked it gingerly. It was Pastis. The rich, sweet, heavily alcoholic beverage fired his taste buds and ignited his need. Making sure no one was looking, he took a swig from the bottle. It was glorious. Fresh, calming and tinged with bitter aftertaste; a drink fit for kings. Ignoring what he was supposed to be doing, he took the bottle and sat at the table. Trembling with his desire to consume, he began to glug at the drink without pause or thought, and was soon laid back in the chair, deliriously oblivious to the world.

Roused from his induced slumbers by shouting from somewhere near, he tumbled to the floor and attempted to look busy. He hid the empty bottle under his own pack and began to pick at items of the floor, in mock parody of concentration.

Sergeant Ardley was a massive man. Muscle covered him like a jumper and protruded from every seem of his uniform, as he strode into the tent. "Put that man's things away and meet me in Colonel's Howe's tent. You'll want to see this, Thaddeus."

He nodded, still attempting to look focussed on his work, and grabbed the empty duffel. After drinking as much water as he could to clear his head, and hurriedly repacking Private York's bag, he straightened his appearance and made his way down the slope.

Outside Howe's tent, a crowd gathered in the late evening sun, parting as he strode toward the entrance. The scene inside was horrific. Colonel Howe was out in his hammock, blood enveloping his face and smothering his features. In his hand was a sheet of paper.

"Notice anything Thaddeus?" asked Ardley.

"Only one thing." he said, as he made his way around the body. "The impact marks are consistent with a large, rounded object. My guess would by a pan or a helmet, although the material is quite soft, so bronze or brass maybe? Definitely not steel. Therefore, that rules either of those two items out. Perhaps a kettle?"

"Impressive." said Ardley, moving to stand at his side. "But that's not what I was getting at. Check the hand."

He knelt down and looked at the piece of paper in Howe's grasp. It was their final output; the detail of why they thought Private York was guilty. "Where is York?"

"Your guy is out trying to find him now. No one has seen him since he left your tent. I have to admit Thaddeus, I didn't have him down as a candidate for this. It looks like you've got your man."

"It's a little late for congratulations. And we haven't got him yet."

"You will. Half the unit has him on a deathwatch by now. He'll be found before long. He'll pay for this Thaddeus, the men will make sure of that."

As he trudged back out of the tent, the men gathered saluted, grateful, even if after the loss of Howe, justice had been served. Little did any of them know how wrong they all were.

Chapter 14

Joshua awoke to the gentle nudging of Walker. Through the mire of cognition, he was sure the man was covered in tea. "What the hell is going on?"

"Livermore." Walker said, almost in tears. "It's… He got Doctor Livermore."

"Fuck." he said, remembering. "Jones. Fucking Livermore is Jones." He stood gingerly and made his way through the downed masses to Doctor Livermore. He sat at the far edge of the main room, lab coat bathed in tea, face down in a bowl. "Four down, three to go."

"So what do we do?"

"First of all," he said, standing to face Walker, "we…" he stopped and stared, his vision clearing. "You haven't moved the body?"

"No. I just woke and spotted him when I was checking around."

"But you're jacket is covered in tea."

"I must have poured mine over me when I fell unconscious. You don't think he was trying to kill me and then picked on Livermore because I was waking up do you?"

"Probably not. Your story is the most plausible. Ignore me."

"Don't do that to me. I nearly had a heart attack."

"Forget I mentioned it. We have bigger things to deal with. We need to make a list of targets."

"We've done that, remember?"

"Not of who has died already, but of who has yet to die. If this guy is following the same pattern, then we can decipher who he will pick next. It shouldn't be difficult."

"Do you want me to wake anyone else?"

"Try to rouse Alison, and the other medic. That way we can leave it to the expert and go and think somewhere where we'll be left in peace."

Ten minutes later, the cursing of Doctor Maxwell still ringing in their ears, the three made their way out of the police station and across to a local diner.

After ordering a round of coffees and a selection of cakes from the display, he made his way back to the table to the smiles of Walker.

"Nice choice, Thaddeus."

"You think so? I just thought we might want something sweet."

"I do. The chocolate gateau looks great!"

"So how do we reasonably decide who will be targeted next?" asked Alison, as Walker launched into the tray of cakes with delight.

"That should be easy. We look at the murders in the institute and then to those picked in the war. It should be simple to generate a comparable list from who is around now."

"And how does the list help us?" asked Walker, crumbs falling from his mouth as he spoke.

"It gives us a list of people that have to be monitored at all times. Our killer has to reproduce things just as they were if he's going to punish me. If we protect the likely suspects, eventually he'll have to take a risk and we'll have our chance."

"So who died and when?"

"That's the part you're not going to like." he said, taking a notepad from his pocket. "Colonel Howe was next in the sequence, bludgeoned to death with a copper kettle stolen from a local house. There's only one match for Howe."

"Houghton." said Alison, shocked.

"Oh my." said Walker, almost laughing. "I want to be there when you give him that news."

"So who was next?" asked Alison.

"The next murder came just as we were approaching the border to Czechoslovakia. We had spent most of early summer trying to track down our primary suspect, Private York. All the evidence pointed to him being the culprit for the other murders."

"Then how come you have never mentioned him before?"

"Because we found him dead when we stopped to prepare the tanks for the final battle with what was left of the German Panzer Divisions."

"But I thought you said he was your prime suspect? Why was he not in custody?"

"Because we didn't know where he was."

"What? Then how did he get from the middle of Germany to the Czech border?"

"Nobody knew. As I said, most of the battalion was on full alert for him. He just appeared out of nowhere; dead as a doornail."

"I take it he had been dead a while?"

"The body was fresh. No more than a few hours."

"That's the strangest thing I ever heard! How does a man stay hidden for that long in a war zone?"

"I don't know to this day. Our guy must have had him hidden away somewhere. Keeping him alive until the right moment to show us what he wanted us to see."

"That would take stupendous planning."

"Not as much as his death."

"Why? How did you find him?"

"He was tied to a metal chair, with car batteries wired to it. You could hear his flesh sizzling against the metal when you got close. But that wasn't the worst part."

"There's worse than being fried by car batteries?"

"His head was sawn off; left on a spike outside the mess."

"Jesus wept." said Walker, shuddering involuntarily. "But at least we have an advantage there. We don't have a prime suspect. No suspect means a none-repeatable sequence."

"Walker has a point." said Alison, placing a reassuring hand on his arm. "And remember, even if we find a suspect who is not our killer, at least we will know who the next target is."

She was right. She was always right. He smiled and placed a hand on top of hers and looked over to the station. "Then we move. We go tell Houghton and then we get to work on our list of suspects."

As he took a five dollar bill from his pocket and slid it under the tray to cover costs and tip, he looked at what little remained of their repast and shuddered. He would not allow himself to be blinded by friendship again.

Chapter 15

Houghton's mood could only be described as gnarly. He sat, smoking as if an Indian's communication attempts were being made within his mouth, as Joshua described everything he knew. At the end of the twenty minute speech, the ashtray was full and his face was furrowed and drawn. "I knew at some point it would come down to me or you, Thaddeus. How did I know I'd be first, I wonder?"

"It's just how it's played out, sir. I never meant..."

"Fucking stow it, Thaddeus!" said Houghton, in a sarcastic, mock copy of his voice. "Boo-fucking-hoo! Look at me. I'm being persecuted by a man who hated my grandfather. He's not actually harming me in any way, just everyone around me, but I'm still upset. I'm a worthless fucking drunkard, who's hardly even aware of the pain and suffering around me, so he's wasting his fucking time in torturing me, but that doesn't seem to stop him. Woe is fucking me!" He stood and paced round his desk, grabbing Joshua by his lapels. "Your piñata moment is fast approaching my friend. I have seventy heavily muscled officers out there who are just itching to stand in line and take pitching practice at your fucking cranium. So you'd better listen to me real careful. If I waste my time protecting myself, and this fucker kills somebody else instead, Doctor Salinger over there will become my primary suspect. The fucking world will know it. That means she'll be next. You got me? You fuck anything else up and you'll have the entire force waiting in line to fuck you over every time they see you. Dealing with this freak will seem like a fucking picnic. Now get the fuck out of my sight and produce me a single fucking name. A guy to drag in here and put in the fucking cells where I can see him. Even if you're wrong, your circus clown has to come in here to get him. And this time, we'll be ready."

"I did not think it was possible," said Alison, as they made their way across to their office. "But I believe his vocabulary has reduced even further."

"Cranium was a good word though." said Walker, with a smile. "He's got to get points for that one."

"A five minute rant in which his Freudian slip was 'cranium'? I think his brain may be wired incorrectly."

When they arrived back, he took a cloth from the table and started walking toward the chalk board.

"What are you doing?" asked Walker. "We need that information."

"No we don't." he said, as he began to wipe. "We need to start from the beginning. We need to draw up a list based on everything we know. Not reduce a previous list based on new information."

"This could take hours." said Alison. "Or days."

"We have until our guy can get to Houghton. And that could be a while."

"Ok Thaddeus. This is your show. Where do you want to start?"

"With our list of requirements." he said, as he began to write. "Our guy has to have access to Masonic tradition. He needs to be related to, or have been given knowledge of the events at the institute and he needs revenge for what happened. He needs to have been involved with the path of the Fourth Armoured Division during the war and now he needs to be here, in Phoenix. This guy also has to have a knowledge of chemistry and have access to, or stolen some

177

chloral hydrate. And lastly, but by no means least, he needs to have recently come into possession of a copper kettle."

"Why recently?" asked Alison.

"Because if we'd accidently gone to this guy's house for any reason and he'd already possessed one, I might have made the link. There's no way he could risk that. The likelihood is he will have bought it, or stolen it, recently. That should be our starting point. We need a list of everywhere in the Phoenix area that might sell one of these kettles and we need to talk to the owners about who has bought one. We also need to search through the recent burglary reports for any that have been reported as stolen. From that list, we dwindle the results going backward; starting with the chloral hydrate.

"Sounds promising." said Walker. "Our last end point is our new starting point."

"I also think we should make our own lists, rather than making a single generic one. That way we can cross-reference our results and maybe find a name we otherwise would have missed. We should also split up. We can make better progress in isolation."

"Are you sure that is wise, Joshua?" asked Alison. "Being by yourself did not do you much good last night."

"I promise to behave." he said, stretching a smile. "I was caught off guard by my emotions to the events. I am focussed on this now. You have my word."

True to what he said, the next three days passed without incident. Reams and reams of information arriving from Alison's contacts in the FBI and even more brought in from their officers in the field.

By the time light was fading on a crisp Friday night, a single box, stuffed with bios, sat in the centre of the desk. To its side, two identical copies sat waiting.

"So this is it. Our shortlist." said Walker.

"It is. All these people tie our criteria to at least a four from five match."

"And we have a copy each?" asked Alison.

"We do."

"Then we should go make our lists and reconvene our discussions on Monday morning." said Walker, grabbing a box from the table.

"After we get some food. If we're still on expenses then we should make the most of it."

"Oh yes. I whole-heartedly concur." said Walker.

After spending another pleasant evening in each other's company, the group dissipated, Alison allowing him to walk her home. The late evening breeze blew warm around his face and lifted his spirits. She pecked his cheek as she left to walk up to her door, smiling as she made her way inside.

He wanted this life.

He wanted to be normal again; to give existence another go. He would not run away from it any more.

Chapter 16

The next morning, refreshed and alert as he had been in years, Joshua made his way to his kitchen to make himself a hearty breakfast. As he sat in his living room and ate, the smell of stale alcohol drifted into his nostrils. He had lived like a pig for too long. It was time to change.

Once his meal was finished, he started to clean. First, he tackled the hideous levels of grime infesting his kitchen, and then he took on the living room. The caustic soda used to scrub the paintwork stung his fingers as it seeped into the cracks around his bitten nails, but it was effective. A yellow sludge, containing the residue of countless cigarettes, clung to every surface. It drooled off the windows as he wiped and filled his bucket with a foulness only generated from the darkest pits of self-pity. He moved to the bedroom, and then the bathroom, the clumps of hair and congealed soap found there a rank and lamentable exhibit of his previous mental state. Previous. The word filled him with pride. He was moving on.

He sat and drank a coffee, from a freshly sparkling mug, and stared around his apartment upon his work's completion. A light wind billowed through the open window and brought the scents of the city with it. The air was fresh and the rotting embers of what he had become were gone; piled neatly in the back alley by the trashcans. With a burgeoning sense of self, he grabbed the box containing the details collated and began to organise the information within on his coffee table.

There were fourteen names. The specifics of each man, his financial records over the last month and even his latest medical documents delicately concealed within individual heavy, brown folders, each bound with cord. The first thing he would check would be their purchases. The kettle, the chemicals, the trappings of lunacy bought to pull off the murders; it would have to show up somewhere. All he had to do was find it.

The afternoon whizzed by in a blur. By the time his stomach's growling informed him too much time had passed since his breakfast, it was nearly seven at night. He stretched and made his way to the kitchen, a forlorn look crossing his tired face as he stared at the meagre fare on offer in his pantry. He would have to find a restaurant that provided a takeaway service. There was an Italian place, mainly serving pizzas as he remembered, sat close to MacAlpine's Coffee Shop. That would do nicely. Grabbing his wallet and throwing on his jacket, he made his way out into the night.

The sounds of the city seemed magnified as he walked down the bustling streets. Smells, many of which he was only experiencing for the first time, wafted round and made him smile. He felt alive. He shook his head as he skipped through the throngs. It was frightening to think about what he may have let slip by, intoxicated oblivion and self-doubt his solitary companions.

Dodging between cars as he crossed the street, he walked outside the opulent frontage of MacAlpine's. The gleaming chrome and red leather combination of its trademark interior was blanketed by the jubilant chatter of its patrons. The smell of its famous, thick, double cream sodas drifted out of its door and dared him go inside. But not tonight. He would eat and get back to work. He would earn his rewards from now on. If his work were completed early on Sunday, he would come back and treat himself to a large shake and one of their glorious cheese and bacon burgers, accompanied, of course, by a healthy helping of their incredible spicy fries and onion rings.

As he turned down seventh, he could see the sign for Mario's in the distance. As he drew closer, the pungent aroma of tomato and basil merged with the background hints of fresh pesto that drifted up the street and made him salivate. He would see if they did an Italian meat special, and top it with extra oregano and anchovies.

As he walked through the entrance, his eyes took time to refocus to the low light in the cosy interior.

"Ah, Mister Thaddeus!" said an Italian male voice, as he made his way toward the counter. "Will you be having the usual this evening?"

He looked up bemused, his eyes picking out a portly man, draped in a chef's apron, stood behind a counter in the back of the room. "I'm sorry?"

"Another long day, my friend? No problem. Please take a seat and I'll bring your order over."

He had no idea what was going on. Was it possible he had been to the restaurant more often than he remembered? Not wanting to question what was happening and cause a scene, he took a seat on an arcing green leather couch, in the shadow of a bay window. "Can I have it to go, please?"

"As always, Mister Thaddeus. Would you like some garlic bread tonight?" asked the chef, as he delicately kneaded a ball of dough into a disc.

"Sure, why not." he said, feeling uncomfortable.

It was clear from the man's manner he had been here many times before. It was also obvious the chef thought he knew him. That was a concern. What if he thought he knew him well? Could he find himself questioned about events of which he had no recollection? He rubbed his hands together and stared out of the window. Maybe if he looked distant, nobody would bother him.

The chef took great care over the preparation of his food, spinning the dough with consummate precision and carefully, almost artistically, applying the topping. After twenty minutes of wait, he came over with a brown bag, containing a large box, a small box, and a bottle. "This one is on me." he said, his round, warm features brimming with cheer as he handed the bounty over.

"Thanks." he said, perhaps a little too awkwardly, as he rose to his feet and accepted the food.

"The wine is a Salice Salentino; a forty six. It is my gift. You must let me know if you enjoy it."

"I will." he said, red with embarrassment.

After a grateful handshake, he wandered back out into the night and looked up toward the heavens. What had he become? How much of his life had passed by without him noticing? He growled under his breath. He had wasted every gift given. A few minutes later, still angry with himself, he sat back down in his living room and arranged the food on the table.

The smell as he carefully opened the boxes was incredible; rich, fragrant and hinted with delicate spice.

His first bite of pizza was ecstasy and his first taste of garlic bread bordered on epiphany. He slumped back in his chair and gazed at the food, so artfully arranged in its containers. Whatever he was, he was definitely well fed. He looked at the wine. It would go so well with the meal. But he would not. He fought back his urge, reached for another slice of pizza, and went back to work.

His list was now just five men long. In addition, one of the names he recognised; Corporal James Carter. His name never came up during their initial assessment. Why? He was part of the unit. Why was he overlooked the first time round? He could not remember, and it infuriated him.

He stared at the wine again. Just one glass. Maybe it would help him relax?

He shook off his demons and tore another strip of garlic bread. He would not lose focus.

Carter was part of the gunnery crew. His looked at his file in Chambrey. That was a long time ago. Why did he discount him? He remembered vaguely something about what he was doing during the first murder. Was Carter working to moor the guns at the time? Did he have an alibi? The information sat at the edge of his memory and dangled tantalisingly out of grasp. It was pure frustration. He addled his mind with alcohol and now he was paying the price.

He stood up and paced across the threadbare carpet. He was missing something. There was some reason this could not be Carter. What was it? Why could he not retrieve the information?

He stared back at the wine. The chef said it was special. It was a gift; surely, it would be an insult not to have just one taste? He was a hardened drinker. One bottle of wine was not going to have that much impact.

He went to the kitchen, grabbed a wine glass, a corkscrew, and sat back down on the couch. He deftly unscrewed the bottle and released the cork with an emotive pop. He licked his lips as he poured a satisfyingly large glass, and then paused. He was weak.

He stood up and paced behind the couch again. How dare he go back against what he was trying to do? He promised himself, but more importantly, he promised Alison. He was to be a better man. What sort of man went back on his word after just a few days? Nevertheless, it was only one glass. And the bottle was now opened. It was a waste to let it rot. Just a taste. Just one taste to go with the food before it went cold. It was a fair compromise.

He fell back onto the couch, grabbed another slice of pizza, and picked up the glass. The crimson liquid swirled in the glass as he took a bite and brought it to his lips. He closed his eyes, savouring the moment, and took a sip. Heaven. No other work could describe the mixture. It was a perfect counterpoint to the spices so lovingly woven into the food. Another bite and another swig. Then a handful and a gulp. Then delight - consumption - delirium - nothing.

Chapter 17

It was only a month before the end of the war. The allies were circling Berlin and CCB were chasing down the last resistance of the German military machine as it tried to find safety in the ruins of Czechoslovakia.

On a chair, sat outside the makeshift garage of the fourth armoured, the decapitated body of Private York still fizzed lifelessly as the power from the massive batteries surged through what remained of him. Behind Joshua and Humphrey, two British Engineer Corps technicians struggled to untangle the numerous wires linking the power source to the chair; no one yet sure if the creation was some kind of bomb.

Humphrey was dumbfounded, lost in thought about how this could have happened. Joshua was no better. Nothing made sense. It was impossible to believe the person responsible for this atrocity could have done this without assistance or without being noticed. As they stood and chatted about what they should do next, Ardley marched up, flanked by an entourage of men, his usual, calm demeanour gone and rage and turmoil written across his troubled brow.

"Looks like we've got company." said Humphrey, turning to face the men as they slowed by their sides. "What can we do for you gentlemen?"

"Lieutenant Humphrey Galloway," said Ardley, as the men with him moved into flanking positions, "You are hereby under arrest for the murder of Private James York and the sequence of murders preceding it. You are ordered to relinquish your sidearm and come with us."

"What the fuck are you doing, Ardley?" said Joshua, moving forward, as a look of dread descended over Humphrey's face.

"I must ask you to stand down Lieutenant." said Ardley, drawing his gun and eliciting the raising of weapons from the men surrounding them. "This is my investigation now."

"What investigation could lead you to this assumption? It's more likely to be the fucking President than it is to be Humphrey."

"Stand aside, sir. If you do not desist, I will be forced to arrest you too."

"Stand aside whilst you take Humphrey off to a drumhead? I think you've got a screw loose somewhere."

Ardley shook his head and waggled his gun, motioning for two burley privates to restrain Joshua. "Execute your duty gentlemen."

"Just stop and think about this for a moment." said Joshua, struggling to free himself as more men grabbed Humphrey and started leading him off. "What kind of lunatic would take up a post with the guy who's tracking him? Humphrey can't be the killer. We're looking for…"

"We're looking for a well-manicured man, about his height and build with opportunity and motive for doing what he's done." said Ardley, walking over to Joshua and staring straight through him. "I take it you are unaware of his early history?"

"What history? He's in his twenties for Christ's sake. How much history can there be?"

"He spent six months in an asylum at his father's request. He tried to kill another child when he was eight. He's mentally unstable, Thaddeus. He's also one of the only men who have been at every crime scene. He matches the killer. In my opinion, he is the killer."

"Don't talk shit, Ardley. I've been with him the whole time. I can vouch that it's not him."

"Have you now, Thaddeus?" said Ardley, scratching his chin and smiling. "Where were you when the first murder happened?"

"In a chapel - in a small room - with Humphrey."

"Really? According to the notes that you yourself have taken, you were passed out after having a drink."

"I may have had a drink, but that's no reason…"

"And what about the other murders? Where was Humphrey when they happened?"

"I… er…" said Joshua, as a dawning sense of foreboding descended on his thoughts.

"You were out cold for all of them. That's no coincidence, Thaddeus. Which leaves just one answer. The killer knew the state you were in. So, that leaves me with just one suspect; your boy Galloway."

That could not be right. It just could not. "Listen, Ardley. You think you're on to something and god knows I can't think of a reason why you're wrong right now, but just think for a moment. Humphrey's a good kid. That's all he is, a fucking kid. I don't care what you presume you know, and I'm trying really hard to find a reasonable out here, but shit man! You can't do this without proof. One child conviction is not that."

"That's no longer your decision, Thaddeus. Maybe if you'd been a stronger man earlier I wouldn't have to do this, but that's it for you. You're done." said Ardley, as he waved a hand to the men restraining him. "Lieutenant Thaddeus is to be kept under guard until I give orders to the contrary, do you understand?"

The men nodded and started to drag him away, as he scrambled to hold himself in place. "Don't do it Ardley. The men want blood and all you're doing is adding another body to the heap. For fuck's sake man! You're wrong. You know it and I do. Don't do this!"

Ardley was not listening. He was turned and walking to where Humphrey was being lined up against a tree. Court was to be held, and the judge had already made up his mind. It was insanity. He yelled, more out of frustration than hope, as the guards continued to drag him away.

Five minutes later, tied to a post and sat on an empty munitions crate in the back of a heavy, green tent, he heard the gunshots. Sentence was served.

Chapter 18

Joshua awoke to the laughter of children. A stick, not sharp enough to pierce skin, prodded his side and he could feel his pockets being rifled. He sat up, the swirling shapes around him taking time to coalesce through the mire of his mind, as footfalls disappeared into the distance, the children startled into escape.

He rubbed his head. It was sore and he was sure it was not just from drink. There was a lump, maybe a bruise, near the back of his skull. He squinted, the bright light making any visual recognition of his surroundings almost impossible. Where was he? He could hear traffic, and his hands squelched against something damp.

As his sight returned, he realised with horror he was no longer in his flat. He was outside in an alley. Lounged like a tramp against an array of trashcans.

He tried to stand, but found his body unwilling to comply with the request and he flopped back into the bags with an undignified tinkle of glass. He reached out to his side, one-half of his body screaming in pain. Through his blur, he could tell he had been in a fight of some kind. His shirt was ripped, and blood was crusted down his trousers from a wound in his abdomen. He gingerly rose to his feet and staggered toward the noise of traffic.

The street heaved with activity. Passers-by, distressed by how he looked, shuffled cautiously around as he tried to discern a location. He was on East Washington Street, miles away from his apartment. What was he doing here? He reached into his pocket, but could not locate a wallet. Either he did not bring one with him or the street urchins just stole it. Either way, it was going to be a long trek back to his abode.

He stared up at the sky. The sun hovered, steady as a rock, in the crystal blue canopy overhead. It was around midday. Was it Sunday? There was no way to tell. He scrambled over to a man in a suit, snatched the copy of the Arizona Republic from his grasp, and stared at the front page. It was Tuesday. The man glowered and shoved him, ripping the paper back before striding off down the street. Two days passed since he had the wine. Two whole days and not a single memory remained. What had he been doing?

He staggered down the street holding his side. It was agony. Whatever occurred, it had hurt him - badly. A couple of cracked ribs and what looked like a knife wound. He could not think straight. He needed to get back to his apartment. He said he would be in work on Monday. He was supposed to be discussing his findings with Alison and Walker. Instead, he was nursing a hangover, a severe beating and he had not even finished his work. He was a disgrace.

As he trudged along the crowded streets, wailing claxons drew his attention to a fleet of cars driving down the road. It was a large police force. He leant against a street lantern and waved frantically for them to stop, as the pains in his side reached fever pitch.

The lead car slowed and swerved into the curb, as the rest of the vehicles continued their thunderous charge across town. He stumbled forward and flopped against the bonnet, his vision almost gone; as a figure flung the passenger door open.

"My god! Joshua!" said Alison, as she ran round the car and caught him before he slid off into the street. "What happened?"

"I don't... I can't..." he said, his voice cracking. "What's going on?"

"Walker." said Alison, helping him to stand. "Neither of you turned up on Monday morning, so we sent out squad cars to your apartments to locate you. The officer had to burst down his door to get in."

"He's dead?"

"I wish." she said, assisting him into the back of the car. "It's him. His house was a shrine to everything we were doing. He had maps, diagrams, photographs. They were all over his walls Joshua. He's been planning this for years."

"It can't be him." he said, as the car set off after the rest of the squad. "Not Walker. Believe me, it's..."

"Houghton was there, stretched over his dining table. His head bludgeoned with a copper kettle. It's him Thaddeus."

"No... Trust me... It's..."

"Your apartment had been broken into. It looked like there had been a struggle. We found a button from Walker's jacket in the folds of your couch and a knife with blood on it by the faucet. I thought you were dead."

Joshua yelped as they screeched round a corner, wilting sideways into Alison's lap. "Are you ok?" she asked, trying to sit him back up.

"I'm fine. Just a little dazed. Where are we going in such a hurry?"

"A note arrived at the station this morning; hand delivered. The desk sergeant is questioning the delivery boy now, but it's clear he was just paid to hand it in. It said Walker was planning to destroy the Railway car barn, with all the workers still in it. I need to know if there is anything you can tell me about where he is holding people. How did you get out?"

"I don't know. I can't remember anything."

She shook her head and hugged him, the warmth of the embrace catching him off guard. "You're going to be ok Joshua. I'm here now."

They pulled in by the side of all the other squad cars, next to a vast, white-walled building, the car's tyres squealing with the force of deceleration.

"Stay put, Joshua, ok?" said Alison, as she stepped out into the light. "I need to go in there and see if I can talk him down. You need to stay still, you hear?"

"I should..." he said, trying to shuffle along the back seat toward the open door, before wincing with pain.

"Just stay right there." said Alison, smiling and placing a hand across his cheek. "There are enough men here to deal with this. You need to stay safe. You have been through enough."

He could not fight her. The pain in his side was making it difficult to focus on anything. He watched as she went over to a large group of men, gathered by immense wooden doors. All the men had guns drawn and were being given orders to fan out around the building. Alison took up a position behind three of them and slowly edged forward, as two other groups walked round either side of the structure and disappeared out of sight.

What had gone on? How could it be Walker? Why was it Walker?

He thought back to the events at the police station. Walker awoke covered in tea, but the drink he watched him make was coffee. Walker, an Ivy League graduate with knowledge of Masonic tradition and easy access to him; it was just too neat. What link did Walker have to CCB, or even the Institute? He needed to think straight. He needed

193

to find the commonality. He needed to locate the one person who held a link to the events at the turn of the century, who was following the path of the fourth armoured during the war, and was now here in Phoenix.

Then it hit him.

He puked, out of total revulsion at the rationale descending through his mind, the officer sat in the driver's seat turning and querying his physical state. Walker's button was not on his couch because it fell off when Walker was attacking him. It was on the couch because… He looked down at his side, the wound location not consistent with an attack of passion or motive. There was only one explanation remaining; self-defence.

He lurched sideways and darted out of the vehicle, stumbling across to the barn. Behind him, he could hear the officer calling him back, as he floundered forward toward the wooden doors. He managed to make it before being caught and stepped inside. Screaming with pain as he moved the doors back together, he reached across to the beam latch and barred the doors shut; the hammering of the officer ignored as he took stock of his surroundings.

The car barn was enormous. It towered above, a vast, arching hall of steel and glass. Wooden framed offices lined the back wall and dozens of streetcars littered the floor, all in various states of repair. He ignored the continued request to open the door, and placed his focus on the sounds inside. He could hear very little, the polarised whirr of a massive generator to his right, making any sense of audible noise impossible. He went to move forward and stopped. The generator. Phoenix's streetcar system ran on electricity. It was a marvel of its age, but here, with his thoughts slowly coalescing, it realised it was a liability.

He scrambled over to the gates shuttering the generator from the rest of the structure and tore them open, his eyes descending on the mass of cables and wires leading from the diesel barrels at its side to the main control panel. It was rigged to blow.

He scanned the mass of cables and wires formed to make the circuit preparing their doom. It was unintelligible. But how could that be? If he was right, he must be able to figure out how it worked.

Conscious of time, he turned to look up at the offices across the building. There, in a glass-fronted room on the second tier, he could see Alison. She was turned, looking out across the space toward him, her hands banging on the glass. He did not want to know what they had found. Nevertheless, in some way, he already did.

He looked back to the mass of wires and traced each one from termination to source. If he could short the generator, he could stop the bomb.

Then a thought hit him, redemption. Was this what was planned all along?

He looked back at Alison and smiled. His demons of drink were gone. However, what they had caused could never be washed away. He had to accept his fate. He was ready for it.

He, the only man who could possibly have committed everything transpired. He, the grandson of Levi Thaddeus. He, the detective assigned to CCB to investigate murders that only started after his arrival. And he, a man who now lived here, in Phoenix. He was the killer. Or, at least, some part of him was. Whatever drink unleashed within him caused all this. His blackouts manifested the evil around him. Either physically or by some freakish proxy of waking hallucination, he was responsible. Now it was time to pay the piper.

He reached out, his nerves on edge at the finality of his actions, as his fingers inched toward the live and earth connectors on either side of the control panel. His end would be brutal. Nevertheless, it was necessary.

As he clasped the searing metal, and instantaneous pain, terror and oblivion enshrouded his mind, his vision contorted down to a single, distant, white spot.

Bang.

Part Three
MEMORANDUM

Chapter 1

Bang.

The halogen strip-lights in the small room fluttered and then when dark, accompanied by a growl of frustration. It was all Gabriel Thaddeus could do not to laugh, as Archibald McMaster fumbled in front of him in the near total darkness.

Gabriel was an average person. Average height, average build, and average looking, neatly cut, brown hair. It was an appearance he enjoyed. It made it far easier for people to forget who he was and, more importantly, what he was capable of.

He was the last heir of the late Viscount Whittingham. He spent his academic years studying at Oxford. He personally bequeathed over ten million pounds to the faculties there, and was handed the keys to the grounds. He studied what he wished, when he wished. It was a freedom of education no one else he knew was afforded. He spent eleven years there. Gathering information as it interested him and never sitting a single exam; the knowledge the only thing he wanted to gain.

Now he was a detective specialising in espionage and fraud. The abilities his education gave him used to root out deviants who transgressed morality in ways normal police would not be able to comprehend. Modern society was riddled with these people, and most of them hid behind the curtain of big corporations. Yet no one seemed to care. But he did. He was the last vanguard against true evil - corporate, money-driven slavery, and theft. A job, which gave him great satisfaction. Catching crooks who believed they were above the law. He had news for them. They were not. And today, his work had brought him to CQIF.

The Centre for Quantum Information and Foundations was located on the campus grounds of Cambridge University. The main entrance stared out like a glass and concrete eye across the neatly tended lawn of the structure. The series of buildings, a striking conformity of layout to the dichotomy of chaos discussed within.

Gabriel arrived just after nine and parked in an open bay off Clarkson Road, taking in the pleasing view of the centres of learning surrounding him. The Cavendish library, the British Institute of Astronomy and the magnificent Churchill College dominated the vista; encompassed by the lush playing fields of the University's many sporting faculties. It was not quite the austere Oxford he was used to, but it still felt like home.

After ten minutes wait in a small office, Archibald McMaster came to meet him. He arrived, carrying a pile of unkempt notes, and sat to one edge of a table, saying hello with a pleasingly firm handshake. He was in his fifties and his attire was a mix of styles; cord trousers, immaculately ironed, white cotton shirt and tan leather jacket. For all the smiles, the handshakes and the air of calm, the visit was not a casual one.

His latest assignment revolved around the UK Physics Research Council. More specifically, how decisions were made to pull almost a billion pounds from the budget. Concerns came to light certain corporations, specifically a start-up called ROS Genetics, were influencing the positioning of large portions of that funding.

"I wonder if you could take me through the reasoning behind your decisions to pull funding from certain projects put forward by the Research Council, Professor McMaster?"

asked Gabriel, smiling as he sat down in one of the uncomplicated plastic seats in the room.

"I thought you were here on police business, Officer Thaddeus?" said McMaster, straightening his jacket and running his fingers over his thick, greying moustache.

"I am investigating possible corruption charges that may be linked to decisions being made. As part of that investigation, I felt it prudent to talk to you."

"Corruption at the Research Council? It was only a matter of time, I suppose."

"Until we talked to you?"

"I'm sure I don't know what you mean." said McMaster, lowering his eyes and absently neatening his stack of papers. "I was given an assignment to underwrite the conclusions of the review committee on budgetary concerns for the Physics Council. That was all. I assume the corruption charges are not levelled at myself?"

"Not entirely. I simply need to understand the logic involved and discuss the matter with the correct people. I thought I should start with the man who signed off the biggest budget cut in British scientific history. So please, continue."

"There isn't much to tell." said McMaster, sitting up and changing to a defensive demeanour. "There were seventeen funding projects on the list of candidates for the Physics Council. If we went ahead with the funding on some of the larger projects, they would have been the only ones accepted. As it is, pulling funding on some of those projects has given the green light to fifteen of the remaining sixteen."

"What was the research grant denied from the list of smaller projects?" said Gabriel, taking notes.

"It was Professor Stallinger's second generation quantum diode experiments. He needed the funding to buy the equipment to begin the work. His proposal, so limited by that lack of equipment, could show no immediate benefit. We discussed it at length, but with so much scrutiny on scientific funding in the UK, we felt spending the little money available on projects that could show advantage to the populace was a wise idea. If times get better, we may revisit his proposal."

"It isn't all just budgetary though." said Gabriel, leading the replies where he wanted them to go. "Private companies add money to the research kitty too, do they not?"

"True. Certain large corporations will add to the grants handed out, as long as the test outputs or technologies devised are shared during progression."

"And did you have contact with any corporations during your decision process?"

"Not at all." said McMaster, clearly insulted. "It is true we were made aware of the funding that could potentially be found from corporate sources should certain projects be accepted, but we never had direct contact with any representatives during the decision process itself."

"Can you provide me with the information you were made privy to during your discussions regarding those companies?"

McMaster noticeably flinched as the question was asked, drumming his fingers on the table as he thought of a reply. "I'm not sure how relevant the information would be. We..."

"It may not be relevant at all, professor." said Gabriel, interjecting. "But I'd need to see it to make that assessment. Can you send it digitally?"

"I'll check through the meeting minutes we assembled. There may be some data in our email trails as well." said McMaster, flustered.

"Good. It may not be pertinent, but it may provide useful at some point. That will be all for now."

"Is that's it?" said McMaster.

"I have just about everything I needed to get from today, thank you Professor McMaster." said Gabriel, as he turned. "Oh, there was one other thing. Have you had any personal contact with any member of ROS Genetics?"

"How…?" said McMaster, his brow furrowed in thought. "They were here only last week. They are majority financing my work on quantum computing. They are interested in aligning it with the work of Giles Eagles on the human brain. His 'Faraday' experiments are an attempt to see if the human mind is a quantum computer of some kind. The have paid up front for another three years of research."

"Can you show me that work?" asked Gabriel, smiling. "I have something of an interest in quantum mechanics and I am intrigued by the possibilities presented by quantum computing."

"I would be my pleasure." said McMaster, standing and motioning to the door.

And that's how he came to be here; stood in a sterile room, in a small corner of CQIF, in the dark.

After a few seconds of groans and muffled thumps, the lights twitched again and sprung back into life.

The room was no more than twenty feet square and lined with racks of equipment. In the centre of the floor, a metallic water-barrel shaped object emitted a light cloud of gas from a vent in its top, as a screen displayed a solitary error message - 'System Failure'.

"You'll have to forgive the flakiness of the setup, Officer Thaddeus." said McMaster, as he pushed his spectacles up the bridge of his nose and couched near the contraption. "Hopefully, with the extra funding I've received, my rig should be much more stable in a few months."

"It's unbelievable to think this bucket of gas and probes can out compute any other computer on the planet." said

Gabriel, watching carefully as McMaster strained with a valve lever.

"Not just any, Officer Thaddeus - every." said McMaster, standing and smiling, his delight evident. "Modern computer chips can have up to sixteen cores, with each core processing at about twenty giga-flops. That's one hundred and sixty billion floating point calculations a second, per chip; and there are millions of them on the earth. If I can get this thing to a point where I can get stability, it will outperform that by an order of magnitude that would make Moore blush."

"What sort of order of magnitude?"

"In relativistic terms, this machine has the equivalent of one times ten the twenty-three cores and each processes data at three peta-flops. To write the overall number of calculations a second possible in inch high numbers, you would need enough paper to stretch to the sun and back."

"That's a ridiculous amount of processing power. Why would a genetics company require that much computational brute force?"

"Gene sequencing." said McMaster, as he reset the screen and a tiny prompt appeared. "Imagine a machine that could break down and analyse every gene in every cell of a sample, interpolating the data against each new result found, and providing a calculation on what genetic markers, weaknesses, or even diseases the sample contains, all in the blink of an eye." He began typing into the screen and soon a command was input, his finger hovering over the return key as he grinned. "In nineteen-ninety-three, IBM completed a computation against something called the Valence Approximation, an algorithm designed to help understand the fundamental principle of quantum chromodynamics. That calculation took a computer, which cost seven-hundred million dollars, over a year to complete. When I press enter,

203

this machine will perform that same calculation." McMaster depressed the key and even before the click registered in Gabriel's ears, the screen updated with a figure and a time stamp.

"That can't be correct." said Gabriel, in amazement. "It's saying it completed in less than a millionth of a second."

"Like I said Officer Thaddeus, this machine will, with the right funding, change the world."

"So what makes it so twitchy?"

"A quantum effect it relies on called superposition." said McMaster. "It's a puzzling ramification of an experiment called Young's Slit."

Gabriel studied some quantum mechanics at Oxford and knew of the effect well. Everything in the universe was made up of little packets of energy called quanta. To determine if the quanta that made up light, which physicists called photons, were waves or particles, a scientist called Young devised a simple experiment. He placed a light source opposite a collection plate. Between the light and the plate, he placed an opaque medium with a fine slit scored into it. If light was a particle, the image collected on the plate would be straight line, exactly the same size and shape as the slit. If light was a wave, it would propagate, like ripples on a pond, away from the back of the slit and the image collected would be bright line with a fuzzy halo. Young saw a halo. Light was a wave. Young then tried two slits, to see if two light waves would interfere with one another as they propagated. They did. With two slits in the medium, you saw an interference pattern of light and dark bands on the plate.

Quantum physicists coined the effect known as superposition when they used laser light. If single photons were sent by a laser to one slit and then the other, with time spacing between them, the interference pattern still emerged. Somehow, either the photon knew where the previous photon had been or there was going to be another photon along soon. That made no sense. The real answer made even less. The single light photon did not go through just one slit. It went through both, at the same time. Superposition said all quanta, light or not, went through all points in the universe at the same time. It was a mind-boggling scientific puzzle. One that only became stranger when detectors were put over the slits to see what was happening. With the detectors turned on, the pattern of interference disappeared, and two straight lines appeared on the plate. Light reverted to a linear particle, unaware of anything. Somehow, watching what was happening changed the result.

"My machine only works if I can keep it isolated. Any contamination - any at all - and the entire thing shuts down. Not only that, but the liquid helium I need to keep the computer below five Kelvin is not cheap. I could really do with another thirty or forty litres."

"It looks as though you could really do with the cash from ROS Genetics if you're going to make this work, professor." said Gabriel.

"Without their funding, I'm finished." said McMaster, his scowl turning to a concerned stare, as he caught the smile on Gabriel's face.

"Thank you, professor." said Gabriel, offering McMaster his hand to shake. "The chat was very enlightening."

"No problem." replied McMaster, his once firm grip now clammy and weak. "I'll get the information you requested over to you as soon as I can."

Chapter 2

Gabriel walked out of the office and over to his car, where a bedraggled looking Oswald Reilly was waiting for him.

Oz, as was his chosen moniker, was his partner. Even after telling his superiors he worked far better by himself, shortly following his appointment, the man's smiling face greeted him when he arrived at work. He was a strange little individual; part human, part sideshow clown. His curly, blonde hair and uneven stubble were only a counterpoint to his frequent pink shirt and tan trouser combinations. His demeanour was effervescent and irksome. He smiled through just about any situation and his winsome attitude was arduous to deal with, let alone comprehend. Many were the occasions he simply left him in the car when he went to take interviews, and rarely was it challenged. He was sure the man was only employed to annoy him.

"Long morning?" asked Oz.

"Just as expected, there's little or no information. But there's definitely something going on." said Gabriel, starting the car.

"Exactly how you like it then." said Oz, his feet placed irritatingly on the dashboard as he tapped his thighs to the beat of an imaginary song. "Where to then, boss?"

"To the nearest decent coffee shop. I need a long, vanilla cinnamon latte, and a blueberry muffin."

The drive was grating at best; Oz's continued patting of his thighs getting more and more fevered, as he continued to play the tune in his head. By the time they sat awaiting the arrival of their repast, the drumming had been replaced by a vaguely out of tune humming.

"Is there any chance you could stop that at some point?" Gabriel asked, with a sneer.

"Sorry boss. Didn't realise it was bugging you."

"Your latte and muffin, dear." said a waitress, as she sidled up behind him and placed them on the table.

"Are you not having anything?" asked Gabriel, as the woman went back to her perch behind the long, glass counter.

"Do I look like I need more sugar in my life?" said Oz, leaning forward and grinning.

Lithium. Oz needed large quantities of lithium in his life; but he was right, sugar was probably a bad idea.

"I don't get your craving for coffee and cake, Thad-man."

"It's a muffin, not a cake."

"Whatever. You go on and on about people wasting the planet's resources and yet here you are, day after day, indulging your own greed. It's a little duplicitous, isn't it?"

He came to coffee shops because they usually bore a quiet and congenial air; respect for the bean. That was probably the reasoning behind them now being found in bookshops. But whilst ever Oz was his partner, he could be sat on the moon; his peace would be shattered. "There are seven billion people on earth. You know that's too many, I know that's too many. One coffee and a muffin each day is not going to tip the balance."

"It will if everyone thinks like that."

Talking about this with Oz was pointless. The world, at best, could support about a billion people in comfort. At the current rate of resource consumption, the planet would be a husk inside fifty years. No fish, few forests, little fresh water, practically no oil, and thus, only a minute chance of survival for man. He savoured every coffee he had; because sooner rather than later, he was sure it could be his last. Not that Oz would understand. He was a great example of what was once called the 'MTV generation'. An entire branch of western civilisation programmed to consume everything in sight, all for the profit of big business. It disgusted him to think about what the world would be like if humanity allowed those people to take over. He smiled as he took another sip of his coffee and contemplated his ignorance. What was he thinking about? They already had.

"So, what's the beef at the council? Budget cuts hitting pretty hard, are they?"

"The accusation is that ROS Genetics has been handing out bungs to ensure certain projects get funding ahead of others."

"ROS Genetics? You had a case with them a while back, didn't you? As I remember, it was a close call."

"The lead scientist on their Faraday project was accused of negligence in the death of one of his test subjects. I still think he may be guilty of it, but there wasn't enough evidence to make the accusation stick. I'm still trying to gather a case, but the trail is cold. It's on my 'to do' list, when I get chance."

"I was right though. It was a close thing."

"If it was my decision, he would have gone down for a very long time for what he did. But it's not. I gather evidence, and bureaucrats make those calls."

"So, after you finish gobbling down your hypocrisy, are we heading over there?"

He stared at Oz and made a point of cramming the last of his muffin into his waiting mouth before individually sucking the crumbs from his fingers. "Why not? It's not like you've got anything more pressing to do, is it?"

Chapter 3

"So your 'Faraday' suspect could be involved in this?" asked Oz, as they drove across Cambridge toward the offices of ROS Genetics.

"Potentially." Gabriel was wary of making quick judgements. Too many times in his early career, his brain led him down blind alleys of reasoning; 'Gumption Traps' he once read they were eloquently categorised as. He now made sure he gathered every available piece of evidence he could before he made a decision. Volume of information was only an issue if the information collated was useless. "I'm certainly not ruling it out."

Oz turned and stared out of the window, seemingly placated by his limited response. He hummed along to the radio, as it continued to play some fatuous, semi-musically literate tune. He hated modern music. It was horrible, soul drudgingly awful pop. Mostly made in sheds by people with no understanding of the mathematical beauty they were creating. Idiot tunes, for an idiot society.

As if it could hear his thoughts, the radio dissolved into static. At first the relent was blissful, but as the whine increased to a screech that hurt the core of his brain and made his vision blur, he could tolerate it no longer. Wincing, he reached over and turned the damn thing off.

"Hey! I was listening to that." said Oz.

Gabriel shook his head. How could anyone listen to that?

The still of the car all the way to the austere building of ROS Genetics was a pleasant break. By the time they pulled up in the haphazardly arranged car park, Gabriel was almost relaxed.

"You don't need me to come in, do you?" asked Oz, as he played with his iPhone.

"Nooo." said Gabriel, as sarcastically as he could. "You keep the car warm. Don't worry about your job, or me."

"You're the boss." said Oz, concentrating hard on his game.

It was like being at work with a ten-year-old child. Whoever paid his wages should be ashamed. However, he was not going to point it out. They obviously recruited the man to get under his skin. He would not give them the satisfaction of knowing they succeeded by moaning about the situation. If they wanted to waste money, let them. He had a job to do.

The crisp, white exterior of ROS Genetics loomed across the horizon as he approached the main entrance. Its exterior was blank and it held the air of a storage depot. It was a truly monstrous carbuncle. A solitary door of steel and glass led to a massive, yet bland foyer, filled with a lone, chipboard and plastic desk. It was akin to a run-down Ikea showroom.

"Good afternoon Mister Thaddeus." said the receptionist, as she put away her pot of nail polish. "What can we do for you today?"

The fact the woman recognised him from his visits came as a surprise. She looked like the sort of girl who spent most of her wages on shoes and found the puzzle section of celebrity driven magazines overly challenging. It was best he ignored the remark and focus on why he was here. "I'm wondering if there is anyone available for a brief chat about some concerns raised as regards funding at the Research Council?"

"Of course, Mister Thaddeus. If you want to take a seat, I'll get someone to come down."

Gabriel turned and stared into the foyer. There was nothing to sit on in the entire space, other than the chair the receptionist was occupying. "Really? I think I'll wait here."

The woman punched up a number on her phone and a few minutes later, an overweight man in suit at least a size too small for his frame came out of the lifts and walked over.

"Officer Thaddeus." the man said, enthusiastically. "It's always good to see you here. To what do we owe the pleasure?"

He recognised the man, but could not place the name. It was unlike him to forget things. He tried again and smiled. It was Kirk Smithson, VP of communications for the ROS Genetics group. "Mister Smithson, thank you for taking time out to meet with me."

"It is not a problem, Officer Thaddeus. We are always happy to oblige your requests."

"Is there somewhere we can talk; in private?"

"Of course. We'll go up to the executive board room. I'll get Sandra to organise us some coffee."

The woman behind the desk smiled at the request, rising from her seat. "Any cake with your coffee, Mister Thaddeus?"

"I'm fine, thank you, Sandra." said Gabriel, wondering if the request was simply kindness or yet more retained knowledge.

As the lift made its way up to the second floor, Gabriel rubbed his brow. His head hurt. Maybe he pushed too hard over the last few months. He had not taken a day's leave in the last year. He deserved a holiday. Perhaps a few weeks somewhere warm, where he could catch up on some reading without the constant irritation of Oz's presence would do him good. When this current assignment was completed, he would rectify the oversight.

The walk to the boardroom filled Gabriel with unease. The stand covers lining the walkway were only four feet high and it was easy to see only a few scant employees working in an office that could accommodate hundreds. "Are you scaling down?" he asked, removing the notepad from his jacket pocket.

"Not at all, Officer Thaddeus." said Kirk, following Gabriel's line of sight. "It's after five. Most of the staff on this floor is administration, so staying late unless warranted is not something we enforce."

Gabriel looked at his watch. It was a filthy, jewel-encrusted reminder of a filthy heritage, and the only thing remaining of his previous life. It was half past five. Of course the building would be empty. "Today has been a little long. Forgive my ignorance." he said, smiling politely, as he was ushered into a board room.

"Not a problem." said Kirk, motioning to a plush, green leather seat at one edge of a large conference table. "What can I do for you today?"

Gabriel sat opposite; placing his notepad on the table and making sure Kirk knew he was taking his time over reading his notes. "I'm here to ask what involvement ROS Genetics may have had in the grant application process at the Research Council; specifically around funding for the LHC."

"Officer Thaddeus, you know we are not allowed to be involved during a decision making phase at the council." said Kirk, smiling broadly and leaning forward. "ROS Genetics upholds the very highest ethical standards. It is our mission to ensure..."

"But you are the primary funder for Archibald McMaster's quantum computing work, are you not?" said

Gabriel, stepping in to quash the company rubbish being spouted.

"We are." said Kirk, leaning back and looking bemused. "Our money specifically allows Professor McMaster to continue his research without the need to apply for a grant of any kind. There was no ethical breach in our decision. We are interested in Professor McMaster's findings. If we wish to fund…"

"And funding his research in no way was an attempt to influence his decision to pull the grants from other research projects?"

"What? I can assure you Officer Thaddeus, ROS Genetics' only interest…"

"I'm looking for a yes or no to my questions Mister Smithson." said Gabriel, looking up from his pad. "Was there any attempt by ROS Genetics to influence the decision process being undertaken, by giving Professor McMaster money to continue his research?"

"Er… I'm not sure that…"

"Yes or no, Mister Smithson."

"No." said Kirk, regaining his composure and buttoning his suit jacket. "Absolutely not."

Gabriel would take that as a possible yes. "And do you not believe that Giles Eagles involvement with Professor McMaster's research is a breach of policy? Specifically, as his case is still under review."

"The Giles Eagles case is closed, Officer Thaddeus. We have a written statement from the chief justice stating as much."

"I'm glad a judge can give you such an assurance." said Gabriel, returning to taking notes. "I was under the impression UK law states that until someone is proven innocent in court that decision remains in the hands of the police. But I'll take a look into your interpretation and get back to you." Gabriel smiled. He could see, just on the periphery of his vision, Kirk cross his arms over his chest. He was scowling. Good. "Just one more thing before I go, Mister Smithson. Can you explain to me why Professor McMaster's research was of such importance to yourself and to Mister Eagles?"

"He's waking up. Dear lord, he's waking up!" the muffled voice blared into Gabriel's head and forced him to snap a hand to his head. It was a female voice, distant and full of fear. He moaned, as the voice melted into a tortured whine, piercing his every synapse.

"Are you ok, Officer Thaddeus?" said Kirk, moving to his side.

Gabriel looked up, confused. His vision was swirling and he could feel something dribbling down his face into his mouth. He raised and hand to his nose and withdrew it in horror. He was bleeding, profusely. "I… I think I…"

However, it was no use. As Kirk attempted to assist him, he lolled sideways and collapsed against the desk with a heavy thud.

Chapter 4

Gabriel awoke to a headache the likes of which he had never experienced. His entire skull throbbed and his vision, what little of it remained, was a twisted horror of shapes and smudged colours.

He rolled onto his side, the cold floor beneath chilling his fingertips and startling his senses. His memory was a mess. He could recall only the most transient of information. A feeling of total uselessness washed over him and exposed fragility in his soul. He felt like crying. But he would not. He needed to keep a grip of his senses and figure out what was going on. He took deep breaths, moaning lightly as the pain in his head came and went, trying to still the panic settling over his actions.

Eventually, his vision began to clear and he sat up to take in his surroundings. He was in a cell. Maybe a few meters cubed. The walls were tiled in white porcelain and the floor bare stone. A solitary, metal riveted door with an iron grille was located to one side of the room and behind him sat a depressing, hessian-covered bed. The only light coming in seemed to drift through the grille in a flicker. Perhaps an oil lantern or candle? He could not tell.

He checked himself for injuries. Other than the pain surrounding his skull, he seemed fit and well. He was wearing a blue jump suit, made from the worst cotton he ever felt. His only item of luxury was a pair of sturdy, fleece-lined slippers. They were comfortable and warm, and the sensation they gave his feet was pleasing.

He moved to the door and tried the handle; locked. He tried to yell through the bars, but his attempt descended to coughing. His voice would take time to recover from whatever malady beset him.

He moved back and slumped against the bed, it was as uncomfortable as it looked. Where was he? Why could he not remember anything? His panic was returning and he fought hard to quell his fears. They would do him no good.

As he sat and tried to regain some semblance of self, he picked out a faint whistling coming from outside the room. The tune was light and chirpy, accompanied by a jangle of keys. Was it a guard or supervisor of some kind? He waited, an unfamiliar trepidation filling him, as the sounds continued to approach. Eventually, the whistling stopped at his door and a vaguely familiar face appeared.

The man was in his mid-thirties, with broad, wide eyes and a neatly manicured moustache. He could not place him, but he knew him somehow. "Who are you?" he stammered, his voice hoarse.

"My name is irrelevant." the man said, as he began the process of unlocking the door.

"What... What am I doing here?" Gabriel asked.

"Is it not obvious?"

"I can't... I do not remember how I..."

"Calm yourself. Do not bother your mind with irrelevancies at this moment. It serves no purpose."

"But I cannot... My head feels like it... What happened to...?"

"You are babbling like a child when its master beats it for misbehaviour. You do not wish to be thought of as a child, do you?"

"I do not want to... I do not know what I am to do... Can you help me?" Gabriel's mind was swimming. He knew this man and he could vaguely remember something about the place. However, the terrified memory refused to appear from its hiding place to assist.

"My dear boy," the man said, as the lock finally gave and the door opened, "I am only here to help you. But first you must help me."

"What must I do?" Gabriel asked, petrified by the sight that greeted him. The man was wearing a doctor's outfit, but the jacket was too small and dirt caked his bare feet.

"You must give me your slippers."

"My slippers?"

"What have I said about babbling incoherently? You are only delaying what you know to be true."

"Why do you need my slippers?"

"Because my feet are cold." the man said, grabbing a handful of his shirt.

The sudden realisation of what was to occur hit Gabriel like a sledgehammer, momentarily stunning his physical response, a lone utterance his only means of relaying his fear. "Please!"

"If my feet get cold," the man said, as a fist snapped from his side and landed across his temple, "then blood will leave my extremities. This trigger is not localized to just my feet, however." the man continued, as another blow slammed into the side of his jaw.

He could feel the bone crack with the impact, and shards of teeth rattled around his mouth.

"Blood will flow from my skin's surface to my core, meaning that I will also lose blood flow to my hands, as my body attempts to keep my vital organs warm." the man continued, as his onslaught picked up pace.

Gabriel could do nothing as the assault continued. As the man's voice slowly drowned back into a hiss of static inside his busted cranium, his mind ran from the horror. Scared and unable to fight back, he found a peaceful corner of his soul and relaxed. His end would take away his pain.

Chapter 5

Gabriel bolted upright and drew his hands up sharply to his face. He screamed, releasing his pent up tension and startling the cordon of doctors and nurses surrounding his bed.

"Calm down, Thad-man." said Oz, sitting in a chair to his side. "You don't want to be busting your stitches."

"Stitches!" said Gabriel, feeling over his scalp and finding a row across his hairline.

"Be careful Officer." said a nurse, as she came across and placed a hand on his shoulder. She smiled warmly and attempted to soothe him, as she removed his hands from his head. "I know this must be very confusing, but you've had a minor cranial bleed. You were in surgery for seven hours."

"What... Who..." Gabriel wanted to ask questions, but they flooded his mind and the words piled atop one another, dulling any response.

"You collapsed." said the nurse, as a doctor in a white lab coat came over and checked his pulse. "You're lucky to be with us."

"I remember..." However, it was a lie and Gabriel knew it. He remembered very little. "I was killed by someone."

"Er..." said Oz, looking puzzled. "You were killed. As in murdered? As in dead? As in, if you were, you wouldn't be talking to me now? That kind of killed?"

"You're probably still dazed from the operation. We'll give you something to help you rest and check on you soon." said the doctor, as he motioned for the nurse to retrieve something from a medical tray at the back of the room.

"I don't need something to relax. I need…" But he did not know what he needed. The nurse returned, and a prick on his arm directed his attention to a needle plunging into a vein. "Really, I…" But the world was spinning again.

"Just rest, Officer Thaddeus. Everything will be better if you just rest."

As the nurse lowered his head onto a soft pillow, his world dissolved away. Hopefully, she was telling the truth. Maybe when he awoke, everything would make sense.

Chapter 6

A week later, Gabriel awoke in his own bed, to an alarm clock buzzing. He slapped the dreadful thing off and rubbed his aching brow, before making his way to his bathroom. After a shower where more time was spent attempting not to wet the bandage covering his forehead than clean himself, he strolled into his kitchen and was startled to see Oz sat at his breakfast bar, reading his paper and eating a round of jam and toast.

"Morning boss. Feel any better this morning?" said Oz, as he munched away.

"Not now I know you're here." said Gabriel, opening his fridge and removing some orange juice. "How did you get in?"

"Doc made you give me a key before he'd discharge you, remember?"

"Not really. Are you sure I agreed to that?"

"You wanted out, he gave a condition. You didn't have much choice."

Gabriel swigged a hearty amount of juice, direct from the carton, before placing it back in the fridge and removing some cheese.

"That's really unhygienic, you know that, don't you?"

"Not now, Oz!" said Gabriel, his head aching to even contemplate dealing with the man at this hour. "You know I'm up and fit. Why don't you go home?"

"Not my choice boss. You got pretty crazy back at the hospital. People are worried and I'm here to check on you. It was no way for a Viscount to act."

"I'm not a Viscount. My great-grandfather was the Viscount."

"It's a peerage title isn't it?" asked Oz, looking up from the paper. "I thought it was handed down through the family line?"

"The family homestead was sold before I was born. There's no land, and thus no peerage. The title is redundant. And I'm not his direct line anyway. My great grandfather was a Thaddeus; not a Whittingham."

"Your great grandfather's real name was Tirney, not Thaddeus. So logically, you're a Tirney and not a Thaddeus; or a Whittingham, for that matter."

Oz was being his stupefying best this morning. It really did not make any difference what the name was. The only thing that mattered was he was not a Whittingham. Therefore, he was not a Viscount. "Are you trying to wind me up and make my headache come back?"

"Just seeing if you're fit for duty. My assessment would be no. So, I'll give that message to HQ and catch you tomorrow morning."

Before Gabriel could say a word in protest, Oz folded the paper and strode from his house into the morning sunlight. There was a downside and an upside to the conversation; he may not be able to go back to work, but he could at least enjoy his breakfast in peace.

After polishing off a half decent Spanish omelette, he lay back on his couch and attempted to calm his thoughts. The images witnessed when he passed out bothered him to his core. They were so real, so vivid. He could not shake them. Tiring of waiting for anything to come on worth watching, he got up and went into the bathroom to assess his scar.

He carefully peeled back the bandage and looked at the surgical work lining one side of his skull. From just above his right ear, across beyond the midpoint of his fringe, a neat, red line was criss-crossed with thick, black stitches. He felt at the edges of the work, the slight contact firing nerve endings and making him retract his fingers. It would be permanent; there was no doubt about it. What worried him more was the doctor told him the bleed was potentially stress related. Both the surgeon and his superiors ordered at least two weeks of bed rest. It was torture. He could not lie about in the hospital. It smelt of surgical spirit and the faint odour of lingering death. He had to get home. Now he was here however, he was just as bothered. He was useless at relaxing. He needed stimulation. There was no other thing for it. He would go out and find some. He would prefer to die quickly, interested, than linger on forever in boredom.

Chapter 7

Three B's café and bar was its usual, bustling self. Office
workers on easy lunches and tourists, many visiting the
Museum sat in the same building, waited patiently to be
served or milled around the tables out front. The structure in
which the café sat was a magnificent example of brickwork;
grey and ochre arcs of form, which pleased the mind and
excited the senses.

Gabriel entered, as he did on many occasions, to a wave
from the barman. After receiving his latte and retiring to a
free table outside, he sat and watched the world go by. This
kind of relaxing he could tolerate. The midday sun was
pleasantly warming and the chatter around him was busy
and easily overheard.

He took pleasure from listening to others; testing his
knowledge against the range of topics discussed. It was a
welcome distraction to the on-going pain lingering in his
head.

As he sat, his mind wandered to thoughts of his youth,
and back to a time when his family was proud and powerful.
Their family home, near Buntingford in Hertfordshire,
reminded him of the building he was looking at. It was
grand and baroque, an imperious seat for an equally
imperious line. Summers were spent running round its
thousand acre grounds or fishing in one of the three man-
made lakes sat within its plush gardens. It was an easier
time, a time for family and friends.

He remembered his hound, more scraggy hair than dog,
lying by the side of his favourite fishing hole, as he whiled

away the long evenings. He loved his dog. The animal may have been an irritating ball of energetic fur that frequently ignored his wishes, but he never answered back. He was loyal, and was always there when he needed a friend, or even just an ear to listen to his ramblings. He was happy back then, safe and content in the knowledge his life would be carefree because of his family's wealth. And his dog, god bless his soul, was his faithful companion through all of it.

Then his grandfather heard of the events in America.

His great uncle, the black sheep of the family, died in an attempt to murder a group of people in Phoenix, in the United States. The police and lawyers frequenting the house that summer, told of his villainy; of his attempts to burn down the rail car garage and how, on some technical legality, their family was to be held responsible. The resulting trial ruined their name and eroded their wealth to a point where assets, including their family home, were sold to cover the costs. It destroyed his grandfather, and eventually it destroyed his father. Yet it turned out to be the happiest time of his life.

Over the years, he had developed a deep sense of loathing in his soul; a hatred for how money perverted the actions of those who held it and how it forced people to want more. His mother, once doting and graceful, descended to drink when the money was gone. His grandfather and father spent hours arguing and he - well he was simply ignored. Left to tend to his emotions, as his closest kin dissolved into self-pity.

He remembered the day it all fell apart as if it were yesterday.

The family had moved. They now lived in the squire's lodgings at the edge of what was once their estate. Tensions ran high, the family forced to live in what his grandfather called 'the meagre shack'. He now realised they still lived in the most grandiose opulence. The shack, if indeed it was one, was a purpose built collection of stone houses sat in two acres of land. Each of the three buildings had at least twenty rooms. Only a fool would call it meagre. Yet, to his family, it was.

The arguments that raged around its high ceilinged rooms were bitter and vengeful. One evening, after a particularly heated exchange, they split up; even his mother sleeping in her own room, far away from his father. It was past midnight when the shotgun blasts echoed out. The first, distant and rousing, came in through his open window. He sprung out of bed, watching as his father made his way back into their home and slammed the door. His mother, still partially inebriated, lambasted his father's actions, and screams, vile noises that still invaded his dreams, filled the house. The sounds ended with a second blast. Running down the staircase to see what was happening, he saw his father. His mother's crumpled form, slumped against the back door, blood flowing freely from the wound in her chest, stopped his heart. He watched, frozen to the spot with terror, as his father, oblivious to his cries of anguish, placed the gun into his mouth and pulled the trigger one last time.

He was only eight years old. With no one left in his family to look after him, he was placed into care. The family he was put with could not conceive children of their own and were generous and caring, almost to a fault.

He spent ten pleasant years with them. They were not poor, but were not in the same league as his real family. They lived in a quiet suburban street, in a pleasingly simple, two-story, three bedroom, detached house.

Living without money was a wakeup call to his upbringing. The world was different, not any worse or better than a life of wealth and opportunity, just different. People acted differently. They put different priorities into their lives, and made different choices. They behaved differently, and when discussions turned to money, they were never about how much they could or should make, but about how much they could save. Money to these people was a gift, not a tool. His grandfather once used the term 'the great unwashed' when he disparagingly talked about people like his new parents. How wrong he was. These people were real - his life before was the fake.

When he came of age and a well-to-do lawyer arrived to hand over what was left of the estate, there was but a small portion of the once great fortune left; a few millions. As sole heir, he soon found a way to rid himself of the burden of money forever. He spent a million on a painting that he left by the door of a charity shop, a few million in direct donations, a huge wedge to his chosen seat of learning to grant him the scholarly freedom he desired, and a healthy gift to his unsuspecting foster parents so they did not have to worry about money any more. It took him just three years to erase the memory of his original family, just as they, in their fits of self-loathing and frustrated greed, had rid themselves of him.

Whilst at Oxford, he researched his past and soon found his line was not what it appeared. He laughed the day he discovered he was not a Whittingham. The irony, after all he had done, tasted divine. So, he changed his name, the ultimate insult to his heritage.

His family died the day the depths of their money disappeared and this solitary action ensured it would remain that way.

He was roused from his thoughts by a heavy clatter to the back of the head. The half-filled cup in his hands tumbled from his grasp with the contact and startled the woman passing by.

"I am very sorry." the woman said, realising she accidently struck him with her handbag. "That was very careless of me. Are you alright, dear?"

Gabriel raised a hand to the back of his skull, placing it over the searing sensation located there. "Just watch where you're swinging that thing. I've already been in hospital once this week." The woman looked shocked as he continued to apply pressure to the impact area. Puzzled by her expression, he withdrew his hand and looked at his palm, there was blood, and quite a lot of it. "I don't believe it!"

"Do you want me to call an ambulance, dear?" said the woman, fumbling to retrieve her phone.

"Don't bother." said Gabriel, taking a napkin from the table and placing it over the wound. "I have A and E on speed-dial."

Chapter 8

Oz sat and laughed, as a nurse cleaned the wound on Gabriel's head and began the process of inserting more stitches into his scalp.

"It's incredible!" said Oz, excitedly, as he looked at the scar. "It goes across your head and meets up with the other one next to your ear. How unlucky is that?"

"Shut up." said Gabriel, his patience gone.

"I'm not saying anything." said the nurse, as she finished the last of the stitches.

"Not you."

"Be careful there, boss." said Oz, picking himself up and walking to the exit. "You don't want to go pissing another woman off. You never know what injury you'll pick up next! Catch you in the morning."

Much to his relief, Oz left the room and set off down the hospital corridor, whistling as he went. As the irritating man disappeared into the distance, Gabriel turned to the nurse and smiled. "Sorry about that. I know it can be very off putting."

"You're not doing anything to concern me, Mister Thaddeus. Just sit still and we'll have you out of here in no time. This is what you get for rushing out of hospital. Two weeks, we said. You were only here three days. You'll have to be more careful."

"I promise to behave."

The nurse was duteous and efficient, and soon he was signing out with the clerk; a fresh bandage at the front of his skull and a neatly shaved line down one side. The stares his peculiar injuries were creating in others were making him feel uneasy and suppressing his usually confident manner. He could understand it. He looked as if he had just been involved in a comedic ball-buffer incident at a bowling alley. If it were anyone else, he would be staring too.

He walked down the corridor, the ache that behind his eyes, a distracting addition to his life he could only assume would remain for some time. Above him, a flickering halogen light, buzzing with every pulse, caught his attention, and forced him to squint. Fzzt - Fzzt Fzzt - Fzzt Fzzt Fzzt - Fzzt Fzzt Fzzt Fzzt Fzzt. How could people stand that? It was a modern version of Chinese water torture.

Not prepared to dally, he made his way to the elevators, and followed them back to the main entrance. Soon he would be outside in the open air and free of his disinfected prison.

"Mister Thaddeus? Mister Thaddeus?" said a female voice.

He spun, his attention drawn to a nurse waving papers as she scurried across the busy foyer. "Mister Thaddeus, do you have a moment?"

No, he did not. However, if he refused they would only drag him back later. "It would be a pleasure to be kept here for longer than I wished." he said, with irritation.

"This shouldn't take long, Mister Thaddeus. We have some questions about your blood results."

"Blood results? I assume you've found something toxicological?"

"It's best we discuss this in private. Please, follow me." with a wave of the hand, the nurse set off toward the lifts.

Gabriel trudged along behind. He hoped this would be quick. He had a burning desire to leave the hospital as soon as he could.

A few minutes later, Gabriel sat in a small office. To the other side of a disorganised desk, loaded down with half-read papers and open files, the nurse who escorted him to the room sat by the side of a surly looking, older doctor. The man fidgeted as he peered up from the collection of papers, looking him over and taking notes on a pad to one side of what he could only assume were his medical records.

"I'm glad we caught you before you left Mister Thaddeus." the doctor said, running a hand across his bald scalp. "I'm sorry for detaining you further, but we need to ask you a few questions about some unexpected results we had returned from your cytological testing."

"Cytological? Why the hell are you poking around with my cells?" Gabriel asked, confused.

"Something came up when we performed your blood tests before we committed you to surgery; standard procedure to understand if you carry any transmutable diseases."

"You could have asked."

"You were comatose, Mister Thaddeus. Besides, many people are unaware they carry certain agents, as they are asymptomatic or not fully developed."

"Not fully developed?" asked Gabriel, swallowing hard. "Are you telling me I have AIDS?"

"Nothing of the sort." said the doctor, laughing. "It was more of a puzzle to us. We assumed we contaminated your sample and thus had errata returned somehow. When you came back to us, we took another sample and conducted more, purely out of curiosity."

"Curiosity of what?"

The doctor stopped taking notes, adopting an almost apologetic air as he slouched back into his seat. "I was wondering if you recently paid for any non-NHS medical procedures."

"Non-NHS? Private, you mean?"

"Not exactly." said the doctor, as he took a pile of charts and turned them to face him. "The sort of procedure that could cause this type of anomaly is not currently legal in the UK. There are very few countries that do not prohibit this type of manipulation."

Manipulation? Gabriel could not understand what he was being asked. He looked at the charts. He knew instantly what they were. They were genetic maps relating to blood type, and there were three of them. Moreover, they were all different. "Why is my name above each chart? These come from different individuals."

"Actually, they don't, Mister Thaddeus. That's our concern. Each map comes from samples taken from you. We wouldn't have noticed the issue unless we accidently checked your blood group; twice. In the first test, you were AB negative. The second test brought you out at O positive. We actually thought we were giving you the wrong blood; it caused us a great deal of concern. What we found this time was equally puzzling. Your blood group today is A positive."

"That's impossible." said Gabriel, refusing to believe what he was hearing. "Blood types don't change. Your equipment is faulty."

"We've redone the tests on three separate machines Mister Thaddeus, the findings are corroborated. You have three separate blood groups and are showing no sign harbouring them is causing distress. That's why you need to tell us if you have had any medical attention recently, other than from us."

"Of course not!" said Gabriel, raising his hands in exasperation. "What makes you think that?"

"After checking your birth records, your blood type was originally A positive. We believe that is your native blood group. The Sulston Scores returned from our tests are very close, Mister Thaddeus. The other blood groups you are carrying are genetically similar enough to…"

Gabriel winced as the room dissolved to static. A buzz, so loud it stood the hairs on his neck to attention, reverberated round his head, forcing him to bring his hands to his ears. He yelled, as the sound flared the nerve endings around his scars and drew delicate agony in strips across his brow. He looked up in terror at the doctor and nurse sat opposite, hoping they would come to his assistance, but they simply sat and smiled, oblivious to his torture. "Help me!" he said, trying to claw for them, as his vision swam in and out of focus. "Why won't you help me!"

"Do you think he's aware of what is happening?" a female voice said, with quiet clarity above the din.

However, the people in the room did not vocalise the sound. It appeared, as if from nowhere, almost as if it were inside his head.

"He's been sedated." said a male voice, in response. "There's no way he could possibly…"

The doctor and nurse leapt back from the table, as Gabriel stood up and roared out across the room.

"Mister Thaddeus!" said the doctor, drawing an arm across the nurse to his side. "I know you are upset about what we are telling you, but you must try to calm yourself."

Gabriel looked around, confused. "The buzzing," he said, trying to remove the anger from his voice, "did you hear the buzzing?"

"Mister Thaddeus. I think the shock of the past few days is causing you mental trauma you may not be able to…"

"I don't need counselling!" said Gabriel, with a snap. "If you don't mind, I'll just leave. I take it there's nothing else?"

"I feel it necessary to tell you I must inform the proper authorities of our findings. This matter needs investigating further. There are potential legal ramifications if you have undertaken any form of genetic…"

"Can - I - Leave?"

"Of course, Mister Thaddeus." said the doctor, noticeably afraid of what might happen if he refused.

Gabriel turned and stumbled over his chair, awkwardly righting it before it toppled, and made his way out of the office. He had no idea what was going on. He needed space. He should get out of this damn hospital and find a quiet corner to think. In addition, even though the thought had never come to him before, he needed a drink; a stiff one.

Chapter 9

It was late evening by the time Gabriel found himself perched on a bar stool back in Three B's. The afternoon shift of workers and museum attendees had dissipated and all that remained were the various personalities of a weekday night's drinking crowd.

He called the barman over and ordered a beer, a light trembling accompanying his hand as he reached over and plucked it from the counter. He had never before imbibed alcohol of any kind. Even during his university days, he only ever drank coffee or tea. Alcohol simply did not interest him. Yet here he was, watching as the bottle slowly moved toward his lips; savouring what would be his first taste.

"With all the tablets you're taking and the fact you've had a bleed in your brain, I shouldn't have to point out how stupid it is to take up drinking now."

Gabriel turned to see Oz stood no more than a stride down the counter. He was looking straight at him and shaking his head. Almost instantly, his willingness to do anything but leave evaporated. "How do you always find me?"

"You're fairly easy to follow, Thad-man. It's not like you skulk around. And besides, how many other people around here look like a half-completed Frankenstein parody?"

"I look like the monster from Frankenstein, Oz." said Gabriel, placing the beer back onto the bar. His voice, usually dull enough to ignore, seemed even more irritating than usual. "It's an easy mistake. Frankenstein was the doctor."

"Sooorrreee!" said Oz, leaning over a grabbing the beer. "So what are you doing here?"

Gabriel watched as Oz tucked into his beverage. He did not want it anymore, but the man should have asked before taking it. His every action was trying his patience. "Trying to find some peace and quiet."

"In a bar?" asked Oz, titling the beer back and taking another swig. "Probably one of the only busy bars you'll find in the centre at this time on a Wednesday. Peace and quiet? Here?"

"That was the plan." said Gabriel, rubbing his brow. "Most of these idiots I can ignore. I'm not going to get either with you here."

"It's unfair to call these people idiots, Thad-man."

"Oh come on!" said Gabriel, exasperated. "Look at that group of women over there." He pointed a clutch of three women, stood round a tall, circular table. Each wore a tight fitting dress and high heels, and one bore the unmistakable skin tone of fake tan. "You can't tell me they have a great deal going on upstairs. One of them is orange for shit's sake! Who in their right mind would go out looking like that?"

Another of the women at the table caught sight of Gabriel's gesturing and motioned to her friends, before making her way across the bar towards them.

"Smooth moves Romeo." said Oz, laughing. "Looks like you're going to get chance to ask one of them in person."

"Aw hell." said Gabriel, slumping his head against the bar. "This is your fault. Do you know that?"

"What would be my fault?" said a sultry, female voice.

Gabriel brought his head up to the sight of the woman leaning over. Now she was closer he could pick out her features. She was impressively good looking. Her cream dress hung closely to her sculpted, porcelain frame and contrasted the vibrancy of her loosely curled hair. Her eyes were radiant and her breasts - well - had he ever seen better?

"If you're done staring at my tits, maybe you could explain what the hell you think you're doing."

"I… Er…"

"Little men, sat talking to themselves in bars are usually freaks or perverts. You're doing nothing to change the stereotype."

"I'm not sat by myself, I'm with…" However, when he turned to look, Oz was gone. He was probably just out of sight, giggling about the situation. "Sorry."

"Sorry?" said the woman, with disgust. "Try growing up. You're not a boy anymore, Levi."

"Pardon?" Gabriel's head snapped up to question what the woman said, but she was already heading across to the exit and her waiting friends. "Wait!" he said, pushing through the bar flies.

The woman stopped in the doorway, the glow of street lamps drifting through her hair as it flailed in a gust of wind pulsing through the open door. Thoughts, like daydreams carried on the wings of butterflies, fluttered through his mind and heightened his senses. His world slowed, and there, just on the outskirts of self, he was sure he knew her. "Mary?" He did not know where the name came from, but he knew it was right. Everything in the bar was still. Time itself stopped, twitching on the verge of forever, as it fought against its slowing. The room was silent, and he was alone with her.

Like a bottle uncorked, she edged through the door into the night and the noises returned. He bounded between tables and found an opening, accelerating and slamming into the exit with his shoulder. She could not be far in front.

As the door opened and the night's breeze tingled along his brow, the dreadful buzzing returned. It careered through his mind, firing synapses and forcing him to buckle. He yelled, as bolts of pain shot down his spine and twisted like knots in his gut. He could feel his legs giving way and he tried to push an arm out to prevent his fall, but there was nothing to grasp. He closed his eyes, as fire tore through his mind and he fought back tears of anguish. He did not know why, but he loved the woman he was chasing. He had always loved her. And somewhere down within his tortured soul, he knew he would never see her again.

Chapter 10

Gabriel collapsed holding his head, to a truly disgraceful sensation. His world was pitch black and whatever he lay upon, squelched with every attempt he made to stand. The smell surrounding him was pungently horrific. It was the stench of death.

He should be in the street. His breathing echoed, and the air was stagnant. He was definitely inside. He fumbled at a crawl, his hand plunging through rotting flesh into the fetid mucus of decomposing forms, in a desperate attempt to understand where he was or how he had arrived.

After an unidentifiable length of gut wrenching searching, his surroundings became a little clearer. He was in a circular room, maybe a hundred feet across, with a perimeter lined with iron bars. He located a door, but without a light source to localise a handle, even though he searched, the door would remain closed. So exquisitely made for its niche was it, that there was no logical way it could be prised open without such a mechanism.

Eventually, in piteous and forlorn acceptance of his predicament, he sagged to the floor and began to weep, there was nothing more to do.

Seconds, minutes, perhaps hours passed by, as he languished in his solitary oblivion, before somewhere, just out of range of full perception, a low rumble began. There it found voice and slowly, insipidly, the noise began to muster in the dark.

It vibrated the floor and crept into a background thrum that pulsed its way around his prison. Thrrm - Thrrm Thrrm - Thrrm Thrrm Thrrm - Thrrm Thrrm Thrrm Thrrm Thrrm.

It was an awful sound. It stood the hairs on his neck and made him feel sick. He tried to cover his ears, but the noise would not be so easily avoided. It sounded off his bones, rattling his mind and dislodging any resistance.

The noise picked up pitch, droning out in long, bellows around the room. It rose to twisted crescendos with each pulse, the reverberation seemingly hanging in the air, motionless.

Then he could see it. Just toward the centre of the room, the noise focussed on a singularity of space. It was an incomprehensible something, flexing on the fringe of his existence.

Terrified, he redoubled his efforts to find an exit, as the sound became so loud it began to interfere with his faltering heartbeat.

Another crescendo, much louder than before, boomed out into the space, accompanied by a flash. It illuminated the dark and provided a fleeting glimpse of everything around him.

He was in a domed room, circled by a series of dull bars. Bodies, many just eviscerated piles of flesh, lined the space. A hundred, perhaps more souls had perished here, their brightly coloured clothing scorched to what remained of their forms. He was alone with the dead.

Most puzzling of all, was the core of the room where three metal orbs dangled in a column from ceiling to floor. The explanation that hit his mind made no sense. Somehow, he had awoken in a giant Van De Graff generator, and it was winding up. He had to get out.

Tighter and tighter, faster and faster, louder and louder. The noise snarled with the force of a jet engine, as he scrambled to find an exit, but there was none. He stared at the balls, realising there was no hope of escape, as tendrils of electricity crawled across their outsides, baying to be set free.

Almost at the point of fracture, the noise blasted out across the room. It froze in the strained space, as a brilliant white shaft of statically induced lightening burst outward. With vile indifference, it streaked across the space and hit him squarely in the chest.

The pain that surged through his veins was indescribable. He could smell his flesh burning. He could hear his veins bursting and feel boiling blood froth from his mouth; he could taste his own demise.

The bolt dropped him to the floor like a rag doll and left him to die. However, he did not fear the end; he welcomed it. Nothingness would set him free.

Chapter 11

"Wakey wakey, Friar Tuck!"

Gabriel blinked and stared out into the brilliant shafts of artificial light that poured down upon him; squinting hard to try to ease the tenderness he felt. "I'm not dead?"

"Not yet, Thad-man. But once you look in a mirror, I'm sure you'll want to be!" said Oz, his voice a confirmation that if he was dead, this could only be hell.

"Just stay still, Mister Thaddeus." said a female voice.

Gabriel tried his eyes again, ignoring the surge of pain and forcing his mind to focus. He was laid out in a hospital bed; again. Stood over him was the nurse who he had seen before. She was smiling, and the heady scent of Dior perfume drifted down from her and startled his fragile senses. He looked at her name badge - 'Jennifer'. It was a nice name, but something about the woman made his skin crawl. He could not place why. "What happened to me, Jennifer?"

"You collapsed as you came out of a bar, Mister Thaddeus. I don't believe that drinking was a good idea with what you have been through."

"I don't drink."

"Your blood alcohol level was point one two, Mister Thaddeus. I can guarantee you were drinking, and quite heavily."

"You've got this all wrong." said Gabriel, smiling as best he could. "I have never had a drink in my life."

"Save it, Thaddeus." said a stern, masculine voice.

Gabriel looked over. There, sat in a chair in the corner of the room was his boss, Superintendent Galloway. "Honestly, I haven't been…"

"We have at least nine witnesses who say you were drinking all night." said Galloway, with ire, his highly polished boots glistening like his eyes and magnifying his stern gaze. "We spoke to the barman. He sold you at least eight bottles of beer and at one point said you were harassing the clientele."

"Honestly sir, he's lying." Gabriel said, trying his best to sit up. "I did not, and have never…"

"Eye witnesses, Thaddeus! Blood alcohol results! These are not paltry pieces of evidence. You were in that bar. You were drinking. You did attempt to incite violence in a public place. You did collapse. And you are suspended until further notice." Galloway stood up and buttoned his jacket. He placed his cap back on and began to walk toward the door. "You are going to take two weeks off and then you are going to sit in front of the board and explain yourself."

"Sir, I…" But it was no use. He could see the disgust welling behind his superior's eyes and knew he could talk his way out of this. "I'm sorry. I honestly don't know what happened. I think I…" His voice trailed off to an unsure warble. He truly had no idea what was going on.

"I don't need to tell you what will happen if this gets out to the press. I'm giving you a chance to get your life in order. I expect you to take it." Galloway's gaze melted with his words, and his tone softened. "You're one of the good guys, Thaddeus. Don't let this turn you into something I know you're not. This type of stress is the ruin of many a man. You just need to wake up and see what's happening. You need to snap out of this, Thaddeus. I'll be here, if you need me."

There was nothing else to say. "Thanks, sir." Galloway nodded and left the room. As his footfalls disappeared down the corridor, Gabriel turned and smiled. "I'm sorry for all this."

"Don't apologise for anything." said Jennifer, as she fluffed his pillows and gently leant him back into a comfortable position. "I've seen far worse, and I'm sure I will again. Now, you just make sure you rest as much as you can." she said, as she took what looked like a woolly hat from a tray to her side. "This should keep your head warm until your hair grows back."

"Grows back?"

"Oh, you're going to love this!" said Oz, still perched on the edge of his seat by the side of the bed.

Jennifer smiled, pensively, and handed him a vanity mirror from the bed stand. He looked into it in horror, the image returned barely recognisable as the man he knew. The scar now encompassed his head. A neat circle of stitches ran all the way round his skull. The dome of his cranium polished, the hair fully removed. All that remained where his once proud hairline inhabited his scalp was a network of grazes and scab encrusted scars. "Jesus wept! I look like I've been mugged!"

"You hit your head pretty hard on the curb, Mister Thaddeus." said Jennifer, taking the mirror back. "You're lucky not have done more damage. If you'd hit the area where your surgery was located, who knows how much additional injury you could have suffered."

"Lucky?" he said, with surprise. "People are going to think I've had my head rescued from a top loading washing machine!"

"Oh dear." said Jennifer, giggling. "It could have been a lot worse."

"Doctor to Captain Picard." said Oz, partially covering his mouth to muffle the sound. "Klingons in the med bay. Alert, Klingons in the med bay!"

Gabriel groaned, trying desperately not to rise to Oz's bait. "It's no laughing matter."

"I know." said Jennifer, carefully tugging the hat on and fighting back a smirk. "I'm sorry." Once done, she pushed the medical cart out toward the doorway. "I'll send Doctor Evesham down in about an hour. He still has some things to discuss from the other day. Hopefully, you'll be slightly more courteous to him this time."

Damn. He could remember that. He was confused, but his actions were out of order. "I promise to be good." Before she left, a stray thought occurred. Something, annoyingly just out of reach, was bothering him. "Just before I forget, is there anything that I should know? I mean, I realise I've been under a lot of stress lately, but I was wondering if there was anything I should be doing?"

"Resting, Mister Thaddeus. We keep telling you to rest, but you don't seem to be listening. Stop fighting us." said Jennifer, as she absently checked her pocket watch and sifted through a tray on the cart. "Do you want something to help?"

"I'm fine." Gabriel said, faking a long yawn. "I think I'll be out like a light in no time. Thank you though."

"I'll come back and check on you in an hour, Mister Thaddeus. If you're still finding it difficult to sleep, I'll give you something then." And with that, she smiled again and made her way out of the room.

As soon as the door closed, Gabriel tore back the bed sheet and flung his legs over the edge.

"Whoa there cowboy!" said Oz, standing to meet him. "Where do you think you're going?"

"The toilet. Why? Do you want to hold my junk for me?"

"You don't look like you want to go to the toilet."

"Would you rather I pissed the bed with the nurse in the room?" said Gabriel, his tolerance for Oz' continued questioning over. "Why don't you make yourself useful and go get me a coke and a sandwich?" he said, shuffling across to the bathroom.

"Are you sure you want a coke? I've never seen you drink coke."

Shit. Bad lie - bad timing. "If I wanted something else I would have asked for something else. I asked for a coke." With mock anger, he turned to face Oz. "Are you here to help me or just to stress me out? I can ask the good nurse to have you removed so I can get some sleep you know."

"Have it your way, Thad-man." said Oz, raising his palms in supplication. "Any particular sandwich you fancy?"

"Cheese salad will do." said Gabriel, without pause. Wanting to make the request seem more real, he added a touch of detail. "No salad cream."

"You're the boss."

As he stepped into the bathroom, he heard the door open and close. Peering round the frame, he scanned the room. Oz was gone, and soon, he would be too.

Chapter 12

After removing his clothing from the bedside cabinet, Gabriel pulled the hat as far over his brow as he could and made his way into the corridor.

Something was seriously wrong. Everyone wanted him asleep or resting. He had not studied as much physiology as he could, but even he knew long periods of sleep were not what were needed. His mind should be kept active and tests should be run on his vision at the very least. There had to be another reason for people's continued insistence to relax. The only logical explanation was what he was investigating. He needed to get out of the hospital as soon as he could.

The corridor was strangely quiet. In addition, the bank of computers next to the small reception in the ward was unattended. His luck was changing. He moved to the back stairwell and descended as fast as he could down the three flights to the ground floor. Once there, he opened the door and peered into the foyer. It was deserted. A lone figure, hunched over a floor buffer, whistled a tune as he polished away, the space vacant of other activity.

Gabriel checked his watch. It was half six. He had never seen a hospital so quiet at this time in the evening. Not wanting to curse his fortune, he snuck out of the stairwell and casually strode toward the exit, holding his head low to avoid eye contact.

Once outside, he looked for a taxi. There were none, and the car park was practically empty. Confused, he spun to look at the hospital building. It was lit, all the way to the top floor, but outside there was not a soul to see. A chill encompassed the grounds and a light drizzle magnified the effect of isolation that drew in.

Pulling his jacket tight, he walked out of the grounds toward the centre of town. As he weaved down the streets, he was relieved to see traffic pass him and the sounds increase. By the time he was approaching a taxi rank, sat next to a greasy kebab emporium, people were buzzing around. The volume of rain falling had increased and the still of a dank autumn evening was settling into night.

He walked briskly to the lone taxi at the rank and reached for the door handle, as another arm came into view. He bumped against the form and slipped off the curb, stumbling backward and landing on his backside in a puddle.

"Oh, I'm really sorry." said a light, warm voice. "I didn't see you there. Are you ok?"

Gabriel looked up to see a woman stood by the cab. She was beautiful. Her high heels accentuated her sleek, svelte legs. She wore a mini skirt, and a pristine, white leather jacket pulled tightly around her frame. Smiling, she pushed back a dangling strand of blond hair from her face. He watched, as a raindrop trailed a curve from her brow and twinkled in the glow of a streetlight, as it arced down her perfect face.

"Are you alright?" she said, extending an arm.

"I'm fine." The words sounded distant, his brain fuddled by the beauty before him. Her voice was delicate intoxication. Her eyes were akin to sirens, pulling him in and preventing his departure. "I... I..." He stumbled, his conscious enraptured.

"Let me help you up."

He took her offered hand. She smelt like heaven. A mixture of exotic honeys sent to trap him like a fly. "Thank you." he said, desperately trying to shake his delirium.

"Don't be silly." she said, allowing an infectious giggle to escape her sculpted lips. "As long as you're not hurt."

"Really," he said, trying to still his beating heart. "I'm fine. Over the last few days, I've had a lot worse, believe me. I'm Gabriel, by the way." he said, shaking the hand he still held, and hoping action would take away his awkwardness.

"Suzanne." she replied, her smile broadening and her gaze falling into his. "Sounds like you've had as bad a day as I have."

"It's been more of a couple of week thing with me." he said, struggling to find the words that would allow the conversation to continue. She chuckled, eliciting a grin, a look of pride at his accomplishment. "You should get out of the rain. You look freezing. I'll wait for the next cab."

"You're soaking wet and it's my fault. You should take it. It's not like I'm in a rush to get anywhere."

"You're forgetting I have my hat. There's nothing keeps you as warm as stout headwear."

Suzanne looked at him, her countenance warm and inviting. "A blue, woolly hat is hardly stout."

"I believe I'm better prepared for the rain than you." he said, with mirth.

She looked down and then back up, his heart skipping another beat as contact was re-established. "I suppose I'm not. I was meant to be going for a meal tonight. Dress nicely, he said. All this to get stood up again."

"Who would stand you up?" he said, awestruck, drawing a blush. "I'm sorry." he said, embarrassed at his lack of control.

"Don't be." she said, re-engaging his look. "Thank you."

Gabriel had never been in a situation like this before. Maybe it was down to the horrors of the last few days, but an impulsion grew he could not ignore. "I know this is an imposition," he said, trying to remain calm, "but I would be more than happy to fulfil that duty this evening."

"I think we're both a little bedraggled to be sitting in a restaurant." she said, pushing her frizzing hair out of her eyes.

She was right. Here they were, stood in the rain, barely knowing one another, and he was asking her on a dinner date. She was probably the sort of woman who refused to go out in public without at least an hours preening, and the seat of his pants looks as if he had experienced a senior moment. It was a stupid request. He hung his head, his confidence shattered.

"A drink would be nice though." she said, softly.

He looked back up. She was smiling at him. His heart was pounding fast and he could feel a wide grin pulling across his face. He could not believe it. She wanted to go for a drink - with him. "There's a good bar round the corner. They do food until late, but it's mostly snacks."

"That sounds nice. Anywhere out of the rain sounds good right now, actually."

Chapter 13

Stepping out of the rain, they found a booth in the bar and settled in, sharing small talk and anecdotes about failed relationships, as they laughed into night. It was bliss. His heart felt like it was flying, carried by angels to his own private little corner of heaven.

Suzanne was enchanting, a creature of pure divinity and grace. He could not imagine a more happy and profound time in his life than what he was experiencing. His skin tingled as they talked; the pains in his head a fading memory.

"Have you never had a drink at all?" she asked, as the barman delivered another large glass of merlot for her and an iced tea for him.

"Never." he said, gazing into his glass. "After seeing what drink did to my family, I suppose I've grown averse to it. Not that there's anything wrong with drinking, per se."

"I'm sorry. I didn't mean to pry."

"It's ok." he said, tenderly. "You had no way of knowing. It's a time in my life that's distant to me now. I don't dwell on it."

"So, what do you do for a living?"

"I'm a detective for a branch of the police." he said, happy for the chance to change topic. "I mostly investigate corporate espionage and fraud. It's a lot more boring than it sounds."

"Ooh!" she said, pursing her lips and making him wish he could kiss her. "That doesn't sound boring at all. What are you investigating at the moment? Anything gossip worthy?"

"I can't really go into the details." he said, trying to find some way of diluting the information. "I'm currently looking into some allegations linking the UK Science Council and a company called ROS Genetics."

"ROS Genetics of Cambridge?" she asked, peering quizzically at him.

"The very same. What's your interest?"

"I'm an investigative reporter." she said, reaching into her clutch and retrieving a black, leather notepad and pen. She flicked the book open, exposing page after page of delicately written script. A few rustled turns later, her finger stopped next to a series of bulleted notes. "Here we go. ROS Genetics, Cambridge. Isn't that a strange coincidence?"

Gabriel looked down the page. Whatever Suzanne was looking into seemed to have something to do with Kirk Smithson and the people who funded ROS Genetics. "So what are you investigating?" he asked, his interest piqued.

"I'm not investigating them directly." said Suzanne, leaning over. "I'm actually trying to do a piece on the life of a man called Levi Tirney. There's an unknown portion of the story that is glossed over. I was trying to track it down."

Gabriel's heart skipped a beat. She was researching his family. "Levi Tirney. I think I know the story; the man who killed everyone where he worked? Nineteenth century, wasn't it?"

"Very good." she said, smiling. "But what many people don't know is Tirney took the blame for everything that went on, but there was another person involved."

"Who?"

"A man called O'Reilly. From my research, it appears without O'Reilly, Mister Tirney could not have done what he did. It also appears it wasn't just a solitary O'Reilly who was involved. It looks as though Mister Tirney's family were, in some way, linked to the O'Reilly's. I think it could be a blood bond of some kind. The O'Reilly clan have been looking out for the Tirney family ever since. But the family tree is not clear."

Gabriel's heart was pounding so fast, he feared it would rattle itself free and fall into the pit of his stomach. He could feel the blood running from his face, as his mind struggled to comprehend the thought that struck him, his brow becoming tighter, and the insidious thrum of buzzing returning to his head.

"Are you alright, Gabriel?" asked Suzanne, placing a hand on his shoulder.

Gabriel held up a finger and reached into his pocket for his phone. He quickly scanned through his contact book and selected his commanding officer. After three short rings, Superintendent Galloway answered.

"Mister Thaddeus. What can I do for you at this hour?" Galloway asked, his usual, serious tone gone and a warm, pleasing mellowness in its place.

"You said you would help me, if I asked sir. Well, I need some help."

"I'm happy to do anything, Gabriel. All you need…"

"This is difficult enough to ask, sir." said Gabriel, cutting his superior off. "I promised I would never make it an issue, but I will have to break that promise I fear."

"What promise is that, Gabriel?"

"I want you to tell me everything you know about Oz, sir. I think he may not be who we think he is." Gabriel's mind raced as he asked the question. Could it be true? Oswald Reilly - O'Reilly. It could be a coincidence, but something deep inside told him it was not.

"I will have one of the desk Sergeants do a full background check in the morning. Don't worry." said Galloway, his voice taking on a soothing air. "What was the name again?"

"Oz sir." said Gabriel, confused. "Oswald Reilly. You hired him. My partner, sir."

"Gabriel, we've had this conversation many times. You've always stated you did not work well with partners. I have always honoured that."

"Sir, please." said Gabriel, beads of sweat beginning to form on his brow. "Don't wind me up. Oz. Short, irritating kid. Was sat in the hospital room with me after I'd collapsed at ROS Genetics."

"ROS Genetics?" said Galloway, his voice full of surprise. "You collapsed after a night of drinking, Gabriel. The ROS Genetics case was months ago."

"Not that case, sir. I'm talking about the UK Science Council one I was tracking down."

"I know the case, Gabriel." said Galloway, his voice becoming sterner. "That was the one I was referring to. You showed that ROS Genetic paid off Archibald McMaster and in turn he swayed funding for the Physics Council. Don't you remember? McMaster killed himself when the scandal broke. That's what made you drink in the first place."

Gabriel's mind was a blur. What was going on? He sat, mouth agape, with the phone slightly pulled away from his ear, as Galloway's requests for response drifted round his head.

"Gabriel?" said Suzanne, dragging his attention back. Her outfit had changed. She was wearing a flowing, white dress and her hair was tied in a bun. "What did daddy say, Gabriel?" She was beaming, expectantly awaiting a response.

"About what?" he said, the words fumbling out.

"About us, Gabriel. Did he give you his permission?"

"His permission for what?" he said, his vision drifting in and out of focus. All he could do was watch, co-pilot to his actions.

"To get married, silly."

"Married?" he said, trying to shake his head free of clutter.

"Of course, married!" said a cheery, male voice.

Gabriel blinked. It was the middle of the day. The bar was rammed with people. A range of drinks was laid out on every table and a smiling, ginger haired man stood directly in his view. He was short, and sported a wispy, unkempt beard. "What...?" he said, almost stuttering.

"Sweet mother Mary!" said the man, in a rich, Irish accent. "You've only had the two, now boy. We've a whole night to be getting you through."

"I'm sorry." he said, desperately trying to hold on to his sanity. "But who the hell are you?"

"Oooh!" said the man, in an overly sarcastic tone. "It's going to be like that, is it? I'm not one of you until you marry my sister?"

"Marry whose sister?"

"What are you talking about?" asked Suzanne, shaking her head and peering across the table.

He looked round. He was back in the bar. His mobile was in his hand, held just away from his ear. Through the tiny speaker, he could hear Galloway asking if he was ok. He pressed the phone to his ear, already reaching for the cancel button with his thumb. "We'll speak later, sir." he said, and ended the call.

"Are you going to tell me what the hell is going on?" said Suzanne, clearly agitated.

"I don't know." he said, as he stood and made his way to the door. "We need to get out of here."

With Suzanne still questioning what he was doing, he stepped outside. As he checked his surroundings, a car sped round the corner, its headlamps on full. Momentarily dazzled, he drew an arm over his face to block out the light.

At the sudden change in brightness, the throbbing in his head magnified and he winced, his world descending into a swirl of noise.

Chapter 14

Gabriel withdrew his arm to a surprising vista. The afternoon sun, high above, blasted down the unmistakeable heat of summer from a cloudless sky. A shadow moved across his view and blurred his vision, as his eyes refocused.

"If you want to go to the mess for some chow, now's your chance." said a rambling, American accent. "We're up at sixteen hundred. That gives us thirty minutes. C'mon Jones, get moving you slouch!"

Gabriel took stock of his surroundings. He was outside a coarse, green tent, surrounded by hundreds of identical ones. Mud, inches deep, covered the ground, zigzagged by the marks of motorized transport. The man talking to him was wearing heavy, cotton trousers, and black boots. His once white t-shirt browned by repeated, failed washing attempts. He scanned around. People crawled everywhere, all of them wearing similar attire. What the hell was going on? Where was he? More importantly, who was he? As he puzzled, a Willys' Jeep pulled up and a man in a blue overcoat jumped out.

"Lieutenant Galloway." said his companion, standing to attention.

Galloway? The man was younger than his superior was, but he could see the familial relationship.

"At ease, private." said Galloway, in an aristocratic tone. "Can I have a word with you men?"

"Of course sir." said his companion, still stiff as a board.

"Forrester, you're first. Then I'll speak to you, Jones." said Galloway, looking over in his direction.

"We were on our way to get food before our duty shift, sir. Is there any chance we can hold this conversation in the mess?" said Forrester.

"These are to be private interviews gentlemen, so the mess is not the place. Jones, if you want to go for some food now, I'll speak to Forrester and then switch when I'm done. That way, I'm not depriving you of sustenance."

Gabriel nodded, to hide his total confusion, as Forrester got into the jeep with Galloway and the pair set off into the distance. Damn, this was not right. He had seen enough movies about military daring-do to know where he was. It was an American camp. In addition, it was sometime during the Second World War. How? Why? The questions came in waves, but no answers followed. Was he hallucinating? He had never taken LSD, but surely, anything witnessed in that state could not be as real as this? He could smell the damp clinging to everything around him, blended with the pungent aroma of gasoline. This was too real. It was just like before. He was in a war zone, and was sure to meet his fate again if he stayed in the open. Perhaps Galloway's idea was a good one. He would find the mess, get something to eat and then question the man. Surely, he would know something. Besides, if he stayed there, perhaps he could avoid the inevitable.

After five minutes of wandering, he eventually found what he was looking for. The large mess tent was open at the front, and rows of benches arranged inside. Other than a few men milling round the outside, there was no one inside. Good. The last thing he needed right now was people asking questions.

He strode through the opening and into the space beyond, spying a pair of large pots on a bench against the far wall. As he approached, a strange man wearing an apron walked up from a side entrance and stirred the liquid inside them. The man hunched over, his face obscured by a peaked cap, but even at a few strides distance, he could pick out the stench of stale alcohol. The man's head turned at his approach and he snapped up a bowl, ladled a healthy portion of broth into it, and shoved it in his direction.

Not wanting his sudden appearance to look out of the ordinary, Gabriel took the bowl, grabbed a wedge of heavy looking bread, and went to find a seat. The bread was dense, more dough than air. As he walked to find a spot where he could keep an eye on his surroundings, he nibbled at its edge. It was caustic and heavily salted, possibly the worst he ever tasted. It was no wonder soldiers were angry.

He sat down and took his first mouthful of broth. Its primary ingredient must be battery acid. He took another couple of spoonful's to put down the hunger pangs in his stomach and stopped. There was no way he could eat this.

So, with nothing else to do until Galloway arrived, he sat and watched the strange man continue to hover over the stores of broth, occasionally adding drops of something from a vial in his pocket and stirring the foul substance. It was no use. No amount of flavouring, no matter how powerful the substance within may be, could possible save the food. It may as well have gone off days ago. It was rancid.

The man turned occasionally in his direction, as if checking he was enjoying his meal. Gabriel kept hold of his spoon, occasionally raising it with a smile, attempting to give an air of enjoyment.

At the last look, a stray belch lurched from his gut and uttered out across the mess. It was a foul discharge of air, heated and sulphurous. He recoiled at the event, piquing the interest of the man, who began to walk over. Shit. He did not need the attention.

He tried to straighten, to take focus away from his actions, as a wave of nausea engulfed him. Something was wrong.

His skin was wriggling and his hands were trembling. He could feel sweat beginning to dribble from his brow, as pain shot through his stomach. He looked up at the man approaching, his face swirling as his vision danced. Did he know him? There was something familiar about his face.

With motor control all but gone, the man arrived at his side and grabbed a handful of his hair. He could not fight. His muscles would not respond. The only thing stopping him from collapsing to the table was this man; this strange, vaguely familiar man. His eyes were bloodshot and a wide grin encompassed chiselled features, as he looked him in the eye.

"Nature or nurture?" the man said, his stare falling straight through him. "It is a difficult question to answer. Who shows the offspring of the cuckoo how to repeat the feat of its parents, if they are not present to teach it?"

Gabriel's mind was hanging by a thread, and the man was torturing him with a theological conundrum. He wanted to strike out, but he was frozen and his conscious mind was failing fast.

"All animals are linked. Nature, not nurture, is the string that binds us together. Do you see? We are all genetically similar, because we are all connected. We have always been connected, every one of us. It is the price of the singularity which brought us here."

The man was staring straight at him; his rancid breath enveloping what little remained of his senses.

"You are running out of time, Gabriel. You need to remove yourself from this place; free your mind and wake up. Do not allow your present entanglement to prevent our salvation."

The man let his head go and he plopped into his bowl of broth, the pungent stew rising up his nostrils and stifling his attempts for air. As he struggled against his muscles, willing them to assist his escape, he could hear the man whistle as he left. To his horror, he recognised the tune.

As the choking liquid entered his faltering lungs and darkness enshrouded his thoughts, he relaxed. Somewhere, deep inside his subconscious, he knew this was not his time.

Chapter 15

Gabriel coughed; liquid rising from his mouth with every choking gasp. He could feel something pouring over his face. He looked up. He stood underneath a broken gutter in the street, the overflow pouring into his face. Still wheezing, he hopped sideways and looked around. Surprised, he rubbed his eyes and rechecked his surroundings. He was alone. The street was empty. He checked his watch; it was half past ten.

He turned and stared into the bar; there was no one. Not even empty glasses remained on the tables. Where was Suzanne? Confused, he ran down the street to an intersection and scanned around. The rain fell heavily from the grey sky and streetlights picked out puddles littering his view, but not a single thing stirred. He scanned the skyline. Other than the faint glow of the city, there was nothing; no movement, no flicker of headlights, not a sound. Everywhere was deserted. Panicked, he ran back toward the taxi rank.

As he made his way under the bridge, the expected smell of kebabs failed to meet his nostrils. Sat in the rank outside the shop was a lone taxi. A cursory glance through the back window as he approached confirmed his worst fears; it too was empty. He arrived at the shop and stared through its frontage. The lights were on and a bedraggled mass of fat and lamb twisted on a spit by the counter, but no one was home. He searched what was once a busy corner of the city, desperate to find signs of life, but the only noise came from a leaky pipe overhanging the street. Drip - Drip Drip - Drip

Drip Drip - Drip Drip Drip Drip Drip. The noise seemed magnified by the silence and tore through his head, sending him to his knees.

As he struggled against the pain, he picked out footfalls approaching. Twisting to the sound, he could see two, white cloaked figures approaching. It was Jennifer, the nurse who was tending him earlier, and Doctor Evesham. They were marching toward him, methodically encroaching into his space.

"Stay back!" said Gabriel, his voice echoing off the bridge.

"Stay calm, Mister Thaddeus." said Jennifer, striding faster. "We need to get you back to the hospital."

"Please come with us." said Doctor Evesham, as he removed the cap from a syringe and continued his advance. "You need to stay calm. The treatment is designed to assist you. It may not work if you resist."

Gabriel stared, terror invading his mind. He would not, could not, go anywhere with these people. He needed to get out of here.

As he turned to run, he noticed the taxi's passenger door was ajar. Baffled, he scanned up the side of the vehicle, and was shocked to see a man's face staring at him.

"Are you going to sit there all night, or are you going to get a move on?" said Oz.

"I... I..." said Gabriel, looking back at the fast approaching medical staff. Where the hell had Oz come from? "I don't know who you are anymore."

"Of course you do, Thad-man. But feel free to take your time. I'm sure Evesham will be gentle." said Oz, shuffling back into the car and closing the door with a clunk.

Gabriel glanced from Evesham and back to the taxi. Whom to trust? A crazed doctor who wanted him asleep, or Oz? There really was no choice to make. Standing and grumbling under his breath, he darted to the driver's side and jumped into the cab.

"Glad you could make it." said Oz, without looking up, grasping his iPhone, as the dreadful hum of a game tweeted out.

Gabriel reached for the ignition and stopped, suddenly realising where he was. "This is my car." he said, bewildered.

"Of course it is, Thad-man. Have you ever seen the inside of a cab from the front seat?" asked Oz, pausing his game. "Of course you haven't. So, this is your car. What part of this isn't making sense yet?"

Gabriel looked into the rear view mirror. His pursuers were closing on them, maybe only a few strides from the back of the car. Instinctively, he started the car and floored the accelerator. The tyres squealed, as he gunned the engine and tore away from the curb, leaving Jennifer and Evesham in their wake. "Who the hell are you?" he said, as he screeched round a corner and made his way out of the city.

"Oh come on, Thad-man!" said Oz, almost mocking him. "Seriously? Even now?"

"Suzanne just told me about you. You're an O'Reilly."

"Suzanne told you about the O'Reilly's nearly eight months ago." said Oz, still playing with his phone, unflustered by what was going on.

"That was tonight! I've only just met her."

"No you haven't." said Oz, his voice annoyingly calm.

Infuriated, he reached across and tore the phone from Oz's grasp, tossing it out of a window into the night. "I assume I now have your undivided attention?"

"Whatever, Thad-man." said Oz, looking over at him. "That was your phone, by the way."

Gabriel patted his pockets. Shit. It was his phone. "How the hell did you get that?"

"How did I get it? For Christ's sake, Gabriel! Try to think, will you?"

Think? All he had been doing was thinking, but nothing was making sense. Had he known Suzanne for months? That could not be true. Then where had the images of the conversation about ringing her father or the stag do come from? In addition, who was Oz? "Just tell me, ok? I'm struggling here. Nothing is making any sense."

"If nothing is making any sense to you, how much sense do you think it makes to me?"

"Oh, that's really helpful Oz." he said, totally exasperated. "Answer my question with a riddle."

"Jesus wept, Thad-man." said Oz, hanging his head. "I can't help you if you won't help yourself."

He looked at Oz, shaking his head and trying to comprehend what reason the man could possibly have for withholding information. "Ok, Oz. I'll play your stupid little game. How do I help myself?"

"That's better." said Oz, grinning. "Where do you think you'll find the information you need?"

"I was going to go to ROS Genetics."

"Great idea." said Oz, looking out of the window.

Gabriel followed Oz's line of sight and instinctively slammed on the brakes. There, looming out of the night by the side of the road was the bland façade of ROS Genetics. "How…?" he said, trying to understand how they travelled from Reading to Cambridge in only a few short minutes. Was he still dreaming?

"The car park looks empty." said Oz, smiling. "You could always get closer to the doors. I don't like getting wet."

Chapter 16

Gabriel pulled up by the entrance to ROS Genetics, turned off the engine, and stared at Oz.

"Are you waiting for me for some reason?" asked Oz, shrugging his shoulders.

Frustrated, he left the car and darted across to the door. The foyer was just as stark as he remembered. "I can't believe the doors were open. The office is shut." he said, as he stood and peered into the badly lit space.

"You think this is really their office?" asked Oz, laughing. "Turn some lights on and let's get on with this, shall we?"

Gabriel twisted toward the door. There, exactly where he expected them to be, were a set of light switches. Understanding only casually why he could remember such a thing, he flicked them on. Above them, the fluorescent tubes shuddered and hummed, breathing life into the dead space.

"The lifts are over here, aren't they?" said Oz, as he trudged off to the far corner of the room.

How could he know that? Oz never joined him in ROS Genetics; not for a single interview. Or had he? Damn it. It was pointless trying to make sense of what was happening. He could not be certain of anything. The rollercoaster was running, and getting off would be suicide.

He arrived by the side of the lifts and waited for one to descend, as Oz simply stood and smiled at him.

"So where is the information kept, Thad-man?"

"How am I supposed to know that?" he said, stepping into the lift and hitting the button for the second floor.

"We're going up though. You know roughly where you're heading."

"I have an inkling. I saw a set of cabinets outside the boardroom when I was here last. I thought I'd start there."

"Excellent." said Oz, chirpily. "I'm sure everything you need to know will be in there."

The lift sounded a gentle ping and the doors opened, only blackness beyond.

"Shit." said Gabriel, stepping out into the corridor. "I need to find a light switch."

Groping along the wall, his fingers searched for something illuminate his surroundings. Eventually, after shuffling down the wall only a few feet, an old-fashioned metal switch, shaped like a drumstick ran across his fingertips. Unsure why the strange switch would be in such a modern building, he applied gentle pressure and flicked the light on.

Before he knew what was happening, a pair of hands clasped around his neck, squeezing tight, and attempting to force him to the ground. He stared in shock at the man holding him, a distant recollection rearing around his startled mind. Where was he? This was not ROS Genetics. He was in someone's kitchen.

He raised his hands to his throat, but the man only squeezed tighter, as he tried to release his grip. He could feel his voice box crumpling under the assault and frantically searched around for something to defend himself with. There, next to a historic looking copper kettle by the side of an American faucet, was a long, serrated, bread knife. He hated the thought of using it, but he had no choice. He was out of time. He could already see the edges of his vision failing, as the man continued to squeeze the life from him.

He reached out and grabbed the knife, and begging for forgiveness for his actions, plunged it into his assailant's side. The man released his grip instantly and Gabriel fell to his knees, gasping for air. He crawled out of the small space and tried to retreat. Where was he?

He was in a neat, but threadbare apartment. The decoration was old fashioned, perhaps late forties. Sat on a chest-table in the middle of the room was a half-eaten pizza and a bottle of expensive wine, a Salice Salentino. How could anyone afford a bottle of wine that expensive and only live in this squalor?

Before his mind could give an answer, a blow landed across the back of his head, sending him sprawling toward the couch. He landed face first, his attacker landing on top of him, as hands circled his neck and began to apply pressure once more.

"You're nearly out of time, Gabriel." said the man, as he continued to squeeze. "I should not have to remind you what is at stake."

He tried to move, but the man was strangely powerful. could smell alcohol. Almost as if, the furniture was drenched in it. He tried to speak, to talk the man down from his actions, but he simply could not vocalise a response. The air from his lungs spent.

"Do you fear life as well as death now, Gabriel? Does vanquishing the corpuscular theories proposed by the dark heretic, take away your inherent propensity for belief? Do you find the inconsequential proclivity toward the nihilistic to be desired above the faint chance of forever? Is that why you refuse to look beyond your reason? Because the infinite is an unintelligible as the nothingness you find transient association with?"

Who the hell are these people? It was the only thought that would resolve in his mind, as his sight funnelled down to a hazy spot. Last time it was cuckoos and now the folly of

Newtonian science. Why was he being tortured like this? What did it have to do with what was going on?

"What does Young's great experiment tell you are the inevitable conclusions of looking for answers, Gabriel? Do you think analysing your situation will free you, or make your assessment irrelevant?"

"Fuck you!" The words blurted out and echoed.

"I'm glad you got that off your chest." said Oz, almost laughing.

Gabriel stood, shocked, his finger pressed against the light switch, motionlessly looking out across the empty second floor of ROS Genetics.

"C'mon. Those cabinets you talked about are just down here."

"Do you…" he said, his voice hoarse. "What is happening to me?"

"That's what we're trying to do, Thad-man. We're here to get you your answers. You've just got to focus and trust me."

Gabriel stumbled, almost in a trance, as he followed Oz to a bank of cabinets against a plain, cream wall.

"Do you remember anything about what was in them?" asked Oz.

How could he remember anything about what was in them? He only vaguely remembered seeing them. They sat by the side of a lone desk, partially covered by a fern of some kind. Now… He looked down at the cabinets. They were bland, grey aluminium with four drawers each. However, they were now alone at one edge of the corridor. The whole floor was empty save for these items of furniture. No desks, no chairs, no plants. It was as if the building had been emptied, save for these two lonesome artefacts. "Has this place been shut down?"

"We're not in Kansas anymore Toto." said Oz, grinning inanely. "Just find what you need and let's leave."

There was no point trying to extract anything meaningful from Oz. His answers switched from the meaningless to the nonsensical, pitched to raise his ire with tactical precision.

He stared at the filing cabinets, unsure of what he would find. A trembling hand reached out and pulled the top drawer open. Inside were ranks of yellow files, stuffed with paper. A plastic tab was attached to the top corner of each, but for some reason, most of the writing on the tabs was smudged. He extracted the first folder, heavy with the weight of paper it contained, its tab illegible. To his horror, the file contained a few garbled pages of rubbish at the beginning and then blank pages. He replaced it back in the rack and thumbed through to another. The same. Just a few pages of random text and blurry characters; interspersed with the odd badly printed chart of graph. Was someone trying to erase the data the file contained? That made no sense. They emptied the office, so why not get rid of this cabinet? It was as if it was left here for someone to decipher.

He searched through the files and located one with a label he could read, 'YTD Financials'. He flipped the cover and to his relief found the text on the front legible. He began to read. Every now and again, a page would dissolve back to unintelligible swirls, but the majority was clear. McMaster was paid off by ROS Genetics. Galloway was telling the truth. The payment trail was last year. But how was that possible?

He placed the folder on top of the cabinet and continued his search. Drawer after drawer emptied, and one by one, all the things Galloway said resolving. Until, eventually, at the back of the last drawer opened, a solitary file remained. Its label reared out and sent twinges of panic rippling down his spine, as he carefully withdrew it from the cabinet.

Desperately trying to still the shaking of his hands, he peered at the neat name scribed on its label; 'Suzanne Thaddeus'. He glanced at Oz. His face was drawn and ashen, his usual mischievous demeanour gone. He fidgeted where he stood, barely able to look him in the eye. What did he know? He stared at the folder, his nerves on edge as he slowly opened the file. The title almost screamed at him, eliciting a grimace, as his mind flooded with recollection; 'Test Subject - 001'. Everything he had learnt, everything he was, and everything contained within this cabinet, blended together. Finally, he understood.

Chapter 17

It was spring. A light breeze blew through the trees and danced apple blossom across a blue sky, but Gabriel could not see it. His world had fallen apart. Behind him in the courthouse, the verdict was returned; not guilty.

He sat against the marble steps with his head in his hands, as people meandered around, and began to weep. He could hear chatter drifting down from the defendant's group, as they emerged into the sunlight to the click of cameras and the applause of supporters. The cheery, defiant vocalisations disturbed his thoughts and forced him to restrain his anger. What he would not give for five minutes alone with the man.

Only a year ago, his life was perfect; he met Suzanne. She was a reporter, assigned after the derivatives crash to do a piece on the fight against corporate crime. It was a chance meeting, based on a freak occurrence in a system largely ignored by people.

He could remember the day she came into the office and said hello. It was as if his world had melted, and all that remained was her. It was love at first sight; every moment gleefully entered into and cherished. Every request met with the same dutiful acceptance. To make her happy was to be happy himself.

After only four months together, a wedding was hastily organised and friends and family from both sides arranged. And in that moment, their fates were sealed. His list of guests was short, only a few dozen and no family members were present.

He never spoke about his family with her; his early life and the history of his line, something he took great care to distance himself from. However, once her interest was piqued by his limited guest list, it was only right she knew.

He told her about his family; about how entrenched they were in so-called 'high society'. He told about the events in America and about his great grandfather's death. Finally, he told of how he gave away every penny left of the once enormous family fortune.

She took the news with grace, never mentioning the details again. Nevertheless, all too soon, he realised her curiosity had gnawed at her. Unbeknownst to him, she began to investigate his history.

By chance, he had taken the ROS Genetics case and, as he often did, discussed it with her over dinner. Little did he know ROS Genetics had also come up in her research. After McMaster's death, she became distant, claiming working pressures were high and placating his desire to know more. How he wished he could go back and change that.

One evening, after patiently awaiting her arrival at home, he received the call that would change his life forever. Suzanne was dead.

He shrugged off his memories and turned to stare at the group, his eyes swollen with tearful rage, as a figure sat by his side and placed a comforting arm around his shoulders.

"You don't need to be going up there and causing a ruckus now, do you?"

Gabriel turned and looked at the man by his side. It was Patrick, Alison's brother. Even through the pain, he was holding a smile; his shock of ginger hair, in deference to its usual state, neatly combed across his brow.

"You be working on a plan to make things better by making things worse." Patrick tightened his grip, the hug firm yet emotive. "But both you and I know that would not

273

be what my sister would want from you. You're a better man than these vultures will ever be. Don't go demeaning your good name now, boy."

Gabriel lowered his head and fought off another wave of torment welling from deep within his soul. "I couldn't help her." he said, the words fumbling from his lips. "I couldn't even punish the man who killed her."

"There is more than one way to skin a cat." said Patrick, his smile widening. "McMaster got his comeuppance. All we need to do now is make sure the rest of the scum hiding behind the veil of ROS Genetics get theirs too."

Gabriel turned and grimaced. Suzanne's research enlightening him to every person he could see stood around the defendant.

He could remember the day after the funeral as if it were yesterday.

People, many of whom he did not speak to throughout the entire wake, making pleasant goodbyes, as they left his house and wandered back to their lives. However, his life was over.

He sat on their bed, littered with the detritus of Suzanne's personal and working effects, and wept for hours. Every new box opened reminding him of some part of the proud and elegant woman who shared his existence for so brief a time, and starting his plaintive howling once more.

Eventually, his wandering through her life's artefacts brought him to her work folders. He marvelled at her organisation. She held a keen mind. Neat, logical, and willing to make the leaps of reasoning required to find even the darkest of secrets.

Almost without noticing, he stumbled across the box that brought him to today, an unmarked container with a faded lid, which looked far older than its contents suggested. There he read about her investigations into his family. How she tracked down the full details of what his great grandfather did, and everything transpired since. Cautiously, he unfurled an enormous sheet, delicately crafted from multiple pages with intricate Sellotape stitches, which showed the timeline of events and all the principle players. Staggered by the level of detail accumulated, his mind raced, as name after name resolved into focus from his life.

Frantically scribbling on top of Suzanne's diligent notes, he began to fill in the blanks she missed, until a single thought resolved. He knew who had killed her and why.

Using every power at his disposal, he began his investigation, ensuring everyone linked was kept as far away from the truth as possible. It was the only way to ensure their safety.

Eventually, he gathered the evidence necessary to make his case and presented it with glee to his superiors. More quickly than he suspected, charges were made and a trial date set. Yet, somehow, the decision was not guilty. He had failed. Not only had he failed himself, but he also failed Alison.

"So, Mister Thaddeus." said Patrick, standing up. "Are you ready to go to the source? I think it's time we paid our man's place of work a little visit."

Gabriel smiled and wiped the tears from his eyes. Playing the game had failed. Patrick was right. It was time for another approach.

-

Back in the offices of ROS Genetics, Gabriel let go of his head, the pain, and the buzzing, now gone. "It's time to go."

With a knowing look, Oz grinned. "Good to see you back as your old self, Thad-man. Where are we heading now?"

Gabriel turned and set off for the lifts, as he began to whistle a tune, much to Oz's obvious delight.

Once called, the doors opened, but not to the interior expected from ROS Genetics. The inside of the lift bland white and the smell of disinfectant greeted them as they stepped inside. Unperturbed, he pressed the button for the basement, as his whistle turned to song. "Because, because, because, because, because... Because of the wonderful things he does!"

Chapter 18

The lift doors opened to a dank and silent corridor. The musky smell of damp clung in the air and stifled Gabriel's continued song. This was not what he expected.

"We're out of time, Thad-man!" said Oz, pushing him into the corridor. "You need to get moving."

Gabriel stood in the corridor and looked toward both ends. To one side, perhaps a few hundred feet down the sterile walkway, a dim light drifted through a window and dispersed against whitewashed walls. As he turned, he caught a sight that stopped his heart. There, not more than fifty feet away, were Doctor Evesham and Jennifer. As they walked, the lights behind them shuddered and blinked out, descending the corridor into infinite darkness.

"A word of your time, Mister Thaddeus." said Evesham, as he removed a syringe from his pocket and continued to advance.

"I've got this." said Oz, turning and smiling.

Gabriel patted Oz on the head and ruffled his hair, finally seeing him for who he was. Oswald, his faithful companion, the dog he grew up with. No more fitting or energetically frustrating a servant could he imagine. "Thanks pal."

Oz turned, scraggy hair and ears swinging as he ran, barking for all he was worth at the enemies approaching.

Gabriel twisted, beginning his dart toward the light. He scrambled onward; ignoring Oz's distressed barking, as he tore down the short strip toward his goal.

Not stopping to look how Oz was faring, he reached the glass pane and stared into the space beyond. His heart skipped a beat as his eyes met the scene; his mind, just for a split second, refusing to accept what he was bearing witness to.

There, on a gurney in what looked like an operating theatre, was his body. He blinked hard, giving his brain chance to re-assess the information it was relaying to his conscious mind. There was no doubt. He was naked, save for a pair of simple looking, blue cotton pants; his hands unbound and a weird, metal, and wire contraption placed over his skull.

Two people stood in the room with him, a female, and a male. Judging from the size and gait of the man, even though his back was to him, he knew who it was.

-

The evening after the trial, Patrick and Gabriel made their way to the Royal Berkshire Hospital. Entering through the old main entrance of the building sat to one side of the more modern construction, they carefully avoided the attention of the numerous staff milling around its ancient corridors and toward a stairwell lingering by a set of outdated offices.

"Where are we going?" asked Gabriel, as Patrick started to head down into the bowels of the building.

"My sister's sources say ROS Genetics have a lab in the basement. You don't think our man is going to be coming to work this evening, do you? So this could be our only chance to break in and find out what has been happening."

"You don't have to come along, Patrick." said Gabriel, stopping him before he could descend any further. "I've got this."

"Oh, do you now?" said Patrick, with a wide grin. "It's my sister you married there, boy. Besides, we O'Reillys hold a bond to your family. And a debt is never repaid until the job is complete."

"You hold a what?" said Gabriel, confused.

"I'll explain everything to you after we do this." said Patrick, motioning off into the dark. "No-one knew they were still active, Gabriel. Not one of us could have guessed you and my sister would end up how you did. Please, Gabriel. We have a chance to finish this. Let's just get it done and I'll tell you everything you need to know."

"Who are still active?" said Gabriel, standing motionless on the steps as a stern look descended over his features. "You'll explain now."

"Oh, for the love of Jesus, boy!" said Patrick, climbing up to meet his gaze. "ROS Genetics! You've read my sister's files by now, haven't you? They surely must have put you onto them into the first place."

"ROS Genetics? I know they're still active. I was in court with them today."

"ROS, boy. ROS!" said Patrick, almost pleading for Gabriel to understand. "R - O - S. Royal Outlook Society! And here's me hoping you're an educated man."

"You mean they're still after my family? After all these years?"

"Who do you think arranged the death of your great uncle that led to the death of those people in the states? Who do you think brought down your great grandfather, the viscount? Who do you think managed to get the company off from the charges you brought against them? You think those are simple things, Gabriel?" said Patrick, placing a hand on his shoulder. "That collection of misguided souls has been after your family for over a century. Now we have them. You have to trust me, Gabriel. You have to help me make amends for what they did to your family, your life, and my sister."

"Why?" said Gabriel, unflinching from his position. "Why my family?"

"Look…" said Patrick, his face contorted as he tried to find a way to explain. "Your great, great grandfather was one of them. He was a banker by trade, but was a dabbler in science in his spare time and promised them something that, once he understood what they wanted to use it for, decided he could not continue. They killed him for his defiance. Then, your great grandfather, under the guises of another man, said he would complete the work his father started. Instead, he turned his device against them and nearly wiped out. They have been out for vengeance of their own ever since."

Gabriel's heart sank. Why did Suzanne not tell him any of this? "They killed my wife, because of something that happened over a hundred years ago?"

"They have killed countless hundreds in their quest for this device. You have to, for the sake of Suzanne and your true heritage, help me destroy it; if they have succeeded, as we fear." Patrick turned and started to jog down the steps. "We must hurry. We are trespassing, and at some point someone will find out we are here. We have little time."

As Patrick disappeared into the dark, Gabriel cleared his mind. Wherever his path would take him from now on, he needed to stay focussed. He did not know what ROS Genetics were trying to create, but if it was worth a hundred years of wait, it must be important. Taking a calming lungful of air, he set off.

-

Gabriel spun to a gruff howl that hollered out down the corridor. Doctor Evesham and Jennifer were now heading toward him, the black, like of giant wave of nothingness, chasing them as they ran. Oz was gone.

"Your time is up, Mister Thaddeus." said Evesham, his voice echoing in the cramped space. "It is too late."

Maybe he was right, but he had to try. Closing his eyes and willing everything in his soul to fight, he searched his mind for his last, true memory. Holding on as the recollection surged to the surface, he opened his eyes once more.

Chapter 19

Gabriel's vision returned to a swirl of brightness that surged into his head and momentarily forced his eyes to close. Re-opening them, he could make out he was on his back in a sterile, white room. He could feel something attached to his skull and could see, through the glare it was throwing in his direction, a medical lamp above his head.

"My my, Mister Thaddeus." said a male voice, as a white blur moved into view and cut out some of the light. "My assistant said you were waking, but I did not believe it possible."

"Should I re-sedate him?" asked a woman, as another white blur arrived at the opposite side of him.

He was sure he knew the voices. Was one the receptionist from ROS Genetics? He was uncertain, but the other one he was definite about. It was the man who killed Suzanne, Giles Eagles.

"I wouldn't worry about that." said Giles, moving away. "I'm not sure how he's conscious, but I can guarantee his mobility is negligible. What he has inside him would comfortably incapacitate medium sized loxodonta."

Gabriel tried to move, to prove the man wrong, but found anything more than twitching his fingers impossible.

"I would not struggle too hard, Mister Thaddeus." said Giles, as he moved back into view. "I think you will find movement would not be in your best interests."

Giles moved in front of the lamp and blocked out enough light so Gabriel's eyes could properly focus. He was a rancid man; short and wiry, with dark, threadbare hair and swollen, dot like eyes. His teeth were crooked and yellow, and his hands stained by nicotine. He struggled against the chemicals holding him down, uttering a guttural growl, as he attempted to get close. How he wanted to hurt the man, to raise his head and bite him.

"Really, Mister Thaddeus." said Giles, noticeably shocked by the effort displayed. "I must warn you that you should not be attempting to move. It would be a shame to damage such a wonderful brain."

Gabriel turned his view to the metal edge of the lamp. Now the bulb was obscured, he could see a reflection of his head in the metal rim. At the glimpse, his heart stopped. The top of his skull removed, exposing his brain to the air. Three rods, each adorned with a silver orb, placed concentrically over the surface of the exposed matter, and wires trailing from each to the floor and an unknown source.

"Ah, the machine." said Giles, catching the look of terror in his eyes. "Myself and McMaster worked very hard to accomplish that which your great grandfather promised us. I find it fitting the first two trials of its effectiveness should be taken with such suitable candidates. Although, I have to admit, the trial run with your wife would have been more effective if I had managed to get the settings right. Burning grey matter is such a unique smell, don't you think?"

Gabriel's thoughts descended to rage. He snarled, desperate to free himself, to close his hands around this vile man's neck and squeeze the wickedness from him. The foul wretch deserved to feel pain, to suffer the anguish of true loss and then die, snivelling for his life.

"It is pointless getting angry now, Mister Thaddeus. That was Mister O'Reilly's mistake." Giles turned and looked to the back of the room, Gabriel's line of sight following.

Even though he could not move his head to get a clear view, Gabriel could see a man propped in the chair. His ginger hair matted to his face, and his head slumped into his chest, a bullet hole oozing blood down his shirt. It was Patrick. He closed his eyes and searched his mind for a solution; he could not allow another death to go unpunished.

"I always hoped you would be cogent, at least of some fashion, for our grand finale." said Giles, as he moved out of view behind him. "It is fitting some small part of your pitiful line is here to witness our great achievement."

Just on the outskirts of perception, Gabriel was certain he could feel the man's fingers play across the exposed surface of his brain, instigating a terrifying tactile response.

"I do so wish you were able to speak, Mister Thaddeus." said Giles, finishing his adjustments and moving to lean over him once more. "It would be interesting to ascertain if we have triggered any memories whilst we have been modifying our settings."

What settings? What was the man blabbering about now? Was this machine the reason for his horrific visions? Gabriel's eyes flicked and settled on Giles', stern and steady, as he gazed through the man with hatred. Did this fiend trigger everything recently experienced?

"Oh, my!" said Giles, his excitement palpable. "I can tell from your response it has. That is wonderful news, Mister Thaddeus! Do you know what this means? I feel I should tell you what is about to happen; it is only fair."

Gabriel's disgust for the man was growing by the second. Not only was he sadistically achieving his goals, but he was now about to gloat about them.

"The human brain processes around three trillion bits of information each second, Mister Thaddeus. A simple calculation into chemical transmission velocity, the bedrock of how the brain supposedly works, tells us this level of processing is impossible based on its size and structure. This leads one to a simple certainty; the brain does not function how we think. It appears, after our research, the brain is in fact a quantum computer of some kind. It is a place where processing takes place at the sub-molecular, or quantum, level, rather than the atomic."

Great. A lesson in basic physics from a psychopathic moron. Hopefully, Giles' drivel would continue long enough for him to find a way out of his situation.

"After careful study of the minute electromagnetic variances within the brain's pathways, it was possible to detect certain thoughts bore certain signatures. The CIA recently developed a lie detector that can tell you are going to lie six seconds before you do; we obviously procured those schematics to help accelerate our own research." said Giles, as he began to pace up and down the gurney, gesticulating as he continued his rhetoric. "From that mechanism, we were able to ascertain a series of such signatures and fed them into a computer for analysis. After enough trials were completed, we were able to build a subset of data that allowed thoughts to be read, much as you can interpret a mobile phone transmission by intercepting the carrier signal. However, we wanted to go further. We wanted to get to information a subject was unwilling to allow to be processed into thought. And that was where McMaster's research was invaluable. Using his quantum computing techniques, we were able to decipher information, directly from the brain itself, with no processing required. And thus, we finally had the device promised to us by your family all that time ago."

Gabriel winced, as Giles turned and nodded to the nurse, a tingling settling in his mind, and sending shivers of conflicting pain signals over his body.

"But do you know what our greatest find was, mister Thaddeus?" said Giles, as he leant over him once more and the disgusting stench of stale tobacco added to his agony. "It was the discovery that somehow, perhaps genetically, memories were encoded that could not possibly be from whom we extracted them. Somehow, we were tapping into history, our very past. Imagine our surprise when we became aware we could extract secrets from a dead man, by reading them from his own lineage. And so you will be our first - well, second if you count our failure - true test of just how far back we can go."

Shock surrounded Gabriel's tortured mind. That was what he was experiencing, the memories of his forefathers. He thought about the scenes, as another terrified realisation engulfed him. The memories were not his, but they also did not belong to his family. In none of the recollections was he a Tirney, a Thaddeus, or even a Whittingham. Somehow, he was accessing the memories of those his ancestors killed.

All his learning, all his reasoning, descended on the puzzle and a solitary result postulated in his conscious. It landed with the force of revelation, fear enrapturing his response, as he finally understood his mind changed the memories to implant the solution, as he was experiencing them. "Yloungh Sleut." he said, the words garbled and hoarse.

Giles stepped back from the gurney, shocked at the sudden utterance.

"Did he just call me a young slut?" said the nurse, arriving at Giles' side.

Young's Slit, you stupid bimbo! The thought snarled as it fought through Gabriel's scrambled mind. He had to make them understand. If he was interpreting their actions correctly, they were going to look directly into his conscious and beyond. They were about to stare at the quantum computer in operation. He could not allow it to happen. That was what his mind was trying to get him to see, as it fought to free him from his coma.

His mind took him back to his conversation with McMaster at CQIF. It tried to have the characters in his memories of the murders he lived through explain what he needed to know - All quanta are linked.

It was a process called quantum entanglement. All quanta created at a solitary source, if forced to interact, will, when separated, experience the same effects at the same time, even if only one of them is localised to the effect. His tutor explained it as two linked tennis balls; one sent to Wimbledon and the other placed on your mantelpiece. When you watched someone serve one on your television, the other would fly off your mantelpiece and smack you in the face. It was the crux of what Giles' machine relied upon. His subjects, through the quantum computers of their minds, were linked to one another; even across time. Nevertheless, his supposition was flawed. All quanta were created, and thus forced to interact, in the same event at the same time; what one of his visions called 'the singularity' - the creation of the universe. Thus, all quanta, everywhere in the universe, were linked; and the terrible fact was, they still were. That was why he had not seen the memories of his ancestors, but those of others. Moreover, that was where superposition became an issue. Once you affected a quantum process by looking at it, it stopped functioning how it should; just as McMaster's own quantum computer had. Now, Giles was about to look at the quantum computer of the mind, and looking would stop the process from functioning how it should. The horror was that due to quantum entanglement, it would stop all linked processes, everywhere in the universe. Giles was not about to see the mysteries of the brain, he was set to end them.

The nurse by the side of him reached over and placed her hands against his shoulders, as his twitching became more violent, slurred words gargling from his mouth. "Youlng Sleet! Yolg Sloot!"

"He's trying to say something, doctor." said the nurse, turning to face Giles, her expression panicked. "It seems important."

"Nothing is important, but the result." said Giles, as he moved behind him.

"Slopp.. Yeongs Slite.. Susperposilssion… Stoop!"

It was no use. He could feel the tingle begin to spread. He could see, just on the edge of his vision, a brilliant white spot appear. His mind screamed to be freed, to stop what was about to occur - but it was too late.

And in an instant, nothing.

Epilogue

Somewhere beyond the reach of normal senses, a solitary, ageless consciousness experienced the end of its great experiment. The delicately crafted beings created, falling foul of their own, gifted intelligence, and their once intricate minds rendered useless by their thirst for knowledge.

Without the beings, the universe continued as planned. The stars burned, the galaxies swirled, and the constant thrum of the black encroached. However, time mattered little. Time could only be experienced by the tangible. The motion of the solid making its perception valid. It was not something that could affect infinity.

As the last twinkling embers of a once vast universe flickered and fell silent, the same confusion remained. What was it to exist? It was a difficult question to answer. When no logical solution of thought would resolve, a solution presented itself by way of a potential experiment. There was no way to recreate the infinite, but could there be a way to recreate the idea, the ever present concept of infinite? Was there a way to retrieve an answer by proxy?

To create a substitute for infinity was easy. It was all a matter of scale. If the tangible was small enough, then infinity was simply more than was comprehensible to it. Therefore, something suitably gargantuan was created. It was a disaster, chaotic and disordered. Something without form.

Therefore, a set of duly complex rules to govern the something was formulated and the experiment started again. Once the system was stable, the beings were implanted to every corner. Once again, it was an unmitigated catastrophe. To make the something real, the system had to allow motions to be unguided. That meant collisions, explosions, and unexpected aberrations in the system's logic were terrifyingly frequent; not to mention the insanity that festered in many of the beings as they developed.

Again and again, the experiment repeated, until a basis of ground rules was formulated. The something must be created, and allowed to find its own order before the beings were supplanted. The beings must also be given the greatest chance of survival, and so a quiet corner of a non-descript system had to be selected from the multitude. Lastly, the beings had to be watched over, guided as they developed, so their own petty insecurities did not spell their doom.

The last three attempts were promising, with the most recent displaying all the characteristics of providing the answers sought for so long. It was true there were teething problems, even in this last variant. The guiding hand was often more divisive than the fears of the beings themselves. Any assistance given seen as favouritism, used to suppress other factions of the beings, and usually those not requiring help. In the end, the assistance was removed entirely. That too caused issues. It took the beings' focus away from the experiment and made them insecure, afraid and isolated; deciphering any advances in their knowledge of self, becoming almost impossible.

Then there was the desire to understand everything. The system was designed to be almost unbreakably complex, but still they tried. Pushing the boundaries of their limitations and frequently hurting each other in the process. It was as though understanding what was not them had become more important than understanding themselves. And with failure, came yet more madness. Present since the start, it manifested as a deep fear of existence, which stemmed from not understanding what was truly important. Quite why so many of the beings spent no time investigating the mysteries of their own existence, was truly baffling.

When the end came, it was almost a relief. It was clear the answers sought were lost to their endeavours.

However, the predicament experienced was still without explanation. It would be so easy to succumb to the same fear and depression affecting the beings, but that would not do. The course undertaken may yet bear fruit.

As an infinitesimally small something, reached out into the nothingness of everything, a solitary thought resolved to action. The experiment would be tried again. And this time, it must not be allowed to fail.

Bang.

Also From the Author

Coincidence Theory

Separated by millennia, a bodyguard of the pharaoh called J'tan and a military specialist named Colonel Christopher Martin, must do everything they can to protect the mysterious artefacts of the Egyptian first time.

As both men strive to deal with powers beyond their control, they take their own journeys of discovery through the heart of the promised lands of old to recover the fabled Ark of Ra and the unbelievable secret it contains.

Hounded at every turn by a secretive sect intent on using the artefacts for their own ends, their faltering allegiances, and misplaced beliefs could be the very things that promote their ultimate demise.

Will either man complete the mission they have set out to accomplish? Or will greed and ignorance destroy one of the greatest archaeological discoveries of all time?

Blending elements of a historical epic with a modern day thriller, Coincidence Theory leads the reader through an alternate version of one of the most well-known stories in history - casting the principle figures in a terrifying new light.

Full of fresh insights and revelations, Coincidence Theory will keep you guessing from the first page to the last.

www.ingramcontent.com/pod-product-compliance
Lightning Source LLC
Chambersburg PA
CBHW020238180626
46810CB00006B/2258